# Tunkumba Creek

Alistair Hume

Published by Alistair Hume, 2026.

This is a work of fiction. Similarities to real people, places, or events are entirely coincidental.

TUNKUMBA CREEK

**First edition. March 9, 2026.**



ISBN: 978-1764587334

Written by Alistair Hume.

To my beautiful family who all helped me across the line in so many ways.

Justice without mercy is no justice at all.

# PROLOGUE

**Havana Cuba**
**August 2004**

Lieutenant Clara Ramirez was a cautious woman. She double checked that the Makarov service pistol was fully loaded, no round chambered, and the safety was on before sliding it back into its holster on her right hip under her shirt. Her badge was in her top left pocket over her breast, a small notebook in the right. She patted her pants pockets, front and back in a silent routine, glanced in the mirror, and pulled her auburn hair back in a ponytail to secure it with a band to keep it out of her face, some loose strands refused to obey. Instead, she smoothed the blue rank epaulettes on her shoulders and wiped a small bead of sweat away from her dark skin.

Clara was fuming that she had been ordered to meet with a Major Colome for a menial customs inspection at this time of night. She sighed; she had no choice; she might be a Police Lieutenant of Cuba's Criminal Investigation, but she was first and foremost a servant of the Revolution after all. Whatever feelings Clara had about this operation she would keep them repressed till it was over. She grabbed her keys off the kitchen table, locked her door behind her, and hurried down the stairs, trying not to stumble in the dark. The internal light was broken again.

Her police Lada was parked out the front on the cobblestones, hemmed in by Zaya Bernal's red Studebaker in front and a pink open topped Chevrolet behind, huge American cars from the 50's, left over from Batista's rule. Bernal's car was his pride and joy, nobody got to drive in that but him. The Chevrolet behind it, however, was a different story, it was owned by the family across the road who used it as a glamorous taxi to drive tourists around town.

There was not much room to get her Lada out of the space, but Bernal, sitting in the doorway smoking, was not going to shift his Studebaker to make it any easier.

Clara opened her car door, and stood with keys in her hand, looking toward Bernal lounging on the steps of the apartment block. Her unsaid question was answered with a shrug; your problem, you fix it.

Bernal was not a troublemaker; he just looked it. He was a 6ft 2-inch part time boxer, bald and muscular; not gym muscles, but ones formed by hard manual labour and endless hours in the ring. Clara had no trouble with her neighbour, but she knew if she scratched his Studebaker getting out of the parking space, she would feel Bernal's wrath.

Clara started her car and opted to nudge the Chevrolet behind instead, using her bumper to gently push it back and give herself some room to angle the Lada out.

She nodded at Bernal as she left. Bernal didn't nod back, but he didn't raise his middle finger at her either. Perhaps he was warming to the idea of living next door to a policewoman.

The unmarked Police car rattled with its throaty exhaust as Clara pushed the ineffectual Lada along the long Malacon sea wall. The moon was a quarter full and gave dancing sparkle to the sea as she drove to Hemingway Marina, 20 kilometres away. She was sure that she had been allocated the oldest unreliable motor vehicle in all Havana's Police force, the price she paid as a woman of rank in the new socialist society. As the Lada protested and belched smoke, she wondered why she had been called. It made no sense; any competent junior police officer could carry out the role of assisting a customs search. Unless, she thought, it involved espionage, but that would be for officers from the Security Division, they would want a juicy case like that, and why not send someone through normal channels, why ring her in the middle of the night? She wondered if it was Alejandro, her arrogant bastard of a watch Captain who would happily put the Interior Ministry on to her, offloading another shit job that he didn't want. She lit a cigarette and settled into the long drive.

She turned off the main road Strata 5$^{th}$ Avenue past the large sign welcoming Cubans to the Ernest Hemmingway Marina; Avenida 3 finger was to her left. It had recently opened, and only a few boats lined the concrete wharf. The marina was one of the ways Cuba was opening up to the world outside. Clara parked just out of view from the complex, behind the Customs office, still raw and unpainted in its newness, the debris of left over concrete and building waste littering the dirt. By the look of it, she doubted that the office was even in use yet, but she cut the lights and got out looking for her contact anyway.

The marina was quiet, no lights or suspicious noise from any boats, only the telltale ting of rigging against the mast as the gentle breeze rocked the boats at their moorings.

Clara circled the dark Customs office, and walked quietly along the concrete edge, identifying each boat as she went. No yacht called *Harmony*. She lit a smoke while she walked back to her car where she pulled out her mobile cell phone, but there was no reception. Cell phone connection was available in some parts of Havana city but out here in the open, the phone was useless. She was concerned that she had missed the rendezvous. It hadn't occur to her that somehow, she had misunderstood her instructions. She silently recounted the phone call in her head.

The dispatch order had said the yacht *Harmony* was located at Marina No.3, which was here. She remembered from an internal memo that the Hemmingway Marina was to be the new point of entry for yachts arriving in Havana. But the yacht was definitely not here, and if the Customs office was not in use yet, then where would the yacht make land? In Havana harbour, at Marimelena, the name given to the eastern cove inside Havana harbour, where a small marina lay next to some warehouses jutting out from shore. It was across the bay from the old town where she lived. Clara saw it every day driving to work, she passed Marimelena cove and the numbers 1, 2 and 3 painted on the side of each of the warehouses attached to the marina fingers. Was it possible the dispatcher meant Marimelena No.3 instead of Marina No.3, both words sounded similar, and both were marina's, though the one in Marimelena, was very old and largely unused. She could have mistaken the directions over the poor phone connection.

She looked around one last time. Well, it wasn't here.

'*Mierda.*' She exclaimed. She was probably in the wrong place and should be 25 kilometres back on the other side of Havana Harbour. She wrenched open the car door cursing herself and sped out of the car park spinning her bald tyres in the gravel.

Clara paid no attention to the sea on the return journey, it was now a dark foreboding place as she pushed the Lada recklessly back the way she had come. Traffic was light at this time of night. Ahead the Malecon wound around down into the tunnel entrance under the harbour. When she emerged, she swung into the right-hand exit past the forts and could see ahead the small Casa Blanca Marina, 3rd finger inside Marimelena cove. Only one yacht was tied to the wharf on the edge of the harbour light. Figures could be seen silhouetted on the deck. She shut off the engine and lights before coasting silently into the carpark next to the white Customs van.

At first, Clara hung back in the shadow of the marina office, watching from afar the tableau of figures, assessing the size and placement of the yacht, watching the way the crew moved and responded to orders, in particular the yacht master and the Customs Officer standing in the cockpit. The Officer seemed to be remonstrating with the skipper while another was moving along the side of the boat, retrieving lines...they were preparing to leave.

She moved out of the shadows and marched out along the wharf till she was level with the wheelhouse, and waited, watching.

The *Harmony* was approximately 60 foot long, fibreglass, one mast, a centre cockpit with small protective bimini, ropes and fenders hanging off the rails, but otherwise neat and tidy. However, the sound of the diesel motor burbling from the rear exhaust confirmed Clara's fears that they were getting ready to leave.

'Turn the engine off I said, you don't go till I'm finished.' ordered the Customs Officer.

The tall thick set skipper reached down to the controls, but the motor stayed on.

'My batteries are low, I may not be able to restart,' he said, his voice a low growl.

'We haven't finished here. This is not what's supposed to happen.' The officer was dressed in the white Customs uniform, displaying the insignia of a Major. Very young to be a Major, Clara noted. There was no one else with him. This was highly irregular she thought. Clara called up to the skipper.

'I suggest you obey the Major, whatever state your batteries are in.' she ordered in English.

Startled, they both turned toward Clara, noticing her for the first time in the dull glow of the light.

'Who are you?' the sailor questioned.

'Lieutenant Ramirez, National Revolutionary Police providing assistance to the Customs service.' Clara raised her eyebrows in question at the Customs Major..

'Why are you here? What are you doing here?' The Officer called. He was young, and agitated, struggling to impose control over the situation. One of the mooring lines was free and the crewman at the bow was about to cast off the second line.

'Don't do that.' Clara barked at him. She calmly turned back to speak to the Major. 'I'm sorry I was delayed. I've been assigned to assist you. Will I come up there?' She asked the young officer, but he ignored her.

'I want to make a full search of this boat.' He pointed at the skipper.

'I already said, there's nothing here to concern you, we're about to leave,' the skipper said. He was a big man standing in the shadow of the wheelhouse, with an imposing voice to match. 'You can't search my boat, we haven't landed. See, no one is on shore. We just stopped here because of the weather. We are on our way to Panama.'

'You are not American.' Clara observed, trying to lower the tension. She placed her hand on the gunwale and looked up at the skipper. 'But you are in Cuban waters, and this is Havana Bay. We have the authority.'

'Yes, I know. But it's got nothing to do with you guys. We were blown in here by mistake. We are not landing here, we are landing in Panama City. We'll be their problem... we don't want...'

'You are not going to Panama yet, I know this. You are using our waters to avoid the Americans, you know they can't board you when you are in our waters, now turn your engine off.' Major Colome raised his voice. 'And get me your passports. Now!'

'You don't want to do this.' The skipper advanced out of the open wheelhouse

forcing the Major to back pedal. Colome stumbled, reached up to grab the boom above his head but missed, tripped and fell in a tangle on the deck. He scrambled at his holster, trying to reach his sidearm.

'Help me,' he yelled.

Clara tried to pull herself up over the rail, but the skipper turned to her, reached up behind his head and retrieved a handgun from the underside of the wheelhouse roof. Clara was halfway up the handrails and off balance. she reached for her own Makarov as he pointed his gun at Clara.

'Bugger off!' he said and pulled the trigger.

The bullet slammed into Clara's shoulder, the pain sharp and intense. She let go of the stanchion wire and fell back, bounced off the timber wharf against the fibreglass hull and slid into the narrow gap between the two.

At first the water was warm and embracing, but as it seeped into the wound the stinging began. She grasped at a pylon, it was slippery and looped with bits of old rope, the current was gently pulling her back out into the light, she jammed her fingers under one of the loops and pulled herself in close to the shadows, sucking in short breathes as the pain ebbed and flowed through her upper body.

Above, a torchlight skimmed the surface, she was too far back under the wharf to be seen, but close enough to hear the voices.

'Fuck, Adam, cast off now. no lights. I shot a cop. You. Major whatever your fucking name is, get off my boat. We're leaving.'

'Not without my money.' Colome shouted.

'No time. No money. It's all gone arse up.'

'But you shot that Policewoman. What do I tell them?' whined the Major.

'Not my problem. Now get off before I throw you off.'

'Not without my money. That was the arrangement.'

'No!'

'Do you know who I am? I can order a patrol boat to stop you at the harbour entrance. You'll never leave here.'

' 'Shit!'

A single shot.

In the space of a heartbeat, the Majors body splashed into the water next to Clara. At first it sunk below the surface, then the current drifted it up against her, but she couldn't hold on to it with her injured shoulder. As the yacht moved off the wharf and motored into the dark, the propellor wash pushed the body away in the other direction.

Clara didn't remember anything much after that until she was rescued from the harbour mud at low tide the next day.

# CHAPTER 1

**Havana. Cuba**
**November 2004**

Clara checked her watch and made her way up the steps of the Ministry of the Interior building. It faced the Plaza of the Revolution and held none of the charm or stonework of the old Havana, it was too austere for that. Even an eight-story iconic image of Che Guevara could not soften the off-white façade of reflected glass. Those inside could look out, but no-one outside could look in, it was perfectly suited to function.

She had been in here before, delivering briefs to Colonel Perez on the third-floor, the administrative office of the National Revolutionary Police force. Perez was the senior officer, who divided his working hours between the National Ministry building and the Havana City Police headquarters two kilometres away near the harbour. It was rumoured Perez kept a mistress halfway between the two buildings in the old part of town, and he used that to his advantage, no one was ever sure which office he was in, or if he was at the office at all.

The coolness of the plaster walls was a stark contrast to the heat that rippled off the Plaza outside. It was her first day back and her uniform felt tight and constrictive, pulling at the light dressing still covering the bullet wound. She shrugged her shoulders, moving them from side to side to loosen her shirt from the clinging humidity before knocking at the door of the Directorate of Criminal Investigation.

The office was lined with dark timber. She stood and waited...and waited, staring over the top of the Colonels head at the Cuban flag. Perez looked up from the file on the desk in front of him and gave her a perfunctory command.

'Sit!'

Clara's chair was cold and metallic, in keeping with Perez's greeting. His voice was sharp, his manner abrupt. Clara had to be careful, Perez had worked his way up through the ranks like her and he was no fool, no matter what the rumours said. Clara knew him to be diligent at running the Directorate and well known for his acumen in navigating the internal politics of the Ministry for the Interior, jealously guarding his authority, as he did the whereabouts of his mistress.

'Welcome back Lieutenant Ramirez. It has been nearly three months. You are healing well?'

'I am thankyou sir. The wound became infected, but it has finally healed.' She answered, sitting forward on the chair, knees together, back straight.

'About time you came back to duty,' he said.

'That wasn't' my decision, sir,' she responded. 'I wanted to come back earlier.'

Perez silenced her with a withering glare. He tapped his finger on the file in front of him. This was not a social summons.

'You come back when you are ordered to. There has been a huge outcry over the death of Major Colome, you are lucky I kept you out of it where I could. Refresh my memory of this Customs operation please, this one you were involved in. From the beginning, the first phone call,' ordered Perez.

Clara shifted uncomfortably in her seat, the shoulder wound itching and demanding attention again, but she ignored it. There was no doubt that this was an investigation, she would have to be careful with what she said, it will always get used against you. Enough to answer the questions but never more.

'I first received the phone call at home from MINIT, the Ministry of the Interior.'

'What time was that?'

'About 8.30, in the evening...'

'And who was it that called you?' Perez interrupted.

'It was from the Ministry, the Office of the Committee for the Defence of the Revolution, Security Division.'

'And who was it that called you?' Perez repeated.

'He identified himself as General Abelardo. He stated that he was responsible for espionage and offences against state security and his rank and Department superseded yours.'

Perez leaned forward just a little.

'Did he mention my name?'

'No sir, he referred to you as my Senior Officer'

'Very well...go on.' Perez looked down at the open file on his desk, making notes in the margin.

'I received the call at home, in my flat in the old town, at approximately 9.30pm. The General stated that I was required to report to the wharf at Marimelena No 3 to aid Major Colome of the Tropos Guarda Frontira, Customs Division in the search of the alien yacht *Harmony* for evidence of illegal activities that may be deemed against the interests of state security and the Revolution. I was to provide a Police presence only in the event of a seizure.' Clara paused before she continued. 'I pointed out that I was a Police Lieutenant from Criminal Investigations and Operations and that I was tired and had just arrived home from a week investigating double murders in the Vinales district, and perhaps an Officer from his own Security Division attached to the TGF and Customs may be more appropriate. He stated that this order came directly from the highest office of MINIT, and as a Lieutenant it was not my responsibility or rank to question his orders.'

Clara fell silent and stared straight ahead at the portrait of Fidel Castro next to the flag above Colonel Perez's head.

'I did not tell you to stop Lieutenant.'

'I tried to protest a second time.'

'You did not think to ring me, to clear it with your superior officer?'

Clara closed her eyes and remembered the MINIT official specifically telling her that under no circumstances was she to notify Police Headquarters of what she was doing.

'No Colonel. Not at the time. I see now that I should have done that.'

Perez finally looked up and engaged Clara with a withering stare.

'Yes, you should have. That was your first of many mistakes Lieutenant. What happened from there?'

'I proceeded to the Inner harbour, to assist the Customs Major in my official capacity.'

'You were in uniform and carrying your pistol?'

'In the holster on my belt, as per regulations.'

Perez looked down at the file.

'It says here when they recovered you from the mud bank the next day, your holster was empty, and your Makarov was missing.'

'Yes sir... I don't remember, it must be on the bottom.'

'Our divers did not find it there.' He raised his eyebrows at Clara, willing her to provide further explanation. Clara remained silent.

'Major Alberto Colome, the Customs officer, was found dead, floating in the water under the wharf with a 9 mm wound to his head. The Makarov is also a 9mm pistol is it not Lieutenant Ramirez?'

Clara stayed silent.

'Your report does not mention the shooting of major Colome, only that you yourself were shot and knocked overboard. I presume you still had your pistol with you when you fell.'

'I did. I had tried to draw it from my holster.'

Perez tapped with his finger slowly on the typed pages in front of him.

'Well, it wasn't there when they found you, and it wasn't on the bottom. So, tell me how Major Colome ends up dead in the harbour, and a Police Lieutenant from my own department who fails to protect him from being murdered, does not draw her weapon, yet has lost it?'

Clara stayed silent. She didn't think to add that she too had been shot.

Perez continued without waiting for an answer, his voice slower, deeper in reverent tone.

'Surely the name has not escaped you, Lieutenant? The papers have been full of it. Major Alberto Colome is the nephew of Minister Juan Ibarrio, Head of the Ministry for the Interior, the third highest office in Cuba. His office is in this building on the top floor.' He let that point sink in. 'What a debacle this is. So, tell me now, how did it happen? And it had better match this report.' Ramirez looked across the desk at her expectantly.

The story she told the investigating officer that interviewed her in the Hospital was the same story she retold for Colonel Perez, she had practiced it enough. She made no mention of her going to the wrong marina by mistake in the first place, nor that Major Colome's presence on the yacht had seemed to be pre-arranged. She definitely didn't tell him that she heard Colome demanding bribe money. However she finished her recount with the clarity of truth.

'I did not see the unfortunate murder of Major Colome, or what happened to the yacht after. I understand it left Cuban waters that night and hasn't been seen since.'

. Perez did not look up at all as Clara spoke, intent on reading the fine points of Clara's written statement. Her recounting of that night was clear, concise and to the point. Exactly as they would expect from a Police Officer... exactly as she had practiced it, double checked against the file on the desk.

Perez flipped back through the file till he settled on one of its pages.

'Many mistakes were made Lieutenant Ramirez, and you were lucky,' he said.

She didn't think that lying in a bed for two months with an infected wound was lucky.

'But for you, it is not yet over.' He continued.

Clara's stomach churned.

'Here,' he remarked, looking closer at the page, 'you said that you felt the man who shot you was not an American, even though the boat was registered in America. Why did you think that?'

Clara paused before answering, looking for double meanings, or a trap.

'His accent was strange, I have a hunch he was not American, he did not speak as I have heard Americans to sound.'

'Be careful Lieutenant, imagination in our job is a dangerous thing, we deal in reality. Hunches and gut feelings are for others. Was he part Cuban? Maybe one of those misguided Marielito's living across the strait in Miami.'

'No. definitely no Cuban accent, Colonel, what I meant to say, was that even though the yacht captain spoke English, his accent was broader, flatter, not like any of the American language I have heard before'

'Would you recognise his voice if you heard it again?'

'But surely you have his description, the one I gave the Investigating Officer?'

'Yes. We do. It wasn't much. But would you recognize his voice if you heard it again?' demanded Perez.

Clara did not answer. Her wound itched; she could feel it beneath the dressing. Her memory of the incident ran wild but eventually centred on the moments before she was shot, the yacht master was holding a gun, pointed at her.

'He said, "Bugger off' when he shot me.' Clara murmured. 'Yes, I'd recognise his voice again.'

Perez watched her closely, as if waiting to make up his mind about her. He glanced down at the file, looked back at her, and eventually closed it. Perez had made his judgement. He leaned back in his chair and pointed to an envelope next to the folder.

'Lieutenant Ramirez, The Minister for the Interior has directed me to appoint you a promotion to the rank of Chief Investigating Officer into the murder of Major Alberto Colome of the Customs department. You are directed to take all steps necessary to locate and deal with the criminal from the yacht *Harmony*. You will be given all assistance necessary from my office in the Directorate of Criminal Investigations, but you will report directly to General Abelardo in the Security Division of the Ministry for the Interior.' Perez pointed upward to indicate that the Office she now needed was located in the floors above. He stared directly at Clara as he held out the envelope to her.

'Here are your orders and confirmation of your promotion to Investigator.' He paused before continuing. 'Of course, all correspondence about your progress will come to me first, before it goes upstairs. Do you understand?'

'Yes,' she acknowledged.

'After this meeting, you will go up to the Office of the Security Division to meet with General Abelardo, where he'll brief you personally.'

Clara's mind was reeling; she didn't know what to say but nodded her understanding. Standard Cuban organization, the higher department will give the orders and take the credit, while the lower does all the work, takes all the responsibility and the blame if it fails. To be fair, Colonel Perez's job was on the line as well. She looked up at him as she took the envelope, and for a brief moment, their eyes locked in understanding of their mutual predicament, his position was also riding on her success at finding the killer. The dead Major Colomè was the Minister's nephew, she as much as anyone understood the need for justice, but only Clara knew how corrupt Colomè was, and if the Minister also knew of that, then this whole investigation was corrupted before it began, and she stood a real chance of being hung out to dry. The justice Cuba wanted to see may not be the truth Clara had been tasked to find.

'You are permitted to leave Cuba for your investigation. There is a passport and signed travel authority in the envelope. Lieutenant Ramirez, you have been given unprecedented freedoms to track down this man...but do not forget, you come from Cuba, you will return to Cuba...for both our sakes.'

'Where am I going?' Was all she could muster.

'The Ministers Security specialists have analysed everything you have stated in your report. The words that were used by the yacht's master before he shot you are very specific. The phrase, "bugger off" is particular to the language of one country.'

'Where's that?' Clara asked.

'Australia!'

# CHAPTER 2

### Monday

Alex rose and fell in the slight swell, sitting up straight, his legs straddling the surfboard that wasn't his, he had rented it. The board was one of those epoxy jobs from a factory in China where desired shape and a traditional fibreglass feel was swept aside in pragmatic indestructability. It floated well, too well, and put his centre of balance higher in the water. All the better to see coming waves he thought. He could hardly blame the board shop for carrying hard light weight surfboards in their rental quiver, one glance inshore at the rocks of Georges Point was enough to know where the majority of them ended up in the hands of novice riders. He might be mid-forties but he was no novice, he reassured himself.

He reached down to his right ankle to check that his leg rope was still attached, then swept his arm back behind him, feeding the cord between his fingers and away from the back fins while he fixed his eye on the approaching set. There were only a few in the line-up, straddling their boards, bobbing up and down in the swell, close packed in a small space and straining to see eastwards for each new wave. It reminded Alex of a seal colony, all acting in unison, bobbing, swaying, alternating between scanning the horizon, and then noting their position in the pack. A ripple of movement, a new set was coming.

He pushed into a paddling position, skirted around a slower paddler in front, and grabbed the inside take-off point just as the peak formed. One, two, three strokes, and he was on. The board floated higher in the water, making his take off angle flatter, more awkward than what he was used to, and by the time he'd got to his feet, the board was skittering down the face, the backside rail barely gripping into the wall, reliant on the fins to do all the work. The board responded quickly to his bottom turn; it pivoted sharply under him and his resulting cartwheel off the front was a wonderful pirouette of arms and legs that brought appreciative smirks from the seal colony watching on. The wave swept over him, taking his board with it.

Alex's head broke the surface, he sucked in a much-needed breath in the brown foam and scooped up his leg rope in his right hand, it came up empty, the break in the cord halfway along. He just had time to glimpse his board being swept inshore toward the rocks before he ducked under the next wave, and began the ignominious swim in. It was a dirty three-foot surf running, the remains of cyclone Kerry that had lashed the coast for the last week, the residue of brown foam made his scramble over the slippery rocks awkward. Alex recovered his board and looked up to see Megan on the sand at the base of the cliff watching him, her hand shielding her eyes from the morning glare, making it so much easier for her to follow his progress. Wonderful, it just keeps getting better, I'm so glad she saw all that, thought Alex. He finished inspecting the board, finding three new dings in the rail. The surf shop owner will be pleased. Alex shook his head and clambered over the last of the rocks ...novice, he thought.

'Nice wave.' Megan remarked, a hint of sarcasm to her voice. Alex would have liked to think it was said as a joke, but their marriage still had a way to go in working out an amicable truce that accepted slights as a shared jest. Alex couldn't bridge that gap yet and fell back on plaintive responses.

'Yeh. Well! I'm a fair way out of practice. It's not the kind of board I'm used to.'

'Excuses! Excuses! A poor workman always blames his tools.'

She tried to ingest some levity, but it fell flat as Alex just stood looking at her. He wiped his hand through his hair and looked back out to sea where the seal colony were cavorting in the waves.

'It's hot. I'm going back to the unit,' she said, shifting her towel to her other shoulder, revealing her bikini clad breast in a provocative gesture. She spun on the sand, and started across the rock platform, heading toward the swimming beach in front of the Nerimbah Surf Club. Alex ripped the Velcro ankle strap off, bound it to the broken leash attached to his board, then picked his way over the rocks after her.

It was her idea to come to Nerimbah with him this time. He was last here three years ago, when he came up from Melbourne to help his friend Beau through his mother's funeral. And didn't that turn out to be a doozy. All sorts of past grief came back to revisit him then, and it has taken him a few years since to reconcile his role in the drowning of an old enemy in the Nerimbah river. He never planned it, it was self-defence. At least that's what he told himself. It was messy, and Megan knew nothing of it. Maybe that was a strong indicator of the state of their marriage. They say honesty is a cornerstone of a successful relationship, but it's not dishonest to withhold information if that information has nothing to do with their current circumstances, is it? At least that's how Alex chose to play it. Megan knew little of that trip, but now that she was here, if she asked him about it, he would tell her...but so far, she hadn't asked.

Ahead, she picked her way through the sand, sashaying her behind as she walked. She looked good for fourty-one and she knew it. Melbourne weather had kept her skin clear and unblemished, the last few days of Queensland sun giving her a light golden dusting, her sandy coloured hair in a tight pony tail. He broke into a trot and caught up with her over the soft sand, their feet squeaking underfoot, forcing them to dig their toes in and sway from side to side as they walked. He looked across at her and glanced down at her flat stomach, trying to imagine what it would look like if she was pregnant. Would it bring them closer? He wondered if she thought the same.

Megan strode ahead and called over her shoulder as she mounted the stairs off the beach.

'When we get back to the unit, don't be too long in the shower. We're going up to see Bonny this morning, remember.'

Alex followed behind, this was Megan's holiday, she was driving the ship, Alex was just along for the ride, and he was OK with that. Bonny was one of Megan's friends from Melbourne who bragged about her tree change in the mountains behind Nerimbah. It was a far cry from the sophistication of Melbourne, and the levels of comfort that Megan was used to, but a holiday in the subtropics visiting a quasi-hippy friend was exactly what it was, a holiday, where you get to go home to what you are used to at the end of it.

'Yeh, I'll be ready.' Alex answered her, as he weaved between the sunbakers.

Across from the beach, a row of high-rise units greeted them. Not so silent sentinels guarding Nerimbah Bay with the beach at their feet. Nerimbah was originally a fishing town, but since the 1980s, it had become a tourist mecca for families and there were now more pleasure yachts in the river than there were fishing boats. It's not to say that the fishing industry was in decline, but it was subject to the seasons and access to variable fish stocks. Tourists, however, could come all year round, there seemed to be no such thing as an off season. Nerimbah had some of the least variable temperatures in the country, and bad weather was just an inconvenience. Retired southerners coming to Queensland were now struggling to find accommodation, the secret was out, and holiday high rise units couldn't keep up with the demand. Alex knew he was the perfect example of new age visitors, cashed up and holidaying any time of year. They were here for a couple of weeks, and Alex had booked them into an apartment on the front, just down from Georges Head. He stepped out of the shower, towelling his hair dry.

'What time are we meeting Bonny what's-her-name?' he called to Megan.

'Don't be rude, you know it's Roachè, with an accent, Bonny Roachè.'

'Yeh right,' he said, as he wandered into the hallway. 'You know she's a fake,' he said in an offhand jibe. Alex couldn't stand her, she was a Melbournite tree changer who felt she must constantly impress on him the moral importance of her choice in life to be at one with the environment. Alex had grown up here in Nerimbah, he already knew about life close to nature and how the environment worked.

'Put some clothes on, I'll see you in the car.' Megan responded as she strode past him out the door.

# CHAPTER 3

**Monday**

The hire car wound its way through the final switchback bends before bursting out on the rim road that overlooked the valley leading to Dunoonan where they had just come from. The views of the coastline twenty kilometres away to the east were spectacular before the road twisted inland and they were engulfed by tall timber, gum trees and the lush undergrowth of dwarf Lillie Pillies and ferns. Alex wound down his window and slowed the car down. The dark shade hid kookaburras and bell birds that rang their calls out from the thick growth at every bend. Alex had to admit, he may not like Bonny, but she knew how to pick a cool place to live.

Cedar Vale was a long-established hinterland community, known for its alternative laid-back lifestyle, but not today. Alex slowed as the farmland gave way to town. The number of parked cars obscuring the main road to the village surprised him, he turned to Megan and raised his eyebrows in question.

'Is it some sort of market day today?'

'Not that I know of. Bonny didn't say anything about this,' she said testily.

Alex parked the car in the red mud and leaf litter to the side of the road. Ahead was the main street, a collection of odd shops and cafes that gave the town its appealing atmosphere. But it was the noise from a gathering crowd near the creek to the right that drew their attention. As Alex drew closer, he could see Bonny in the centre, arms gesticulating wildly, her voice calling out in protest.

When someone like Bonny Roachè injects herself into a community, it can have mixed results, Alex knew this from his work on Current Affairs programs. In some instances, the injection of cash and ideas revitalises these older established communities, making up for the loss of youth migrating to the cities seeking further education and higher paying jobs. Other times, the new arrivals use their power to affect community changes in the way they would best like, regardless of the consequences to the locals. He was not sure which side Bonny belonged to or if indeed she was a mixture of both.

'Megan, Megan,' Bonny called out, spotting them both across the heads of the crowd. She pushed her way through the gathering until she could grasp Megan in a warm embrace. 'Glad you made it.'

'Me too,' Megan replied, leaning back and taking in her friends' appearance. Bonny's hair was dishevelled, her cheesecloth shirt adorned with bold jewellery, designer jeans and dirty R.M Williams boots finished her ensemble. She had taken on a true tree change persona. It was a stark contrast to Megan's chic summer print dress and expensive sandals.

'You should see what they're trying to do here Megan,' Bonny exploded. 'Those bastards are going to fill the creek in, push a road across for a new development, a housing estate...here...in Cedar Vale,' she said, pointing at a bulldozer parked next to the trees. 'I didn't come here to live in the suburbs. That creek's full of platypus, they've been seen in that creek, really. It's against the law isn't it.' Megan hadn't got a word in, which wasn't unusual, at which point she noticed Alex for the first time. 'So, you came up too Alex,' she said.

'Hi Bonny.' Alex mustered a lame greeting. Though, after observing the creek and the menacing bulldozer ready to pounce on its beautiful surrounds, he thought maybe Bonny deserved a little more respect than he had granted her. 'Anything I can do to help?' he asked.

Megan looked expectantly to him, a quizzical look on her face. Bonny however jumped straight in.

'Alex, you were in News. Can you get a camera crew here, confront the developer, get footage of the bulldozer and our protest.

I tried, but they wouldn't come just for that. Maybe if we lie down in front of the bulldozer.'

'I don't do that anymore Bonny, and it's too late for a crew, I think they are about to start anyway.'

'Well, what can you do?' Megan asked of him expectantly. 'We can't just stand here and look.'

Alex watched the driver finish inspecting his dozer and put a drink bottle up on the caged-in seat. Ahead of him a group of protesters stood between it and the lush environs of heavily ferned creek bank. Alex thought for a moment.

'What's the developers name?' he asked.

'Terrence Dittman... they call him 'Tiger' for short.' Bonny spat.

Alex moved off in the direction of the dozer, Megan and Bonny a short distance behind. He weaved his way among the protesters till he confronted Dittman remonstrating with a tall elderly protester, tempers almost frayed on both sides. Alex interjected by wedging his way between the two, facing the shorter man.

'Excuse me Tiger,' he offered pleasantly. 'I know you have a job to do, and so have I. Just wondering if you have the right permit for the Angiopteris Evecta?'

'What?' Dittman snarled.

'If you have, no problem, I'll leave you to get on with it.' Alex continued, raising his eyebrows expectantly, and starting to back away.

The developer stood planted in place, his beefy hands locked into his belt. Alex was taller, and maybe 20 years younger he thought, which put Dittman into his early-sixties. Short in stature with a ruddy complexion, but still fit and ready for a fight.

'Look,' Alex continued, 'Just show me the permit and I'll get out of your hair,'

"Who are you?' Dittman growled.

'Donald Horne, Lucky Country Investments, we're interested in your development, hoping to replicate a similar one down outside Byron Bay. Plenty of Angiopteris Evecta there, but without a federal permit, each plant destroyed invokes a fine of $5000, and I figure there's about $100,000 worth of plants in your path, and nearly twenty mobile phones ready to record their loss.' Alex jerked his thumb behind him at the protest group for emphasis.

'Bullshit.' said Dittman, 'I don't know anything about a permit for Angio... whatever it is.'

'I'm just doing you a favour mate, a permit for each plant. If you've got them, I'll report back that you're the man for our next development...if you want the job.' Alex held his gaze; he didn't flinch or waver. Normally he was no good at bluffing, but in this, he had had plenty of practice working in media production.

Tiger Dittman equally held his gaze, obviously trying to work out if Alex was legitimate, or if he could take the chance on him not. Alex stared back.

'Shit!' he exclaimed and turned away. "Wrap it up Clarry,' he called to his dozer driver. 'We're finished here for the day until I find out what this clown is on about. What did you call that stuff?'

'Angiopteris Evecta, King or mules foot fern. It's protected fauna, I thought you would have known about it.'

Dittman marched back to the bulldozer where the driver jumped up into the seat and began to lock everything down. The protesters gave a disjointed cheer and began to break up and drift away, a few patting Alex on the shoulder. He walked over to survey the creek that he had just ostensibly saved, Megan and Bonny joined him.

'What do we do now?' asked Bonny. 'What's our next step if he gets the permits?'

'What permits,' replied Alex. 'I made all that up. The King fern is the only plant I know the scientific name for, and as far as I know, it's only grown on Yindiba Island, just north of here. I don't know what these ferns are, but I'm pretty sure they are not Angiopteris Evecta.' He looked around at the lush plants ringing the creek bank and nodded. 'It was all bullshit.'

Megan looked at him appreciatively.' You did well,' she said.

'He'll probably be back tomorrow,' Alex remarked. 'The next step is your job Bonny, I don't know what you're going to do, that's up to you. I just brought you a day's reprieve.'

'Yeh...well, looks good for the moment.' She turned to a couple of the protesters, waved and called out that she would talk to them later to discuss tomorrow's next round, then turned back to Megan. 'Anyway, we've got a lot to catch up on, the creek can wait for the moment, I think we can do lunch. Follow me,' she said. She grabbed Megan's hand and marched off in the direction of a café festooned with Buddhist bunting.

Bonny had adopted Cedar Vale as her own and was proving she was ready to fight for it. He looked at Megan and wondered briefly how much he, or Megan, would fight for what they loved, if the love was still there.

# CHAPTER 4

### Tuesday

Alex didn't have a particularly elegant swimming style, but he could get through the water at a respectable speed. The oily swells undulating into Nerimbah bay were pushing at him, they hadn't broken yet but were on the verge of tumbling over themselves and giving the host of board riders the reason for being out there.

There were few ocean swimmers in the bay today. Two grizzled old men swam passed him in the opposite direction, arms laboriously striking the water heading back toward the rock wall, they must have started before dawn, he thought. The storm that had lashed at the southern Queensland coast had moved on four days earlier, but the ocean was still turbulent, and undercurrents swirled and reached for Alex with every stroke. The corner of the bay was protected by Bayman Headland, dulling down the size of the waves, but the swim was still uncomfortable. He just needed some exercise to stretch out and clear his head.

When they had got back from Cedar Vale the previous night, Megan had complained of a headache and promptly retired to the bedroom, leaving Alex to drink by himself in front of the TV. He caught up with some local news, taking note of the story about the reinstatement of the shark nets after they dragged during the storm surge. Cyclone surf had also broken through the dunes at Hideaway beach, uncovering a body that authorities believed had been buried there for many years. Some Current Affairs show, and a late-night Samurai movie completed his evening viewing. The alcohol helped him to sleep.

Alex was first awake at sunrise. He rolled across and looked at Megans sleeping form, stroked her bare back with his fingers, and slowly made circles around her shoulder blades, drawing imaginary lines over her silky night shirt down her spine to where her buttocks began to form. Megan had responded with a sharp pull on the sheets, forcing them between their two bodies, tucking them under her. She wanted to sleep in, it was her holiday after all, she jokingly said, but he wasn't so sure it was a joke. Alex had swung out of bed and changed into his board shorts for a swim.

As he pounded past the surfers, stroke after stroke, he tried to enter that space where repetitive exercise stripped away the consciousness of time and effort and allowed him to ponder 'what if's' in recreative thought...the famous meditative state. But today wasn't one of those days. Instead, Alex felt every stroke of his arms in the turgid water, slapping at spray tops when he delivered a poorly executed stroke, his goggles gave him a view of the world below the surface, which today was brown and tinged with yellow from the weak sunlight that penetrated the surface, hiding whatever had been washed or swam out the river mouth. Alex had to force himself to not think about what may be below, sharks are always there and not interested in you anyway, he said to himself. Alex stopped and treaded water. He looked around, taking stock of where he was. The second lifeguard tower was only 50 metres away.' Have I only swum that far?' he murmured aloud. Looking inshore, the board riders disappeared and reappeared with each passing swell, waiting for the sets that were sliding in behind him. They regarded him with some sort of curiosity, but ultimately, he was just another mad swimmer. He turned and began to make his way back to main beach.

The beachfront shower stripped away the salt and sand, swirling it around his feet. He dried himself off and smiled at early morning dog walkers, slipped on his T shirt and looked up at the balcony of his unit. No movement. Megan must still be sleeping in. He retrieved the unit and car keys from his hat and slung the wet towel over his shoulder. Across the road were a string of cafes under the high-rise apartments, all offering coffee and breakfasts. Most had some customers, sitting in couples or small groups, deep in intimate discussion or sharing laughs over their coffee. He ordered a takeaway and headed for the underground garage and his hire car. Breakfast could wait, a sticky beak at the gap in the sand dunes at Hideaway beach and the discovery of a body, now that was far more interesting.

He drove up the ramp and swung right to follow the esplanade alongside the river, heading for the bridge. Same fishing houses as were always there, but newly built riverside mansions dotted among them now. He deliberately avoided the section of river front where it had happened. Megan still didn't know the full story. He'd spoken about his friend Beau often enough, and she understood that his return to Nerimbah three years back was problematic, tied up with both their pasts. But he had deliberately kept his involvement with Janice and her daughter Elizabeth vague, skirting the main issue, the one that continued to haunt him, that he had drowned a man to save their lives. He knew it was naive to think he could forget about it. He couldn't. All men were capable of great evil, justified or otherwise, and he had forgiven himself for it, but could not forget it. It would be callous for him to do so. He still sought the wisdom to accept that in himself. What he wasn't sure of was if Megan could. He shook his head and turned up the music on the radio, crossed the bridge to the south side of the river, and turned at the sign for Hideaway Beach.

In terms of development, Hideaway Beach was a recent suburb. It stood on the opposite riverbank to Nerimbah township, and although fishermen had built shacks there for many years, it had remained a flood plain of swamp wattles till the 70's when the rickety bridge built to get there from town was replaced with a more substantial structure. This opened the way for more fishermen, developers, surfers and girls who used to sunbake topless on the weekend. As a teenager, Alex often found an excuse to go there for a surf. He wondered if the breakthrough was at that stretch of beach below Bayman Heads where there had always been a weakness in the sand dunes, ever since they had been once flattened to make way for ocean views in the early 80s.

Close to the dunes, near the beachside housing estate, a row of cars and their attentive onlookers partly obscured a cluster of police vehicles. In the dunes beyond, a police gazebo had been set up, and blue and white bunting was woven between the trees surrounding the site. Alex parked nearby. Underfoot dirty sand and debris from the powerful surf that had broken through still smeared the bitumen. He picked his way through the cars till he could see the police site clearly.

Like all forensic sites, the pace of activity was slow and methodical. He watched two men in white coveralls working their way around a blue tarpaulin that denied the crowd a view of what they were interested in. Alex could guess what was behind it, the news this morning was fairly clear. It was the remains of a body buried in the dunes for many years, uncovered by the storm surf, and discovered yesterday evening by a dog walker, but no more details than that. It was not a recent death, so the urgency was not there, the police had just begun their forensic investigation. It will be days before more information would come to light. They were like that.

A uniformed officer stood chatting with some onlookers nearby. Alex scanned the crowd; a gaggle of locals either dressed for the beach or a walk to the shops. Among them, an elderly man held a dog on a short leash, Alex wondered if that was the dog that found it, a black and tan Australian terrier, good at digging up bones. The owner kept reaching down to scratch the dog's ears and pat his ribcage as if congratulating him on his stellar performance. The dog looked up at him lovingly, one ear flat the other attentive, a snaggle tooth giving it a lopsided grin, the tail beating side to side.

Beyond the group, further along the road, standing at the open doorway of a Holden utility stood Tiger Dittman. Jeez, thought Alex, I only met the prick a day ago and here he is again. On the other side of the car stood Dittman's bulldozer driver, Tiger had called him Clarry. Alex wondered what they were doing here, shouldn't they be up the range, pushing in the embankment in round two of the great platypus creek debacle. Instead, they were deep in conversation, Tiger nodded every now and then in the direction of the dunes and the police. Alex looked nonchalantly over Tigers head at the wispy clouds still juddering across the sky, left-overs from the recent storm.

He looked back down at Tiger Dittman and realised he was staring straight back at him. Tiger slammed the door shut, gestured for Clarry to follow him and they marched directly over. He stopped close to Alex, enough that no one else would hear the exchange. Clarry, standing to Tigers left was clearly a head taller than his boss. Alex remembered that the traditional side for the enforcer to stand was on the left. According to Hollywood gangster movies, the right side is reserved for the second-in- command, the one with brains. He wondered if he would point that out to Clarry but wisely decided against it.

'Good morning, Mr Horne,' said Dittman. 'If that's your real name.'

'Mr Dittman.' Alex responded, nodding to them both.

'I couldn't find Donald Horne among Lucky Country Investments, because it doesn't exist, neither that name nor the company, but there's a book you know, and a writer, but nothing to do with you I reckon. Whoever you are or what you're on about, I don't care, and there is no such thing as that precious fern you were talking of yesterday.'

Alex was impressed, Tiger had looked him up and uncovered the ruse. Maybe Tiger was no fool, and the crusty persona that he projected needed to be handled carefully.

'Mr Dittman, I assure you that the fern I was talking about yesterday is real, endangered, and needs a permit to be removed.

Perhaps I was mistaken with the appearance, all the different types of fern fronds look very similar, a bit like environmental groups really.'

'Don't be smart.'

'Look, Mr Dittman, I don't know what you are doing up there at Cedar Vale, but perhaps you might need to pause before you go ahead with wrecking the creek.'

'I've got permission from Council, that's all I need to push that road through. Greenie protesters I can do without, or people from outside sticking their noses in.'

'Maybe times change and any adverse media coverage of what you hope to do wouldn't get the development onside with the locals, or anyone else for that matter.'

'The locals aren't my concern. I've found that the media focuses on who makes the most noise and misrepresents the truth for their own ends, or for whoever pays them the most. That would be right wouldn't it Clarry?'

Clarry didn't respond, he was too busy watching what the forensic team was up to in the sand dunes. Dittman glanced over Alex's shoulder, following Clarry's gaze.

'What are they doing Clarry?'

'Looks like they're bringing the body out,' he said.

All three of them turned to watch the forensic team lift a stretcher from behind the blue tarp. The body was masked in a white sheet that had been tucked in around it. The watching crowd were quiet as the remains were brought down, united in a sense of communal respect, each lost in their own thoughts. One of the men stumbled in the soft sand as they wrestled the stretcher over the uneven surface toward a white van parked rear up to the police tape. A policemen followed with a large garbage bag tied at the top with a label attached.

'Must be evidence.' Alex murmured.

'He's been there a long time,' said Tiger Dittman, in a quiet voice.

'I wonder how long they've been missing?' Alex mused.

'Twenty-three years,' whispered Clarry.

Alex stood silent, watching the stretcher disappear into the back of the panel van. There were no markings on the side, but an attendant was behind the wheel, and drove away slowly, the crowd silently stepping aside to give a clear passage through. He watched it drive all the way down to the first intersection, where it turned left and was lost from view. Alex turned back to Dittman, but he was already heading to his own car, gently pushing Clarry ahead of him.

As he watched Tiger Dittman and Clarry drive away, Alex was puzzled as he drove back to his Nerimbah beach unit. Perhaps he had missed an update, but he was acutely aware that the news report that morning did not mention anything about whether the body was male or female, or for how long he had been buried.

# CHAPTER 5

**Wednesday**

Villi Tanoa and Alex bickered their way along the hospital walkway, the Brisbane skyline distant through the windows, until they entered the closed confines of the main ward. Before them were rows of rooms with patients and closets full of medical equipment on both sides.

'I gave up a day of my holidays to drive you down here,' said Alex.

'Yeh, but you weren't doing much anyway.' Villi countered.

'You're just lucky Megan has gone up the mountains for the day with Bonny.' Megan had decided it was time to get in on the fight to save Cedar creek and had left Alex at a loose end. Alex paused to re-read the signage. 'Villi, are you sure your cousin is in ward B, on this level?'

'I told you, they said Level Three, ward B, room 27' stated Villi.

'I thought it said Maternity back there.'

'See, that's your problem Alex, you don't know how to read. Didn't they teach you anything at school?'

The two men continued to stride along the corridor, glancing up, to the side, even behind, not sure that they were in the right place.

'What's his name again? I can barely pronounce yours let alone his.'

'Geeze you're a racist bastard,' Villi quipped. 'Its Kamisese Rauluni, everyone calls him Kami. He's Narina's sisters' husband's nephew, that makes him my cousin, or uncle...I don't know which one, anyway he's a doctor now, looks like me too.'

'No one looks like you Villi, life is too short for anyone to look like you.'

'Don't piss me off Alex, or I won't take you home with me.'

Alex scoffed. 'I'm the one who drove you here, I'm doing you the favour, remember.'

Villi chortled as he strode further along the hallway, scanning left and right for his cousin's room. The big man was a long-standing friend from Nerimbah High School days, and even though Alex had spent most of his adult life in Melbourne, they still carried on like teenagers. Perhaps that was why Alex sought to reconnect with him after so many years. Villi Tanoa was of Fijian ancestry, his parents still lived at Dunoonan in the Nerimbah coast hinterland, but Villi was born for the sea and ran a successful boat chandlery in a set of shops facing the Nerimbah River. Alex never tired of his company and his constant twist of any conversation to work in his favour.

'There it is. See, I told you I'd find it.' Villi sped up, marching toward the door, the hobbled gait from his left foot a reminder of the accident that kept him ashore. He reached the door, pushed it open and stopped dead in his tracks. Alex looked over his shoulder, inside the room was full.

A young Fijian who Alex presumed was Kami, was sitting up in the hospital bed, but there were three others present, crammed into the small hospital room, and none of them were in hospital scrubs. All four looked expectantly at Villi and Alex, but it was the tallish older guy in the suit who immediately reacted and strode over to the door, pushing at Villi and Alex to back out into the hallway. He stepped out with them and closed the door behind him.

'Who are you?' protested Villi.

'I could ask you the same,' the suit retorted.

'I'm Kami's cousin, come to visit,' Villi replied and made to push past him, reaching for the door.

'Look, you can't go in yet, there's an interview underway.'

Villi stopped and looked quizzically at him.

'I'm Agent Hughes, Australian Federal Police...Deputy Commissioners Office for International Affairs.' He opened up his wallet so Villi could glance down all too briefly at his credentials before they were whisked away into his back pocket. 'Look, we are busy here now, but won't be for too long, it's just a formality. Maybe if you ducked downstairs for a coffee while you wait,' he said not unkindly, but Villi wasn't having a bar of it.

'What do you mean the Federal Police?' Villi bristled, 'Has Kami done something wrong?'

Hughes tried to pacify him by waving his hand up in Villi's face. He was tall and trim, his suit was a little loose on his frame, he was close to 50 and had the haircut of a policeman.

'No, nothing like that. But there's some people from the Cuban Consulate here wanting to talk with him. Nothing serious, OK!'

'Cuba? What's that got to do with Kami? He's not Cuban you know, he's Fijian, like me, can't you tell?' Villi didn't wait for an answer. 'He's a doctor in Nandi for God's sake, only here for an operation on his leg, not to invade Australia. Alex, this bloke has got him bundled up with a bunch of Cubans.' Villi once again made to push past Hughes to get into the room.

'Look Mr...what's your name?' Hughes inquired.

'Tanoa, the names Kai-Villi Tanoa, and that's my FIJIAN cousin in there,' Villi voice raised in protest, he pointed at the door over Hughes shoulder. Villi in full flight was a terrifying and belligerent figure. Alex gripped his arm, and gently squeezed it, not that Villi would have felt it the mood he was in. Alex leaned in close to Villi's ear as he tried to pacify him.

'Mate, perhaps we want to hear what he has to say first, OK?' Villi turned to Alex then back to Hughes, but Villi didn't back off, he stood inside the man's comfort zone, Hughes was up against the door, he had nowhere to go. To Hughes credit, he didn't flinch but spoke clearly and succinctly.

'Mr Tanoa, your cousin, Dr Rauluni, was training in Havana under a Cuban Scholarship program that finished only a month ago. When he was there, he may have witnessed a crime that the Cuban Police are interested in. They are merely wanting to find out what he may have seen. Dr Rauluni is not under investigation himself, alright. I'm here to assist the Cuban Officials, no more, that's all.'

Alex stayed close to Villi, keeping his hand on his shoulder, gently pulling him backwards. Villi started to respond when the door opened, and the two Cubans stood in the doorway. Villi was having none of this, his usual polite façade had taken a hit that morning and he pushed passed all three of them intent on seeing his cousin, showing no interest at all in the Cubans. Alex wisely chose not to follow. Villi slammed the door shut behind him and left all three in the hallway. From inside the room, came muffled greetings from Villi's booming voice.

'Well, that went well, don't you think?' Alex said to the Federal policeman.

Hughes ignored him and turned to the Cubans. The man was dressed in a tight grey suit, shiny black shoes, neat dark hair slicked back, an attaché case held tightly in his fingers. Now that's a Cuban, thought Alex, no faded dungarees and revolutionary flag draped over the shoulder for this one, a career diplomat if ever he saw one.

The woman standing next to him was quite tall, similar to his own height, with fair auburn hair tied up on top with a ribbon in the colours of the Cuban flag. From the brief glance he'd had of her seated next to Kami's bed he thought she was young, but now up close he figured she was closer to 40, dressed in jeans and a long sleeve cotton shirt, he wasn't expecting that. She must be the detective. He didn't know much about Cubans, but images of her in green army fatigues popped into his head, and that did seem to fit.

'Mr Hughes,' said the diplomat, 'Investigator Ramirez has everything she needs. We won't be requiring your assistance anymore. It was a mere formality, and it hardly needed the presence of the Australian Federal Police to chaperone us. However, if we require anything further, I'm sure you will be of some use.' The Cuban emphasised the word *Some* which made even Alex flinch. 'I'll be returning to Sydney on this afternoon's flight, and I'll pass on to the Consul General the pleasure we had of your company, even though we hadn't requested it.'

'Mr Souza, I'm glad to have been of help,' Hughes responded, his voice slow, methodical, diplomatic. 'I hope you got what you required, for a...what was it? A third Undersecretary of the Translation Department of the Cuban Consular Services?'

Good for you Hughesy, thought Alex, nice come back, you're not such a washed-up old copper after all.

'I'd drop you at the airport, but I'm not going that way.' Hughes continued. 'I have some important work at the George Street office in the city. Do you need directions on how to get to the airport, you can call a cab from downstairs easily enough.'

Alex smiled, sink the boot in Hughesy. By the look of Souza's scowl, he deserved it. Souza turned away and gestured for Inspector Rameriz to follow.

'Come,' said Anton Souza, third Undersecretary of the Translation Section of the Cuban Consulate, if that's what he really was. She in turn, nodded to Agent Hughes and turned to follow Souza, casting a glance over Alex as she passed him, probably wondering where he fitted in to all this.

Alex turned to Agent Hughes, but he was already marching off in the opposite direction.

He opened the door to Kamis room and stuck his head in. Kami was sitting up in bed, his leg propped in a sling suspended from the roof. He was deep in conversation with Villi who was sitting close to him, his head leaning in, their voices low in confidentiality.

'Heh, Villi, I'll be having a coffee downstairs when you finish here.' Alex called.

Villi raised his hand in recognition but didn't turn from what he was saying to Kami. Alex withdrew, closed the door after him and set off for the elevator at the end of the corridor. He heard the ding of the doors opening just as he rounded the corner and saw the two Cubans enter the lift. Two quick strides and he squeezed between the closing doors to end up facing the Diplomat Souza and the policewoman Ramirez.

'Hi again,' he smiled.

Souza turned his back on Alex and spoke to Ramirez in what Alex presumed was Spanish. The language ebbed and flowed, from one to the other, till Souza opened his attaché case and handed her an envelope which she glanced at but didn't open. A quick demand from Souza was met with a defiant shake of her head.

The lift hit ground floor, Alex stepped out, Souza strode passed him, heading for the big glass entry doors. Alex meandered across the foyer to the coffee shop and looked back at Investigator Ramirez, standing just outside the lift doors, deep in concentration as she read the sheet of paper from the envelope, a large soft travel bag at her feet. Alex watched her finish, fold it into her pocket, deep in thought. She glanced at her watch and looked around as if trying to make up her mind. On the front footpath, the Diplomat was trying to wave down a taxi with little success, she was making no move to join him. Alex smiled at her and pointed at the Italian coffee machine on the counter. She shrugged, picked up her bag and walked over in Alex's direction.

# CHAPTER 6.

**Wednesday**

Alex had finished placing the order for two coffees when Clara Ramirez sidled up next to him and reached into her small shoulder bag. Alex swept some change off the counter into his pocket and turned to her.

'You looked like you could use a coffee, so I've taken the liberty of ordering you a double shot. I've found two shots a safer bet in hospital cafes.'

'Is a double shot like two espressos?' she asked.

'Something like that, made with milk, like a latte. This brand is not bad, Italian. Shall we take a seat, they'll bring it over.'

He led the way through the cluster of small tables to one that was pushed up against a wall of glass, looking out at an indoor fernery. They both sat and looked at their surroundings, waiting for the coffee to arrive to ease the path into conversation between strangers. The café was half full, a mix of visitors and nursing staff on their breaks. Alex was surreptitious as he studied her, glancing in her direction as he rearranged the tables condiments, making room for the cups. She had dark skin with a hint of makeup, strong features for what he would have described as a handsome woman.

The waitress navigated her way between the tables and placed the two coffees on their table. He made a show of twisting off the end of a packet of sugar and stirring it in. Clara, opposite him scooped a small teaspoon full of foam into her mouth before taking a sip and putting the cup back down.

'It tastes good, I didn't expect that,' she remarked. 'I'm used to our Cuban coffee, it is much darker, and stronger. We call this a Café Con Leche in Havana.'

'Is that where you are from?' questioned Alex.

'Yes.'

'Sorry, its rude of me, I'm Alex Holmes,' he said, putting his hand out.

'Clara Ramirez,' She briefly returned the handshake.

'I'm a friend of Villi Tanoa's; it's his cousin you were interviewing. You met Villi as he barged past you into the room'.

'Yes. I think his shoulder introduced itself to me. I'm an Investigator with the National Revolutionary Police of Cuba.' Her voice displayed a confidence in speaking English but there was no escaping the differing pronunciations that revealed Spanish as her native language.

'So, what brings the Cuban Police to Brisbane?' he enquired.

'The coffee of course,' she quipped back, deflecting that line of enquiry, Alex noted. 'I usually have a Cafecito, some call it Cubano. It is sweet, strong and very milky. Its traditional. My mother used to make it after dinner as a treat when I was young. We lived in the mountains near Cienfuegos, where it would get cold in winter, and a Cubano would warm us up.'

'Cold? In Cuba?' Alex asked incredulously.

'Yes. Of course it is. The mountains are cold in February, especially when it rains. You do not know much about Cuba, I think. Coffee is good to warm you, but you are right, it is not something we usually need to do in Cuba, maybe only in the mountains.'

'Couldn't agree more. In the Himalayas, the Sherpas brew this dreadful stuff called Mustang Coffee. Spoonful of instant coffee in melted butter, milk and rum, then stir in mountains of sugar. It's supposed to warm you up at night. Now they need it.'

'Ergh! Coffee with butter! Sounds horrible and you would drink this?'

'Only when I had to, and smile while I did it.'

'I think you are a brave man.' She joked. 'My mother would whip the sugar and milk into a foam, it's called Espumita, before making a layer on the espresso. She would add some drops of the espresso to the foam to make it brown and creamy. Cuban coffee is better I think.'

'You get no argument from me there.' He was enjoying this; she was very easy to talk with. Her command of English excellent and she understood the nuances of what he said. Clara, in turn, was sharp enough to counter any of his probes.

You aren't' going back to the Consulate with your friend?' Alex asked.

'I'm not with the Consulate.'

'Oh yes, that Federal Policeman said you were following up a crime from Cuba.'

'Mr Hughes says too much.'

'I'm sorry, I didn't mean to pry,' Alex apologised, totally meaning to pry.

'And what do you do Mr Holmes?' Clara switched tack again.

'Please, call me Alex. Can I call you Clara?'

'Of course.'

'Good. I'm in Media production in Melbourne; I produce a TV program about past criminal cases that haven't been solved.'

'So, you are also a policeman?'

'No, not at all, but we do uncover some interesting things in our investigations which we pass on to the police. It's called *The Cold Cases*.'

'We have had that television in Havana, it was called *Caso sin Resolver*, very similar. But of course, there are very few crimes that are not solved in Cuba, we have a very high success rate. Ours mostly centre on crimes before the Revolution, more as a history lesson. And you do this in Melbourne? It's a city in the south, yes? So why are you here? One of your programs?'

'Not at all, I'm on holiday, up the coast at Nerimbah. I just drove Villi down today to see his cousin.'

Clara seemed to sit up a little taller in the chair, immediately interested.

'And what is at Nerimbah, is it a holiday place?' she asked.

'Nerimbah is on the beach, white sand and surf, it has a river, lots of boats, lots of sunshine, a typical Queensland beach town. Bit like Havana I guess.'

'Maybe not as old,' she observed. 'And is there a harbour?'

'Very much so. Fishing boats, yachts, we have the best beaches. I grew up there. The beach is a big part of Australia, it's a life, a culture, I'm not explaining this well, it's what many of us dream of, to live near the ocean. If you've got time, come up and have a look, I'll show you around, that would help explain what I'm getting at.'

She had a natural air about her, it was refreshing. For a Police Officer, she was not as officious or direct as he thought she would be. Alex looked at her, trying to gauge how genuine she was with her reactions.

'I grew up on a farm,' she said, taking another sip from her coffee. 'I saw the sea for the first time when I was nine, it was at *Bahia de Cochinos*...you might know it as the Bay of Pigs. The water was beautiful, clear and warm where we swam. My father wanted to show it to us, it was where the Americans invaded in 1961 but were beaten back. My father was a policeman then. He fought at the Bay of Pigs alongside the army, he even got to drive an armoured car, there was one just like it at the Museum de Playa Giron. That's the beach where some of the Americans landed,' she added, for his benefit. 'I'm sorry. I'm talking too much,' she said, and brought her coffee to her lips.

'No, not at all,' remarked Alex. 'Please go on, I love hearing about it.'

'He was so proud when I said I wanted to become a policewoman, to serve the Revolution, and one day be able to defend Cuba like he did, because it is the greatest honour.'

'Is he still alive?'

'No. he passed some years back.'

Clara turned to look out into the fern garden, lost in thought, the sound of cups, cutlery and low murmured voices in the background. Alex sat back and let his mind wander as he waited patiently for her to return. He could spend all afternoon talking with this woman, he thought. Megan would have criticised the coffee and café they were sitting in now, she could be exhausting when she opted to play the privileged Melbournite. Clara however, enjoyed discussing differences rather than find fault in them, and she was certainly unlike that Cuban diplomat, now he was a pretentious little prick.

'Did you know there is an Australia in Cuba?' Clara broke the silence.

'Nooo!' Alex drew out his reply in mock indignation.

'There is, and it's quite famous. It's a small town near the Bay of Pigs. It's where Fidel set up his base to defend Cuba from the Americans.

'How do you know all this?'

'My father showed me...and we learned about it at school and again at University. History is very important to Cubans.'

'I'd like to think it is for us as well.'

'So maybe our countries are not so far apart, we both have Australia.'

'That settles it, you must come up the coast, see our beaches. How long are you here?'

'I have nine days, but for some of that I will still be working. Do you sail Mr Holmes?'

'Yes, I do,' he answered, taken aback at the shift in conversation. He leaned forward and lowered his voice. 'Are you working now?' he asked cheekily.

'No,' she was adamant, recoiling from his question. Alex however, thought otherwise, but decided to leave it there and put it away for later.

'I like to sail when I can,' he said. 'I don't own a boat, but I might be able to get you a sail on one if you come up. Would that entice you?'

'I've never sailed before, and I will not get many opportunities to sail on a yacht in Cuba. You know, I like the thought that yachts can come and go as they please, whenever they like... from all over the world, they have a freedom. So yes, I would like to taste a little bit of that freedom.'

'If you don't mind my asking, what is to stop you from just staying here in Australia if you wish, when you finish your work. I mean, in the 70's, every Communist sympathiser wanted to hijack a plane to Cuba, but surely there are people who would want it the other way around, want to get out. The last two decades proved that more people today want to leave Communist countries that get in. I know travel is very difficult for Cubans, and the United States has sanctions on your country.'

'Don't get me wrong Mr Holmes...'

'Please, call me Alex.'

'Of course.... Alex. Please understand, I am a Lieutenant, a Chief Investigating Officer in the Cuban National Revolutionary Police...there are not many women like me in Havana, or all of Cuba. It has taken me a long time to get to that, and to be allowed to leave my country...and allowed to return. No. There are not many like me. I love my country; I believe in our Revolution. It is not a perfect system, I can say that here, but I am first and foremost, a Cuban.' She took the last of the coffee in one gulp and stared straight at him as she placed the cup firmly on the saucer. Take that, thought Alex, shame on you for even hinting at her not going back, let alone asking for political asylum. Clara Ramirez lowered her eyes and her voice. '...and my family still lives there.'

Alex stared at her, she looked up, their eyes locked momentarily, and he nodded his understanding of the complexity of her allegiances. She leaned back in her chair, sighed heavily, and placed both hands on the table, their time here was coming to an end.

'I don't know why I tell you this, Alex Holmes, but I think you are a good listener, and you have done this before. You would make a good Policeman.'

'No one has ever accused me of that.' Alex laughed. 'But seriously, I'll give you my phone number. Come up the coast and if you want to taste freedom that much, I will find a sail for you. I have connections, I have a Villi Tanoa.'

'What's that?'

'You met him earlier.'

'Oh him!' She laughed, pulling at her hair and standing, brushing her shirt to neaten it before departure.

Alex handed her one of his Media Production cards with his number on it. Clara pulled out the crumpled envelope from her top pocket and slipped the card into it. She held out her hand to Alex, which he willingly took, he thought he'd played that well, sure in the knowledge that they will meet again.

'Thank you for the coffee and conversation. I'll be here tomorrow, but then maybe I can come up to your beach and see if it lives up to your boasting, see if it is a match for Varadero, she said, referring to the beach resort close to Havana. 'Maybe I can call you on Friday.'

'That will work for me. In the meantime, I'll persuade Villi to find us a sail on someone's yacht, he can be very persuasive.'

'That would be a pleasure. Until then.' She promptly turned and strode toward the doors.

Alex watched her all the way before sitting down to finish his cold coffee and ponder over the last half hour. Particularly the point when she stashed his card into the envelope from her breast pocket. Part of the sheet inside was reversed, revealing a few typed lines. Ordinarily Alex wouldn't have taken any notice if wasn't for the last word on one of the lines...Nerimbah. Why would she have a letter from the Consulate that mentioned Nerimbah, a coastal town, his coastal town. He wondered who was playing who?

# CHAPTER 7

### Wednesday

Villi was unusually quiet on the drive home to Nerimbah. Sunset over the range of mountains inland from the highway cocooned them in soft evening light, headlights briefly illuminating them each time a car passed in the opposite direction.

'Kami's operation went well?' Alex asked.

'Yep, the surgeon reattached the fine nerve ends that the silly bugger ripped in the fall.'

'So, you can report back to Nerina that all's well.'

'Yep,' he replied, shortly.

'What about the other, that business with the Cubans?'

'What of it!' Villi said testily.

'You didn't tell me why they were there?'

'Oh, that,' said Villi, as if it was an afterthought. 'Kami may have been a witness to a murder in Havana while he was studying there. He was renting a room that overlooked the harbour where some customs officer was shot on a yacht, and apparently the landlord dobbed him in as a possible witness.'

'No kidding. And was he? Did he see it?'

'Nah. Not a chance, if he wasn't out chasing girls in a bar, he'd have been flat out on the bed sleeping. Didn't see a thing he told them. Wasn't even sure he was home that night.'

'A long way to send an Inspector just to ask a few routine questions. That guy from the Consulate could have done it without sending a policewoman specially from Havana. It's not as if Kami would be involved with anything illegal is it?'

Villi looked sharply at Alex. 'Why do you say that?'

"Well, a Fijian boy, in Cuba, on a student scholarship to become a doctor is hardly the criminal element. Kami looks like he wouldn't hurt a fly.'

'He's a good boy Kami, and I wouldn't want to hear otherwise.'

'He was in Havana, though,' chided Alex, prodding the bear. 'Those sexy Cuban girls and a tall, handsome Fijian boy... just saying.'

'As long as that's all he did. Which is what it is, nothing more, alright? Nothing's going to get back to Nerina or her family about anything that didn't happen, OK?' Villi warned seriously.

'OK Villi. I get it. Nothing but a bit of cultural exchange.'

'That's right.'

'Was he wearing a condom?' Alex blurted out laughing.

'Shut up man, you talk too much,' Villi grinned back.

'I'm not the talker, you were in there with Kami long enough, what did you guys talk about?'

'Nothing much...family gossip...that's all.'

They lapsed into silence for a while, the steady thrum of the tyres on bitumen threatening to put Alex to sleep. He gripped the wheel a little harder and shuffled his butt in the seat in an effort to stay alert while he drove.

'Speaking of Cubans, did I tell you how much I enjoyed coffee with Clara, the Police Investigator this afternoon?'

'Yeh, twice now.'

'Her father was at the Bay of Pigs.'

'Yeh, you told me that too.'

'Right.... well, she might be coming up on Friday, and I need you to find me someone with a yacht that I can take her out on. You must know some yachties, they're your best customers after every race. They love breaking gear. Is there a race on this weekend, or a sail out around Dinnan Rocks or Florette Shoals?'

'Has she sailed before?'

'No. I'd go with her, keep an eye on her. There would be two of us.'

'What about Megan?' Villi asked pointedly.

'Oh, she'd come too I guess,' Alex said, as an afterthought.

'So that would make three extra crew.'

'I guess so,' admitted Alex.

'I'll see what I can do. There's a guy owns a yacht always looking to go for a sail. He keeps buying little bits for his boat. Came in last week wanting an ice maker, I don't stock that sort of thing, but I'll certainly charge him for the one I've ordered in. He's coming in tomorrow to pick it up, I'll ask him when he's going out next, or if he's interested in taking you out for a sail. An extra three people on his boat wouldn't make any difference, there's plenty of room. I'll let you know.'

'Thanks Villi, you're a champion. You're not at all like what everyone else says.'

'Get fucked Alex,'

'That's what I like to hear.'

'Are you sure Megan won't mind you taking a good-looking Cuban woman along for the ride?'

'I don't know yet. That one remains to be seen. You reckon she was good looking?'

'I tell you what, I would have hit the roof if Nerina came home with a Cuban bloke, telling me he's just a friend she met, and she wants to take him sailing with her. Are you sure you know what you're doing?' questioned Villi.

'Mate, she's a Policewoman from Havana visiting for a few days and I'm helping her to understand what life is like in Australia compared to Cuba. Think of it as advancing International Relations.'

Yeh...sure Alex, you just keep telling yourself that.'

For some reason, Alex didn't tell Villi about her envelope, or how Nerimbah was written on the letter, and coming up was probably already on her agenda before he invited her. That she had already had a brush with Villi's family was obviously a prickly subject with Villi, he saw no reason to advance that area of thought any further today. He flicked his indicator left and moved across a lane to turn at the sign pointing the way to the Nerimbah coast. Only another ten minutes to home.

# CHAPTER 8

**Wednesday**

The taxi dropped Clara off outside the Brisbane Best Hostel near the city centre in The Valley district. The hostel had been booked by Colonel Perez's office back in Havana, and they clearly had no idea about what they were booking. Clara only knew a few people who had been outside of Cuba, and no one she knew of had ever been to Australia, this was the other side of the world, and she thought that this hostel was the cheapest part of it.

The driver looked over his shoulder and gave her a look that bordered on reproach.

'Are you sure you want to get dropped here? Is this the right place?' He offered in fatherly reproach.

Yes, I'm sure,' she said.

'You're not from here are you love?'

'No.'

'By the look of you I'd have thought that.' He tapped at the meter and took note of the numbers.

'So, where you from?' he called over his shoulder, counting out the change to her $50 note.

'Havana, Cuba.'

'Here on holiday?' His eyes looked at hers in the rear-view mirror, awaiting the answer.

'Something like that,' she said, sliding across the back seat with her bag in tow. The footpath was hot and dusty, shops along the sidewalk were mostly food take aways, others were vacant, partly boarded up. It was that kind of place.

The Hostel was next to the Fortitude Hotel, the entrance marked by the neon *B & B* letters above the door. A secondary door in the foyer led directly into the ground floor bar where a few old men sat sipping on their beers, leaning on the polished countertop. The bar smelled of stale beer and smoke. The hostel was part of the hotel, so Clara got the key to her room from the middle-aged woman tending the counter, fairly disinterested in the whole process. Clara pushed through the dark wooden door and up the stairs to the first landing to find her room. It was just her luck that it was directly above the bar.

It was small but neat and clean which surprised her, and she had her own bathroom with a toilet that flushed first time. Clara heaved her bag up on the bed and shuffled onto the pillows leaning up against the bedhead. She took the envelope from her pocket and searched for the folded sheet of paper Sousa the Consulate official had given her. Alex Holmes' card fell onto the bedspread.

The first part of the letter dealt with an update on phone contacts for the Consulate that were to be used to pass on progress reports each day to the Ministry of the Interior in Havana. She also knew that Police Colonel Perez wanted private reports each day as well. No fucking chance, she thought.

What drew her immediate attention was a report on the arrival in Nandi harbour of two yachts matching the size and description of the *Harmony*, but only one had indicated a forward passage to Australia. The yacht was called *Cosmos*, and the time frame and passage fitted the profile of the yacht she was seeking, and although it had a different name, it would have been easy enough to have changed it and fabricate papers to suit. Maybe the same yacht, but a new name. It had passed through the Panama Canal and stopped briefly in Fiji before departing for Nerimbah, Australia 14 days ago. She had no idea how long it would take to sail that distance, or when to expect the yacht, but she knew someone who would.

She picked up the card Alex Holmes had given her and noted his role as an Executive Producer of Peninsular Media in Melbourne, with a cell phone contact. He had invited her to go sailing at Nerimbah on Friday, that will get her to the place she needed to go, give her a local contact and put her around lots of yacht people. She glanced between the letter and the card, now that is progress, she smiled to herself, Investigator Ramirez, she liked the sound of that.

Clara loved the Police. She loved the structure and the processes of her work every day. Her whole life had been secure in the sanctity of the state, in its cocooning presence, and the Police force was an extension of that security. She believed in Castro's socialist state and revolutionary equality, no matter how often it was abused. She pinned her own morals to upholding the laws of her country and knew only too well the highs and lows of protecting that society. If nothing else, her loyalty to Cuba was undeniable.

She re-read the last line. *Your mother and brother are in good health.* Fuck. It was nothing but a thinly veiled threat. Why did they write that? Why did they feel it necessary to threaten her? It wouldn't have been Perez...strangely enough, she trusted her superior. It had to have been General Abelardo, something his Security Division would come up with. Unless she obeyed her orders and returned to Cuba, her family would face consequences.

Her brother Raul? Good luck with that, he was an anarchist. He'd already been jailed once for anti-government sentiment. Clara had used what little influence she had to get the magistrate to go easy on him, citing his youth and ignorance of the goals of the revolution to gain a more lenient sentence. It nearly cost her job. Perez had hauled her over the coals for that one, pointing out that she obviously didn't understand Cuban law or its close relationship with the National Revolutionary Police Department. Family members were not absolved from this ignorance. It was only when Clara declared that she would be responsible for Raul with promises to curb her brothers' activities, that got him a slight reprieve. In a place where every transaction in life could be linked to black market spending, or corruption, knowing that laws protected everyone in society allowed her to uphold her beliefs, to be a moral compass for her family. That was her fall-back position.

Raul in turn hated her for it. He told her she was interfering in something far bigger than Cuba's petty socialist experiment. It was time for change, and he was starting a black-Market economy in protest, there was no room for politics, or the police who were just lackeys of a corrupt state. He didn't want her to come near him again. She wasn't sure where Raul was living now, he had cut off all contact with her, but sure as hell, the Ministry of the Interior Security Division would know. The Security Division would also know that she had risked her career to protect her brother once but may not do so again. She and Raul were both realists and understood the human cost of being on opposite sides of the revolution. Raul had chosen his.

Clara's mother, Valerina Consuela Ramirez on the other hand, needed all the protection that Clara could give her, and was the perfect candidate.

Valerina was oblivious to reality, so she just ignored the revolution. On the surface, she dealt with the scarcity of food and the shortages with masked criticism, but deep down, Valeria Ramirez was a bitter woman. She was 19 when Batista was removed. Castros revolution had stripped her of the life of glamour that the Americans had brought to Havana, the music, the bars, the movie stars, these were the things she had been born to. The Revolution put an end to that. She hated the modern Cuba, the socialist state that Clara had sworn to protect, and she took it out on Clara at every opportunity. To her, the new Cuba was an abomination. Her husband was once a policeman who should have used his position for the privilege and perks that it brought, like it did during Batista's reign, but instead he upheld the law, and was proud of his role in defending Cuba's ideals. To Valerina, the Cuban missile crisis and Bay of Pigs were only an opportunity to admire Jacqueline Kennedy's dress on the cinema newsreels. And now her own daughter had joined the Police... to dress like a man. Why couldn't she be more like Raul, who came around once every six months with some embargoed American perfume that Valeria thought was reminiscent of the grand days of Havana. Instead, Clara visited every week with fresh vegetables, and washing powder whenever she could get it from the markets, only to be told it was of poor quality or the wrong brand. Clara was the embodiment of everything that was wrong in Valerina's life. She was the target of her mother's bitterness, but without her, she was lost. The Security Division would know that too, they had leverage over them both. Tomorrow she would ring the Consulate.

She threw the page on the bed, stripped off and squeezed into the small shower cubicle, luxuriating in the constant stream of hot water, washing away the 36 hours of plane travel. With a towel wrapped around her, she perched on the edge of the bed and opened the shutters that gave her a view of the Brisbane skyline as the lights began to come on. She marvelled at the brightness of their colours. It seemed that they didn't have water or power cuts here.

One by one, the lights around the inner-city blocks twinkled on and merged with the sunset to bring a life to the darkness, and a different world from the daytime. It happened like this in Havana too, but previously she hadn't taken as much notice of the beauty, certainty she could never take it for granted. Each night at dusk, her neighbours sat in doorways or leaned out shuttered windows, waiting expectantly for the darkness to be replaced by lights before they went inside to start the nights alternate life. Sometimes, it just didn't happen, and the darkness was replaced by more darkness. Clara would light candles and postpone her dinner and shower as she waited for the power to come back on. When it did, it came suddenly, as if to taunt her that she should be more patient in the future, to stop trying to outguess if she would be left with dirty dishes in the sink and no water to wash them. She would look in the fridge and formulate plans for dinner the next night in expectation, but it was never a certainty. Even when she had power, the water in the shower only dribbled from the nozzle.

She changed out of her towel into fresh jeans and a bright floral peasant top with a neckline that took advantage of her figure. She brushed her hair out and looked in her bag for some high heels. A cold beer and perhaps some conversation was on offer for a single Cuban woman among the reveller's downstairs in the bar. At night the place came alive with music and shouting that meant it was useless to try and sleep before the bar closed, so Clara retired to her room around 10, but didn't get to sleep before 1pm when the young American backpacker left.

# CHAPTER 9

### Thursday

The Thursday had started well. In the morning, Villi rang to ask Alex to come for dinner that night, and to say that he had found someone for a boat on Friday if his Cuban friend was still up for a sail. Clara had rung shortly after, and they had arranged to meet at the Yacht club the next day. Alex jumped at all three invitations, smiling as he looked forward to a day to himself while Megan took the car up the range.

She had tracked down an article about Tiger Dittman for Bonny, who promptly labelled him the 'Cedar Creek murderer'. She was going to have signs drawn up to say so. The two of them would visit the local paper and point out all the shortcomings of the Cedar Vale development on the environment, and Tigers distinct role in perpetrating the outrage. Bonny had a point, thought Alex, he was keen to see how it would play out. Bob Browns Franklin River protest was a blueprint for environmental protest twenty years ago and the subject of many documentaries since. There was a lot to be learned in his perceptive use of the media for his cause. Megan and Bonny were also going to canvas the Cedar Vale community to shore up the various plans of action. She was in her element, she was good at this, and she could talk a formidable argument.

Alex lazed the morning away, reading the papers, trying to make sense of the war in Afghanistan and the government's stance on sending asylum seekers to Nauru. It was coming up to a year since the Boxing Day Tsunami in Indonesia, and the photos brought back all the horror of that event. He decided to go a bit closer to home and reached for the article on Tiger Dittman that Megan left for him.

The story focused on Dittman's backfilling wetlands near Brisbane for a housing project gone wrong. He mulled over the comments Clarry the dozer driver had let slip at Hideaway beach about the dune body, trying to make sense of that too, but didn't get anywhere beyond the sinister undertone that they already knew who it was and how he died. Just another piece on the shelf to take down later if or when he needed to use it. However, he was here on holidays and the surf beckoned. He felt game enough to get another board for a paddle in the small waves.

This time he hired one from the same surf shop as last time, only a little larger, a 7'6" Na Papa fibreglass mini-mal with a thin wooden stringer down the middle. He negotiated the rough path down the cliff at Georges Headland and slid across the mossy shelf to the water's edge. He flipped the board over to protect the three fins and leaned on it for stability as he gingerly picked his way over the submerged rocks in shin deep water, slowly making his way deeper. When he was up to his waist, he flipped the board back the right way up, and launched himself over a small foam breaker, paddling strongly out to the line up off the point. It was the middle of the day and had most of the small waves to himself. The legion of tradies had left the water, engaged in keeping the economy going in the building industry. They usually surfed from dawn till 8 am, swamping the breaks with each other and fighting off school students until both were required at their respective places of work, leaving the surf to vacationers like Alex, and a few hardened old fellows who hadn't given up on the sport with retirement.

The surf had settled down and was running at a clean two foot wave that behaved itself well enough on the mid tide. It would start to get a bit shallow and faster as the tide dropped, but Alex knew he would be long gone by then. Just off the point, where the last rocks of the wave cut platform disappeared under water, he turned the board and swept onto a small right-hand break. It took a bit longer getting to his feet, but this board was more stable and once there, all the freedom and joy came back as the board moved effortlessly beneath him. Pushing back with his right leg and aiming higher on the face rewarded him with more speed, enough to thrust far in front of the breaking lip, out along the mounding wall till he pushed down hard with his back foot and twisted his body to the left, carving a neat spray of water as the rail cut into the wall and brought him around in a smooth arc back to the peeling edge.

He immediately reversed direction and set himself up to repeat the same manoeuvre. He did it a second time and was in the process of the third, when he noticed that the depth of water had shallowed considerably. At this point Alex needed to flick out immediately and save the board and himself from running aground. He couldn't help himself, against his better judgement, he continued the turn and ran the board straight over the shallows, slamming the fins into the rock shelf. Alex pitched forward as the board stopped dead, cartwheeling in an ignominious fall from grace into the shallow water, bruising on the barely submerged rocks. He struggled to his feet looking for dings on the board, then flipped it over, revealing the left-hand fin had been ripped from its mount and was dangling by a few threads of fibreglass.

'Shit!'

When he returned the board to the surf shop, the owner looked quizzically at the damaged fin then glanced at Alex's last board in the rack, different coloured fibreglass patches showing where it had been repaired from his last effort.

'You're not here for the surfing are you mate?' he remarked dryly to Alex.

Hubris had brought him undone again.

When Megan arrived home that afternoon, she was full of purpose, revitalized and eager. Alex's injured pride had recovered enough by then. They had a swim together and shared the shower in the unit before making love on the bed, luxuriating in the cool breeze from the open window that dried the sweat and moisture from their bodies. However, it was over dinner at Villi's house that it all began to unravel.

At first, the conversation ebbed and flowed around Villi and Nerina's children, their family, and the media and chandlery businesses as both couples learned about each other. Alex explained how he hadn't known Villi much at high school. They moved in different circles until the end of year 9, during the Xmas holiday break, when Alex tried to teach Villi how to surf. It was a failure all round, but they became friends over a lot of laughter. Villi just wasn't built for riding the waves, he was much more at home on top of them in a boat.

Alex watched Megan size up Nerina. She was well-practiced in the art of social subterfuge, he knew the signs, the subtle inflictions of tone designed to reveal weaknesses that she could exploit in later conversation. In Nerina, she would find an honest and powerful adversary. You don't get to raise four children to adulthood in a small fishing community like Nerimbah unless you earn the respect of the people around you.

Villi was as expansive as usual, his body shaking every time he guffawed at his own jokes while he retold stories. Nerina was smaller in stature, but no less impressive, organised and efficient in running the dinner gathering, she certainly complimented the imposing presence of Villi.

She issued instructions for the serving of dinner to Xavier, the youngest of the four children who had failed to find an alternative escape route for the night and been cashiered into acting as waiter for the evening. He was only sixteen but was well on the way to matching Villi's physique. Xavier went about his tasks with a pretend objection, complaining that he had much better things to do with his time, like cleaning his room. This brought Villi to fits of laughter. Xavier brought two more beers from the fridge to their table. Villi tried to tickle him, to his son's obvious embarrassment, but the episode ended with grins from both sides. An act that had been played out before. Xavier would end up like his old man, a true force of good nature.

'And don't you try to take one of those beers for yourself, you're not old enough to drink.' Exclaimed Villi. Xavier winked at him with a sly grin as he disappeared into the kitchen. Yeh right, thought Alex, he could hear the opening of the fridge door from where he sat. Alex looked around again as he sipped at his can. The dining room wall was a mix of photos of family and fishing boats amid various curved and highly polished wooden implements from Fiji, warm, friendly, nostalgic.

'What's that?' Alex asked, pointing at one of the tools on the wall, no idea what it could be used for.

'Don't change the subject,' said Villi, returning to a previous conversation. 'You knew your mate Beau was already here when you came to the shop three years back. Pretending he'd been drowned all that time, acting all innocent like. And you let me prattle on about how Beau deserved to drown for being so stupid to go fishing in a storm with those two other halfwits.' He turned to Megan. 'Have you met Beau?' he asked her.

'I have,' she replied, with little enthusiasm. 'He showed up in Melbourne in an old yellow Monaro, thinking Alex would drop everything and go surfing in Western Australia with him.'

'Typical,' snorted Villi.

'When I was here last time, I couldn't say anything about Beau. We were here for his mother's funeral,' he explained for Nerrina's benefit,'and Beau had been presumed dead for the last twenty years.'

'Why was that?' Nerina queried.

'Long story, won't bore you with it.'

Megan butted in. 'I don't even know, Nerina, there's a lot of things Alex doesn't talk about, doesn't tell me till after it's happened.' She pointed out, looking at Alex.' I only ever get half the story.'

Alex was under attack from all sides, but it was Nerina who saved the day. 'That's all in the past I think Villi, don't badger him. There's lots of stuff in the past that should stay there.' She pointed good naturedly at Villi.

'Don't be like that,' protested Villi, the smile disappearing from his face.

Alex sensed a chance to change topic and waded in.

'What do you think about the body in the dunes?' asked Alex.

'What body?' said Megan.

'The one at Hideaway Beach, I told you about it. There was a body recovered from the sand the other day. That storm surf uncovered it; been there for a long time the Police said.' Alex explained, deflecting the conversation away from himself.

'I didn't hear about that. Did you know about that Villi?' Nerina enquired.

'Yeh, I heard,' he said seriously. It's been in all the papers.'

'Well, I never get to read them till after you've finished with the sport section,' she accused Villi. 'What did they say?'

'Only what Alex said, that they don't know who it is yet, you know how the papers are.' He turned to Alex. 'Are you right for tomorrow?' he asked, switching topic.

'What time?'

'11.30 at the Marina. It's a yacht called *Cheetah*, owned by a bloke called Glenn Bertlemann, he'll come and pick you up at the end of B finger. Meet him there.'

'Are you going sailing?' asked Megan, raising her eyebrows at yet another piece of newfound knowledge.

'Yeh. I organized it on the way back from the hospital the other day.'

'Is your guest coming too?' Villi asked pointedly, staring straight at Alex.

'What guest?' Megan flicked between the two men. 'Do you mean me, am I going?' she asked.

Alex mentally composed how best to explain it, but before he got a word out, Villi marched right in.

'Alex met a Cuban Policewoman at the hospital on Thursday,' he explained, pretending innocence. 'He's invited her to go sailing with him tomorrow.'

'What do you mean she?' asked Megan, turning the heat back on Alex.

'Clara is an Investigator from Havana, here for a few days, and I thought it would be good for her to see the coast,' he explained, as if it was all perfectly above board. 'We had a coffee together, that's all.' And that made it worse.

Megan said nothing in response, sat quietly, readjusting to the indignity at finding out something that everyone else at the table already knew. The look Alex got from her was as cold as the white wine she was sipping. That was when Nerina stepped in to try and salvage the dinner party.

'Who wants dessert? She asked gayly, but the night was already lost. Neither had much to say after the dinner party, Megan was silent for the drive home.

Alex and Megan stood just inside the verandah door to their third-floor unit overlooking Nerimbah Bay, together, but apart. *The Breakers* was only two years old and next door to *Sailfish Bay* where he had stayed three years ago. In truth, he couldn't tell the buildings apart, the high-rise holiday apartments all looked the same, sporting grand entrances and shopfronts facing the beach, with tall glass facades encased in white stucco reaching ten stories above the shorefront. He had tried to rent a house on the esplanade overlooking the river, but Megan had wanted something newer, with a view of the beach. At nighttime the lights from the park splayed out over the sand, and lit up the edges of the advancing surf, outlining the white foam as it marched its way inland with the incoming tide. A soft rhythmic crump of the waves breaking and surging ashore drifted up to the units lulling the occupant to sleep in the evenings. But neither Alex nor Megan were listening to that tonight.

'You didn't tell me you were taking a Cuban woman sailing!' Megan said quietly, staring out at the inky blackness of the bay. 'Am I coming too or were you planning on keeping this one to yourself?'

'It's not like that Megan, of course you can come, I just didn't think you'd be interested, you've never really expressed the desire to go sailing when I've gone before.'

"'Well, that's not your decision to make.'

'True. I know that now.' Alex mumbled apologetically and lapsed into silence.

'You should have known then. I'm going to bed,' Megan announced with finality, closing the bedroom door firmly behind her. That hadn't gone well, in fact the whole evening had ended up a disaster. He went looking for the rum bottle.

# CHAPTER 10

**Friday**

Alex woke on the couch; his head skewed up against the oversized cushions. Megan was leaning over him, shaking his shoulder. He sat up and looked out at the early morning sunlight and a seagull strutting back and forward on the verandah railing.

'What did you sleep out here for?' Megan asked.

'I thought you had locked the door.'

'Well, I hadn't. I don't know what made you think I'd do that.'

Alex didn't say anything, he had a fair idea what it had been, but perhaps he was the one over thinking it now.

'Come on, what are you getting me for breakfast? We're going sailing today,' she said cheerfully. 'Going to need something in our stomach, that's what you do isn't it?

Alex was bemused. Silence and an awkward shuffle around the kitchen were what he expected until relations thawed enough to discuss the menial tasks. This was different, in one way he was relieved at Megans conciliatory approach, but he was still wary that it may be a ruse for later retribution.

Megan sat at the café, coffee and a fresh juice in front of her, while Alex steered away from the big breakfast with bacon, and opted for raisin toast instead. Fatty foods were to be avoided, even though the yacht would hardly roll in the gentle swell today. Megan chatted about what they would need to take for the day, food, drinks.

'This woman you're bringing, she'll probably like a white wine. I'll introduce her to a Sauvignon Blanc, she wouldn't get that in Cuba, something light and fruity for a day like this.' She pointed to the side of the café where the sun was creeping along under the awning, lighting up the tables and chairs, forcing a couple to seek the shade.

'Maybe she wants rum. The Cubans practically invented the stuff.'

'Don't exaggerate,' she said.

'It's the Caribbean. Boats, Cubans, rum, they're all made for each other,' Alex said expansively.

Megan had stopped smiling. He realised he'd pushed it a bit far.

'She's getting white wine.' Megan said with dead pan finality. 'Did you read that article on Tiger Dittman that I left you yesterday? The one about his draining the wetlands.'

'Yeh, it seems he's had plenty of practice filling in waterways to make land for building. Those houses never stood a chance in the floods, why the council let them develop that land in the first place I don't know, it was always a floodplain to begin with.'

'We talked with one of the residents, they've started legal action against him. I got her name from the paper, she's suing the developer, but that's not Dittman, he was just the blunt implement, the tool that did it. Turns out the developer was a Singapore company that paid him for it. How do they get to do that here?'

'I read that they couldn't get Dittman for that one, it wasn't illegal. So if you want to get him, you have to find something illegal to get him on, something that's against the State or Federal laws, or creates enough public sentiment that the Council is able to put a stop work order on it till it's been investigated, and they can come up with something in the law to use. Otherwise, people like Dittman just ride over the top of you. Has Bonny found anything she can use about platypus in the creek?'

'No, nothing yet apart from usual wildlife conservation in general. Its only just started.' Megan dug into her handbag and brought out another article on Tiger Dittman, smoothing out the folds and twisting it around so that Alex could see the headline and photo in the top left corner.

'But we did find another story on Dittman, an old one.'

'Where did you get this?' The page was yellow with age and torn down one side.

'Back issue from *The Weekly*, the regional newspaper at Dunoonan.'

'Did you rip this out of the paper? From their archives?'

Megan looked defiant.

'Well, it's pretty old, and not like anyone else needs it.'

'You sneaky thing.' Alex smiled at her.

The headline read *Terry the Tiger of Hideaway Beach*. The large black and white photo showed a younger Dittman making some comment off camera with his arm disappearing behind a tall blond woman in a low-cut evening dress holding a martini glass. She was looking straight at the camera, laughing. Nothing shy about her. The caption read *Terry and Gloria Dittman celebrating the opening of their fashion studio 'Gloria' at Hideaway Beach.*

'Who's holding up who up in this photo?' Alex pointed.

'Not too much holding her in either. She looks drunk.'

> 'Gloria, that's an old-fashioned name, you don't hear it much these days.

Maybe she's an old-fashioned girl?'

'Hardly,' said Megan, 'look at that photo, she's mutton dressed as lamb, a fair bit older than Dittman I think. Looks exactly like one of those hangers-on in Melbourne, got nothing, want everything.'

'Now! Now don't get catty.' Alex leaned in closer to read. 'Says here Terrance Dittman came to the coast in early 1973, at age 27. Started work for Forrests as a salesman at Hideaway Beach.' Alex turned to Megan to explain. 'There wasn't much there before then, an old log bridge over Nerimbah river, just a beach track off the road that led to the Passage, on the way to Brisbane. But council built a new bridge about then, and that's when Hideaway took off.'

Alex turned back to the article and read on, before explaining it. 'It says here, Forrests started with a sales office for a modest housing development near the beach, but it was Dittman who had the bright idea to flatten the dunes so that prospective house buyers could see the ocean. The estate took off, and sales soared. It seems that Dittman got his nick name 'Tiger' from this, his aggressive marketing of Hideaway beach...pity about the dunes. It didn't matter that the place flooded, was full of mozzies, or was miles from the nearest shops, if you built here, you could see the ocean, Tiger made sure of that. Apparently, he and Forrests made a mint.'

'Bastard!' said Megan. 'Him and his bulldozers. Bet that was popular with the locals.'

'Yeh well, I didn't mind it too much at the time. It was the unofficial carpark for Hideaway. You could drive straight up onto the flattened dune to see the waves. I used to go over there with Beau for a surf, it was near a spot where the girls used to sunbake topless, a great place for parties too. Went there a few times in Senior.'

'What were they like? The parties I mean, not the girls?' Megan asked seriously.

'It was a long way to come from Nerimbah on a shitty road at night. Sometimes a few of us, sometimes a lot. Bit of a fire, sitting round getting drunk. Not as romantic as you think, not like those ones they show in the movies, like Gidget. Hideaway is an open beach, the wind comes in there from the southeast all the time, even at night. I mean, when there wasn't much wind, we could sit around a fire and drink goons of wine, or rum if we could afford it. I remember one bloke kept bringing Blackberry nip because it was cheaper than his petrol to get there. But if the wind was up, you couldn't do a fire, sparks would go everywhere, and the wind would coat everything in sand. The green timber off the dunes would set off a ball of smoke that would choke you to death.'

'So why did you go if it was that awful?'

'You never knew what it would be like till you got there, besides sitting in the dunes drinking with the girls wasn't too much of a hardship'.

'Did you have a girlfriend then?'

'Yes and no.' Alex wavered.

'Did you get serious with anyone?'

'It wasn't like that.' He objected. 'Well, maybe it was, but not for me. We were young, the parties were good regardless. Between the bands at the pub and parties on the beach, and surfing all the time, it was a pretty good growing up here.'

'Did you go there with Beau?'

'Yep. It was great being around him, the girls couldn't keep their hands off him. He was everything that I wasn't.'

'What about Villi? Did he go to the parties too?'

'He was famous for his half a coconut cup full of rum. He'd try and sing Fijian war chants when he was drunk. Wasn't very good at them... but maybe he was, and we just didn't know. Made us laugh though.'

'I like Villi,' Megan confessed. 'He's honest.'

'Yeh. Good mates, he and Nerina.'

'Nerina's very good at what she does, runs the house, the kids. does the books for Villi, bit too perfect I thought.'

'Is that just you being jealous again?'

'What do you mean by that?' she bristled.

'What I mean is, is that coming from our own view of life?' Alex asked cautiously. 'That when you have children, you operate in a bit different way from people that don't. Them having a family is different to our situation, so we view and operate in a world differently to them.'

'I don't think so. That doesn't affect honesty'.

'Well, we don't know yet do we?' Alex ventured.' We haven't had children.'

Megan didn't respond. She made no move to answer, nor did she look away. In fact, Alex couldn't tell what she was thinking. She pushed some hair back behind her ears but didn't look Alex in the eye at all. He had hoped that coming up to Nerimbah would reignite some passion in their marriage. When he was up here at Nerimbah three years ago, Megan had stayed in Melbourne, and their marriage had bottomed out in a makeshift plateau of recriminations. It had been a slow climb back, and the possibility of starting a family might be what brings them back from the brink. However, he was still in the dark on how Megan felt about it, and nothing yet had brought them any closer than when they had first arrived. The only thing Megan seemed to be passionate about was nailing Tiger Dittman for environmental vandalism.

'Ahh, it doesn't matter.' Alex tried to dismiss it, but the thought just buried itself deeper to be resurrected at another time.

'The parties dropped off as everyone got a bit older and moved away, like me. The old school networks started to fragment, like they do. Besides, we started going to the bands at the International Hotel on the northern beaches instead. I got into that when I came back here after I finished Uni'.

'It says here that the council ordered Dittman to fill in the dunes, fears of waves breaking through in heavy storms.'

'I remember hearing about that, but I wasn't here for it. Apparently, the old river mouth used to break through there once, as well. Putting the dunes back probably put an end to a few beach parties.' Below was a black and white photo of a bulldozer in the dunes, Alex leaned closer, squinting at the figure with his back to the camera directing operations. Alex couldn't tell if the sand was being taken away or put back.

'That looks like Pitman there, and his mate Clarry, up in the dozer, Clarence Woods it says.' Alex pointed at the photo and turned to Megan. 'They're younger there, but they were both at Hideaway the other day, watching the police remove the body. It says here that Gloria married Dittman in 74'. She came from New South Wales. Doesn't say where. She was a fashion designer and wanted to bring high end fashion to the coast, was looking forward to her venture with Dittman in building a studio at Hideaway beach.'

'Studio!' spat Megan, 'that's just another name for a shop. Is it still there?'

'Doubt it. I can't imagine that it would do very well. Most people who brought at Hideaway were young working families, or retirees from Sydney who weren't interested in high end fashion, more boardshorts and thongs.'

'Sydney?' Megan queried.

'Forrests advertised with some big firms down there in a marketing campaign, even had advertisements in London papers. Someone was rumoured to have sold a block near the river that went underwater at high tide, to a Sydneyite who brought it off the plan, sight unseen. Bet you that was Dittman. They never pinned it on him, but that, with the sand dune fiasco, was probably too much for Forrests I imagine. He and Forrests parted company in 1980. It says that since then, he's been sole owner and managing director of Dittman Developments.'

'Nothing here we can use on him to stop his current development?'

'Maybe...maybe not.' Alex sat back and smiled. 'You've got a good chance of stopping him with an environmental angle, use the platypus. Buy a plastic one, stuff it in a hole in the bank and take photos of it. Better still, let it float around the creek, it would be like the Loch Ness Monster, the only proof of its exitance is some grainy photo.'

But Megan wasn't smiling. 'This is serious.' She sat back in her chair and stared at Alex. 'You always make a joke of what I do.'

'I was only having some fun.'

'No, you weren't.'

'I was making a joke about what Bonny could do then.'

'No. You were making fun of me. You do it all the time, and I just don't appreciate it. It would be nice if you had left that all behind in Melbourne, but obviously you haven't.'

Alex didn't respond to that, he couldn't, it was true. He was joking about the only thing that Megan was interested in since they came. He knew that he often made fun of Megan's ventures, but to be fair, they were usually in some frivolous exercise in the Melbourne fashion world. Bonny was living proof of that, the two of them were ferocious in the social circles of the Melbourne cliques. The parties, the races, not unlike Gloria Dittman he thought. Fuck, he's doing it again, how did he just think that. No wonder Megan was writing him off. He stared out to sea, silent, next to him Megan was doing the same, together, but apart. They looked just like the many couples that Alex criticised for their lack of engagement, and here he was, just as guilty of it.

At the next table sat a young woman, people watching while her partner read the paper. Front page held high, *Boy in the Dunes Identified,* the headline read, but his face was probably buried in the page three pin up girl, ignoring the real one in front of him. How did we get here? So lost in ourselves that we can't even make idle chatter, enjoying the moment together, he thought. Instead, we spend our time ignoring what's in front of us and go looking for each other's mistakes instead. He glanced at Megan, but she hadn't looked back. Maybe the fault was his as much as he thought it was hers, wasn't going to matter much to that kid in the dunes, he's out of it all now, no more navigating relationships for him.

'Shit! I wonder?' exclaimed Alex, as he pushed back his chair, rose to his feet and marched across to the couple's table.

'Excuse me, but would you mind if I borrowed the front page of your paper for a minute? I'm interested in that lead story.' Explained Alex, pointing at the front photo. After much shuffling of paper and removing of segments, Alex returned to Megan with the page he was after. Behind him, the reading had been abandoned the young pair were chatting. Good deed for the day accomplished, thought Alex, got those two talking. Now for his own mess.

Alex read through the article, digesting the main points. Barry Crinns. Missing since 1978. His age estimated at late teens, from Sydney originally. Very little known about him. The story outlined the process of recovering the body, but little else. Limited Identification had been found on the body. Foul play had not been ruled out. That was the job of the coroner. So how did Clarry and Tiger know that the boy had been missing for twenty-odd years. Did they know who he was?

'Megan, what if there was something you could pin on Tiger Dittman that cast doubt on his reputation, that you could use to link him to a crime, would that be enough?'

'What are you talking about?'

'If I could link him to this body in the dunes, would that stop his development?'

'Well, if it was splashed across the papers, he might not be able to go ahead, the Council wouldn't want that publicity and might put a hold on his workings.'

'Help me here will you. What does that say?' Alex pointed to the photo of the bulldozer, his finger next to the writing on the door. 'What does that say there?'

Megen squinted, looked in closer, trying to make it out.

'It says Walls...no ... Wallace Earthmoving.'

'Excellent.'

Alex looked around, spotted a phone booth in the distance.

'Be right back,' he said. The phone directory in the cubicle was badly ripped, but enough remained for him to find Wallace Earthmoving, Dunoonan. He returned and pulled out his Nokia. Alex rang the number, only to be told that there was no Clarry Woods working at their company.

'What about in the past, maybe twenty years ago?' Alex asked.

'Before my time.' Came the reply.

'Well, is there anyone there who might know or remember.'

'Hold on a minute, I'll ask Maureen, she's been here forever, does the books in the other office.'

Alex tapped his fingers on the table and smiled at Megan expectantly. He was secretly pleased that she smiled back.

'Hello, you there?' the phone squawked. 'Apparently, we did have a Clarry once, he was the main dozer driver on the Nerimbah rivermouth project in 77, 78. We had the contract to extend the rock wall. Left us to go full time working for Dittman Developments, but that was long time ago.'

'Do you know his address?'

'Maureen says he lives on the road to Kenilworth, out the other side of Dunoonan, in an old house on a block near the big nursery.'

'Can you be more specific?'

'No mate, sorry. Good luck with that.'

Alex thanked him, flipped the phone closed and turned to Megan.

'Tomorrow is Saturday, if Clarry Woods is home, it will probably be over the weekend. I don't want to see Tiger about this yet. I got the feeling that Clarry is more open to it. Ill drive up and see if I can find him tomorrow or Sunday. Will you be right without me for a bit?'

'Let's see how todays sailing goes first.'

'You're right,' he said, nervously gathering his phone and car keys from the table. Out to sea, the ocean was turning on a spectacular day, light winds, sunshine and an azure that he hoped would rival the Mediterranean or the Cuban West Indies for that matter.

# CHAPTER 11

### Friday

The bus trip up from Brisbane to Nerimbah the evening before had been an eye opener. Clara hadn't expected to travel through pine forests so close to the highway; it made her think of the photos of Europe she had seen in the library books when she was at school. The setting sun flicked between the trees, strobing the light till she was forced to put her sunglasses back on. More than that, the strong scent of eucalyptus assaulted her senses whenever the bus pulled up and the door opened to let someone off. Clara wasn't sure if she liked it, it reminded her of the hospital in Havana, she had spent long enough in there and didn't want to repeat that. The trip up to Nerimbah had one thing in common with Cuban buses, they took forever to get anywhere.

A fast-food hamburger for dinner on the front overlooking the beach was all she needed. The sun had set, and the tourists around her were eagerly devouring food and cold beers. It reminded her of the beach side resorts of Varadero, two hours from Havana, full of Russian and English tourists on cheap packages from their cold northern winters, come to the tropics for warm water sun and sex. It was Cuba after all, and at times it suited Clara perfectly. Maybe Nerimbah was a bit like that, she mused.

Although the Nerimbah backpacker hostel was clean and tidy, it was noisy, but the room was cheap enough for her expense account. It wasn't a dormitory, but she shared the room with a young Swedish girl, Eva, staying here while looking for holiday work. Eva had invited her to the bar further up the road, a pub, she called it, a very English name for a bar, to meet up with other backpackers for Thursday night drinks, but Clara declined. The next day she was meeting up with Alex again for a sail and a chance to find out more about the port of Nerimbah. She wanted to be clear headed and the thought of embarrassing herself with a queasy stomach on the water was too much for her.

By Friday morning, she was glad to be up early and out walking, stretching her body and using muscles that needed a bit of a workout. The manager at the backpackers had told her to stay on the esplanade road, past the old ice works on the corner, heading to the river mouth, there she would find the marina. Ice works? What Ice works? There was no fucking ice works, why tell someone to turn where there used to be a building that is not there anymore. She shook her head in wonder on the corner of the esplanade...where a heritage sign told her the ice works used to be. It didn't matter she could see the yacht masts ahead over the tops of the holiday houses on the river bank.

She stopped outside a fishing Co-Op to watch a large truck reversing into the bowels of the shed, doors opened at the rear, where a small loader was scurrying back and forth from the concrete jetty to the back of the truck, stacking large orange bins filled with ice. From one of the bins a dark grey fish tail protruded, pointing dejectedly into the air, and as it was loaded into the truck. The bin lurched to the side spilling ice and a fish from the top layer. It hit the floor with a crack and skated effortlessly across the concrete out into the morning sun to stop at Clara's feet. She reached down to touch it. Frozen solid, dark silver and black, no scales, sleek and powerful yet round in the middle with a crescent tail. Tuna, a meter long. A young fisherman shuffled over in his heavy gum boots, plastic apron and elbow length gloves to retrieve the escapee.

'Gidday,' he said to Clara, 'just getting the one that got away.' He looked her up and down before bending to retrieve the fish.

'Where are these going to?' she asked.

'Japan mostly,' he replied, heaving the weighty fish up to his shoulder.

'I am looking for the yacht club.'

'Well, you don't have to go far, its next door.' He pointed with his free hand. 'Not looking for a drink, are you? Cos' the bar won't be open till after ten.' His eyes darted across her face, then flitted down to her T shirt.

She didn't react but held his gaze until he looked up again and it was apparent that he had been caught out ogling her.

'No,' she replied, pausing without further explanation. 'You should take your fish inside before it thaws out.'

He didn't say anything more but turned away and retreated to the shed.

The yacht club next door was an equally large building, but the small sign proclaiming it as Nerimbahs Premier Yacht Destination. The building was in need of a repaint and was seriously underwhelming. The front door was closed, but a side gate was open and led down to one of three floating yacht fingers. Waiting on the dock below was Alex and a woman she didn't know.

The marina was larger than Hemingway's in Cuba, more yachts than she had seen in one place before, but that was to be expected. Havana didn't really encourage yacht owners from the US, and although there were thousands in Florida across the straits, few of them sailed to Cuba, they were heavily restricted by their own government. She walked along the concrete finger passing the rows of boats, the stern names revealed a plethora of ports of origin from all over the world and sent a thrill of excitement through her. Fremantle, Hong Kong, Miami, Panama. Clara stopped, and backed up, looking at the boat from Panama. It was a little dishevelled, a colourful beach towel draped over the wheel, two surfboards strapped to its rails, plastic tubs and a spare gas bottle lashed to the back rail. It wasn't the boat she was looking for, but it did remind her of why she was here.

Alex greeted her warmly. There was no hiding his excitement at the coming days sail, and he was as open as he had been two days earlier. He fussed about her briefly, making sure she was prepared for the day ahead. The woman he was with stood a little to one side, staring down the river at an approaching yacht, till she finally turned to face her.

Megan was pleasant enough when Alex first introduced her. She was shorter than her, with blondish hair tied in a ponytail. Her figure was trim, gym tight, a bright bikini top showed beneath a large white linen shirt, with expensive blue sailor shorts below, chosen to enhance her firm thighs no doubt. Clara had to admit that she was beautiful, but her eyes gave her away for something more, they were reserved and calculating, and her lips too narrow to be generous. Her handshake was firm, but her straight arm held Clara at a distance. She released her grip and grabbed Alex by the elbow possessively, quickly dismissing Clara, to point at the incoming yacht.

The white bows swung in from the channel, revealing a sleek 10 to 12 metre boat. The sails were laying folded over the boom, and a mooring line draped from the stanchion at the rail ready for retrieval. The boat slowed and nosed in gently at the dock. Alex reached across and grabbed the rope, guiding the yacht in until he quickly flicked the rope over a cleat to pull it up to a stop.

'You must be Alex,' the skipper called to Alex. 'Don't tie off too tight, we will be away as soon as you're on. Well, don't wait,' He waved his hand, encouraging them, pointing toward the gap in the rails.

Clara quickly reached up to the stanchion and pulled herself up. She turned as Alex handed her the soft esky and a bag of towels before helping Megan up. The skipper jumped down and deftly released the line before hopping aboard himself. Alex followed as the yacht slid past him and pulled away from the finger. The water burbled at the rear as the engine revs increased, pushing the boat back out into the main channel.

'I'm Glenn,' the skipper called out from the wheel. He was suntanned, and jovial, his head moving from side to side as he scanned the water around him and pointed the bows toward the river mouth. 'Put your things down below when you're ready.'

Clara had trouble determining his age, a craggy lined face, his hair bleached and wind-blown dressed in what Clara could only describe as well-worn sailing gear, all atop a pair of legs like tree trunks planted firmly to the deck. Clara liked him immediately. She looked down at his bare feet and took own her shoes off.

'I'm Clara,' she called out.

'Villi told me I'd be taking Alex and a friend sailing. I take it you're the friend.'

'That's me.'

Megan chimed in, not to be outdone. 'Hi, I'm Alex's wife, Megan,' she said, settling into the yacht's cockpit.

'Sorry. Got that mixed up.' He turned back to Clara. 'You're not Australian, you sound Spanish, we get a lot of backpackers here, especially from Spain, I often take them out for a sail. They love the sun, just like home.'

'She's Cuban,' announced Megan, her voice dropping an octave as if that explained everything.

Clara shot Megan a withering look. She didn't take kindly to someone answering for her, especially when it came with a hint of condescension.

'I don't think I've ever met someone from Cuba. Here on holiday?' he asked.

'Something like that,' Clara replied, still smarting from Megan's interjection.

'Hope you enjoy it,' he said. 'Megan, if you want to put your shoes somewhere, give them to Alex, he'll stow them with your gear below.'

Clara noted the veiled command for Megan to take her shoes off while on the boat and smiled to herself. Glenn was no fool.

She turned to look at the boats tied up as they passed. Fishing boats with their steel gantries were backed up to the wharf, while the long rock wall leading out of the harbour protected the yachts and attentive dinghies tied up to timber pylons.

As they burst from the river mouth, Glenn turned into the wind and Alex helped raise the sails, winching the flat white dacron up the mast. Ropes whisked past Clara's ankles and wound onto the winches, handles blurred as the ropes were tightened. Glenn brought the nose of the boat around for the wind to fill the sails and the flapping and noise subsided as the yacht settled into a steady rhythm and began pushing through the gentle swell. Alex tightened the main headsail as Glenn turned the motor off, and like a sigh of relief, the wind took over.

She had never sailed before, mainly travelling in small motorboats and a tourist ferry around the Bay of Pigs once, but nothing of that had prepared her for the feeling of delight that enveloped her today. The yacht balked and she reached out to steady herself on the coach roof as she adapted to the different motion.

'You'll get used to it pretty quick,' said Glenn. 'Just keep one hand for holding the boat when you move around, it's a gentle day today, no real worries. If you go downstairs, hold on with both hands.'

'Is it often like this?' Clara asked.

'Days like today are pretty good. It's quite inshore where we are, a bit lumpier out there.' He nodded toward the open sea. The wheel moved effortlessly in his fingers, letting it float back and forth without fighting the wind and waves pushing the boat around, but the bows stayed steady in the direction of a small island ahead.

'What is it like out there?' She pointed to the east, the horizon, the deep ocean.

'Oh, that's a different matter.'

'Could you sail this boat out there?'

'Of course,' he said. 'I've taken this to Tahiti, Samoa, Fiji, all across the south Pacific.'

'What's it like?'

'Like you're free from the rest of the world. Alex, can you go downstairs and check that the fridge is on and working. There should be cold water in there if you want some. I noticed you had some wine, Megan, and there is beer in there as well.'

'Can I go forward?' Clara asked.

'Sure, remember, one hand for the boat.'

She smiled warmly at Glenn and made her way out of the cockpit along the rail, hanging on tight as the boat lurched and bounced.

Clara was enchanted. The yacht swept past the headland and aimed for the open sea to the north. On her left stretched the Nerimbah coast, as far as she could see, which Alex informed her was only about twenty kilometres. There was very little swell running, but it still surprised her how often the bows fell into the troughs. They were running sideways to the swell from the east and though the bows remained steady, they rose and fell more than she expected, but Glenn was right, she was getting used to it. She stretched out on the deck at the front, leaning back against the cabin roof and jamming her foot against a hatch cover to stop her sliding sideways with the motion. The front sail shaded her body while the sun baked her legs a golden brown, and the wind swept into the sails pushing them along with a rhythmic swish of water against the hull.

It would be perfect, if not for that bitch of a wife that Alex had brought along. She turned her head back to look aft, where

Alex stood chatting with the skipper, while Megan sat opposite them sunning herself, her shirt discarded to show off her bikini clad body beneath. Clara looked back to the front and sneered. Right from the start, Megan had started this joust, but Clara was determined that she would finish it. She won't let her spoil the day.

Alex shuffled past her up to the bow and bent down to loop a loose line back through the anchor chain and secure it to the cleat. Now Alex was a different matter. He seemed oblivious to Megan's jibes, but then most men were, it wasn't their fault, they were just men. But he was bit different to the machismo she was used to in Havana. She didn't mind studying Alex as bent over the bows, he might be married, but plenty of her work colleagues had testified that meant nothing on a hot Havana night. He looked good, about the same age, and definitely had an interest in her, she could tell. After all, if I had a wife like his, I'd be casting around too, she thought. Alex suddenly turned and looked at her, his expression motionless, then his lips spread in a mischievous grin. Damn, she was sure he had caught her out in what she was thinking. She blushed. Shit, how did I let that happen?

Alex crab walked back to her and settled onto the deck beside her looking forward.

'Is this what you expected, I mean, how you thought the sailing would be?' he asked.

She smiled at him. 'Yes, thank you for this. It's better than I thought.'

'It's a quiet day today, not much swell. If it gets any more than this though, we'll have to go back to the cockpit. You'll get a bit wet up here.'

'Do you want me to go back now?'

'No, I didn't mean now. Only if it gets a bit stronger. For the moment, this is glorious. Is it satisfying that freedom bug you've got?' He chided her.

'Freedom. Yes... I couldn't think of anything freer than this at the moment. What about you Alex? What does it mean to you?'

Alex looked ahead, then turned to face her, suddenly serious. 'This! And to make choices in my life without fear of retribution.'

'But all choices have a result, a retribution you say. You cannot just make your own decisions without it affecting others.'

'I didn't say it wouldn't affect other people, but it is whether the effects of your choice will come back to hurt you or another person. Meaning that you are hoping others respect your freedom to make choices without retribution as well. Take politics, the political freedom of choice without retribution. I can vote for whoever I want without it coming back to bite me, not quite the same in Cuba I imagine.'

'That is a very simple way of looking at freedom. Not simple, but the English word to use for when you don't know any other way, for when you trust too much, like a child.'

'Naive. You think I am naive?'

'I don't know that word, we would say *ingenui*, but if you believe too easily without seeing or knowing anything else, then maybe that is the word.'

Alex pursed his lips; he clearly didn't like being told he was like a child.

'Alex, I don't think you are...naïve, but perhaps if you came to Cuba, you would see different freedoms. It is easy to criticise my country for its political freedom, however, it is what I believe in. But we did not come here to talk politics, that's boring, what other freedoms do you have without fear of...retribution.'

'I've been able to make choices about my life, my education...career.'

'Did you choose your own education?'

'Well, not at first, I went to the local high school, like everyone did. It's just in there, behind that hill.' He pointed toward Dunns Point at north Nerimbah, level with where they were sailing now.

'Same for me, but you had to go to school, you had no choice?'

'Of course.'

'So where is your freedom of choice there?'

'I didn't have to go to that school; I could have chosen another school. Some days I chose not to go, mainly when the surf was up.'

'And the retribution... when you missed school? The teachers, your parents?'

'The idea was not to get caught, but we would have it recorded on our report cards, that's when my parents would find out and then there would be hell to pay. I'd be grounded,' he chuckled.

'Me too. I used to skip school and go into the tobacco farm nearby to feed the horses in the morning and swim in the lake, then come home for lunch pretending I had been at class. When my mother found out, she would chase me round the house with the broom.'

Alex laughed. 'Mine would tell me to wait till my father got home.'

'My father was a policeman, he never got mad, he was kind. He was the one who told me I could do whatever I wanted, and not let anyone get in the way, not even the government. And believe me, that is not an easy thing to say in Cuba, or as a policeman.'

'And what about you, do you let anything get in the way of what you want?

'I'm here, aren't I. I get to choose who I wish to be with and where, like now.' She glanced surreptitiously over her shoulder to where Megan was still sunning herself, wine glass in hand, watching Glenn at the wheel. She turned back and leaned in close to face Alex. 'Don't you wish you could have the freedom to make that choice, to reach out and have what you would like, without fear of retribution?'

Alex stared wordlessly back at her. The bow cutting through the waves, forcing the water along the hull never sounded so loud to her.

'That was what you said was freedom, wasn't it Alex?' She had grown up with sexual freedoms and was used to conversations with undercurrents of sexual inuendo. The revolution had little time for the staid approaches to sex and formal relationships, they were a trademark of the older religious order. 'Do you practice it? Those freedoms without retribution Alex?' She leaned in close, searching his eyes for mutual understanding.

'Touché,' he replied. 'And here I was thinking that you were only here for your investigation,' remarked Alex. 'Why did you came up to Nerimbah?'

Clara was taken aback with the sudden shift in conversation. She pointed ahead and changed the subject.

'What is that island ahead?'

'That? Dinnan Rocks,' he replied. 'last time I went fishing out there was over twenty years ago, when I was back here after I finished University.'

'I thought you said you lived in Melbourne?'

'I do, but I came back here while I was waiting for a job.'

'So, you became a fisherman?'

'No. I can't fish for quids. I'm hopeless. But when I was twenty, I did a favour for a mate that involved some fishing out here. Well, it was more than fishing, I got in with some bad stuff, drugs and stuff like that.'

'Alex, tell me more. You surprise me.'

'You don't want to hear it.'

'I do. I love hearing about it, investigating the past, I'm a policewoman remember, but only in Cuba.... not here. Please tell me.' She pleaded, batting her eyelids in a mock schoolgirl like flirt. 'I promise not to arrest you.'

'It's not pretty,' he said. 'I had some friends who were mixed up with drug trafficking, back in the 80's. There were some bad bastards involved, particularly an American. It came to a head with a bomb that was planted to kill police investigating their drug ring, but it claimed the life of an innocent girl. That was awful. I'd had enough. I left and so did my mate. We all thought that would be the end of it.' Alex paused and looked out to sea, then continued. 'There were a lot of deaths at the time, but it doesn't matter now, that's all in the past. I came back up here three years ago, for a funeral, and to see some old friends. Villi, that big Fijian you met at the hospital was one. He organised the sailing today. Anyway, I loved being back so much I brought Megan with me this time. Well, that's not quite true, it's really her holiday and I'm just along for the ride.'

'You like the sailing?'

'I like all water, I grew up here, it's hard not to.'

'Have you ever sailed to Fiji?'

'God, not that far.'

'How long would it take to get there?'

'No idea, maybe a couple of weeks, it would depend on the size of the yacht, the weather, lots of things.'

'Have a guess,' she proposed. 'What if it was a bigger boat than this one? Which way is faster, or slower?'

'Wow. Now you're getting into stuff I don't know, it would be faster coming from Fiji, but by how much, I have no idea, and it does depend on the winds. I'll go ask Glenn.' He made to get up, but Clara reached across and held his forearm.

'No, stay, find out later. Tell me about that island. Does anyone live there?'

Alex settled back into his spot.

'No, it's uninhabited. Though there is a small stone shelter on it, and kids sometimes stay there overnight for fun, surfing and fishing. The locals call it Dinnan Rocks, after the indigenous name,

Mindingman. There are two outcrops. Means something to do with water and spray in the local dialect, something like that, but I can't be sure.'

'We are sailing there today?'

'Looks like it. We're definitely heading in that direction. You can swim there, on the northern side, but I haven't done it, too much of a chicken.'

'Why is that, Alex?' she asked in earnest.

'Sharks. Simple as that. There's a tiger shark that hangs around there, chasing turtles and surfers mostly, and stealing fish. I saw him once, scared me to death. Came up under the boat and tried to bite the motor.'

'Really. Do they do that?'

'Sharks feel with their mouths, they've got no hands,' he said, waving his arms around and gnashing his teeth to lighten the conversation. Clara laughed. They leaned closer to the side, looking down at the water sweeping aft, as if they would suddenly spot the offending shark.

Clara turned to see Megan steering the yacht, while Glenn stood closely next to her, guiding her movement with his hand next to hers on the large wheel.

'Would Megan swim there?' She asked innocently.

Alex looked aghast at her suggestion. 'God no. She tries not to swim in anything that's not chlorinated.'

'Perhaps she would like to try something new? Out here, at the island.'

'You have pretty evil thoughts for a policewoman, Miss Ramirez.'

'Its Investigator Ramirez to you.'

'I'll try to remember that. I'd better get back,' he sighed.

'I'll come too.'

Clara let Alex help her to her feet and felt him place his hand gently in the small of her back, guiding her along the rails till they reached the cockpit. She jumped down onto the deck to prove her sure footedness, but Glenn quickly reprimanded her for jumping; if it was wet, she would end up on her arse or worse, a broken leg. Megan smirked, lost concentration at the wheel, and rounded the bows up into the wind, losing way in a burst of flapping sails and tilting deck. Glenn quickly stepped in and pulled the wheel downwind to get the boat under way again. After a moment of chaos, forward momentum returned.

Clara couldn't resist a jibe.

'Megan, I did not know you could steer, you are doing so well.' She quickly turned away before there was a reply and addressed Glenn. 'So, Glenn. You steer from the back, but I have seen some yachts where they steer in the middle of the boat.'

'Right,' he said, checking Megan's progress before answering Clara. 'The ones with a centre cockpit are often bigger than this, and maybe you don't get as wet, you are higher up from the water. A bigger, wider boat, but you can't see how the sail is going from there.' He pointed up at the curve of the sail and swept his hand downward as if to replicate the shape.

'So, you could carry more on that kind of boat, more weight?' She asked.

'I guess so, more water definitely and food, but I think it might be slower, and it's really a preference for what you think is more important, speed or weight. More yachts these days have the open cockpit at the back like mine.'

'Are there any of the centre ones at Nerimbah, at the moment? Ones with a cockpit in the middle?'

'Sure, Joel Roberts has one stashed up a canal, but he barely sails it. There are a couple in the river, but most are...'

'You sailed from Fiji? Straight across?' Clara interrupted.

'Yep, two years ago. Took 16 days, it was a good trip, fast, the wind was right, it was boys' trip, only three of us on the boat.'

'And does anybody official see you when you arrive?'

'Of course, there is customs and immigration, they're sometimes here at Nerimbah, or will come up from Brisbane when they have to.'

'Could you arrive without anyone knowing?' Clara asked in a quiet voice.

'Depends,' he said. 'If you come into somewhere like Pelican Point behind Yindiba Island it might take a day or two before they catch up with you, but you are bound by law to check in on arrival in our waters.'

Clara saw Alex looking at her quizzically, his eyebrows raised. She quickly switched tack and asked innocently, 'What about today, will they look at us today when we come in? I'm from Cuba, maybe I'm an illegal refugee, trying to sneak into the country to steal your secrets.'

'Hardly,' Glenn chuckled out loud. 'I'll vouch for you. Besides, the worst secret you could steal is how to make beer. Time to swing around and head for home. I think I can hear a beer calling my name.'

He relieved Megan from the wheel and began the instructions on turning the yacht about. Just ahead, Dinnan rocks looked calm, peaceful. Some low vegetation grew on its summit. Clara could just make out a mound of stones, which must be the shelter. A small wave broke along its southern rock face, just beyond she could see the second set of rocks with half a dozen fishing boats bobbing in its protection, anglers leaning over the side. The outcrops didn't project any of the menace that Alex gave it credence for.

Clara sat quietly on the return, wedged into the corner, rising and falling with the stern. Glenn had said it took him 16 days sail from Fiji, but the wind was good, a fast trip he said. That idiot from the consul said the yacht had departed from Fiji over two weeks ago. But where in Fiji? And how accurate was the report, was that information already old? If that was the case, the yacht could be close, already here... or not. Nothing she could do about it at the moment. She looked across at Alex and Megan sharing a beer can on the opposite bench.

The wind was stronger on the return leg and Megan had covered up at last.

She seemed to have stopped staring daggers at her, in fact, she looked a little uncomfortable, queasy maybe, and Alex was working hard to distract her from the motion of the yacht. She smiled to herself, leaned her head back, revelling in the cool breeze washing her neck and drying the stickiness from her cheeks. She closed her eyes and felt the rhythm of the boat, unwinding from all her demands. The Cuban Ministry of the Interior was a long way away and couldn't touch her here. Now that is freedom, she thought.

It didn't take long to secure the yacht and tidy the boat before heading to the yacht club for a drink. The sun still had some sting in it, and the Marina did not attract any breeze to cool off. A cold beer was a welcome thought.

The club bar had seen better days, and like the sign out the front, desperately needed a makeover. But they served cold beer in the bottle and according to the chalk board, offered a range of snacks, which by this time of the afternoon was reduced to a couple of sausage rolls in a hot glass cabinet. Alex pointed them all to a vacant table while he headed to the bar. There were a few drinkers, most of them off the yachts as far as Clara make out from the way they dressed, clones of Glenn, but with beards. Alex returned briefly with a plate and four beers.

'Anyone for a sausage roll?' he asked after taking his first sip.

'Do they always look like this?' Clara asked, leaning back away from them in mock horror. The sausage rolls were anaemic, wrinkled and flat as if all life had been pulled from their pastry. 'We definitely do not have these in Havana.'

'No. No, try one,' said Alex. 'They are an institution here.'

'I'm sorry, but they look like a reason for me to become vegetarian.'

'No problem there,' quipped Glenn. 'I doubt there is any meat in them anyway.'

'Your loss,' said Alex, as he squirted tomato sauce along the length of the pastry and he held up his beer. 'Anyway, thank you for today, Glenn. Great day, I enjoyed it, but I think Megan is still getting over it.' He draped his arm across her shoulders and pulled her in close. She shrugged some resistance but smiled and raised her bottle to Glenn as well.

The beer was wonderful, cold and slid down her throat with little resistance. The smiles all around were genuine, this was a delightful end to a day on the water.

'What about you Clara?' Glenn inquired. 'Will we see you down here again looking to crew, scrounging a passage to Fiji? Have we converted you?'

She thought about it for a moment and responded with all sincerity.

'Today I have tasted a freedom that few in Cuba get to experience. Every time someone goes out offshore in a boat from Havana, the police think you're trying to sail to Miami and arrest them. So, thank you for the sail Glenn, and thankyou Alex for giving me this moment.'

'My pleasure,' Alex replied. 'Now who wants another?' He pushed back his chair and headed to the bar before anyone could say otherwise. Clara looked around her, trying to avoid eye contact with Megan. The sausage rolls remained untouched on the plate. The sun was beginning to filter between the yacht masts as the voices at the bar got louder and more boisterous. Behind her a chair crashed over to the sound of broken glass, and a voice roared out in anger.

'Bugger off'

Clara froze. She knew those words, that voice, she had come halfway around the world to find the owner.

# CHAPTER 12

Glenn and Megan were looking over their shoulders at the bar to see where all the noise was coming from, but Clara refused to turn. She desperately wanted to see what he looked like without drawing attention to herself, to see if he matched her vague memory of him. It had been only three months but all she could conjure were his big meaty hands holding the gun. She couldn't be certain that the Skipper wouldn't recognize her. The night he shot her and Alberto Colomè in Havana harbour it was dark, and she was largely in shadow on the quay, while he stood in the shadows of the cabin roof. But as she tried to climb the side of the yacht, it brought her face into the glow of the light, while he remained a dark silhouette. He had looked directly into her face before he pulled the trigger, but all she remembered was his hand and the gun. No, she couldn't take a chance on being recognised. She put her cap on and wouldn't look back, yet.

Alex dropped down into his chair next to her and handed around four new beers.

'What was that all about?' Megan asked.

'Prick,' said Alex. 'He was standing on a chair trying to reach across the bar but fell and knocked over one of my beers...well it was yours actually Glenn, you nearly didn't get another one.' Alex joked, but the glance he gave back toward the bar showed no humour in his eyes. 'I tried to give him a hand up, but, well, you heard him. So, fuck him I say.' Alex added defiantly. 'Do you know him?' he asked Glenn.

'Nope. Never seen him before'. Glenn glanced back over his shoulder. 'Looks like he's off one of the yachts. Hello, here he comes.'

Clara sat rigid, whatever she did, she mustn't look directly at him. She grabbed one of the new beers off the table.

'Now there's a thirsty girl,' the voice behind them declared. 'That's what I like to see, a girl with a bottle in each hand.'

He stopped next to her. Clara couldn't believe it, she was so focused on not being seen, she still had her empty bottle in the other hand. A rookie mistake. Without looking up, she placed the empty on the table and made to drink from her full one, holding the bottle high to her lips, pretending to drink, blocking most of her face with her hand while she quickly studied the newcomer.

He stood tall, over six foot, she remembered his size, his commanding presence, he had sandy coloured hair under a bleached St Kitts cap. But what stood out to her most were his big features, and his voice...exactly as she remembered it, coming from deep inside a gravel pit.

'Look mate,' he addressed Alex, 'sorry about before, here's a couple of beers as a peace offering.' He placed two more beer bottles on the table.

'What were you doing trying reach over the bar anyway?'

'Now that's my business mate, not yours. There's a couple of beers, alright?'

'Yeh,' said Alex, 'no problem.' Alex looked around at Glenn, Megan and Clara in turn, as if seeking acceptance of the gesture.

'Yeh, sure,' said Glenn. 'Happy to accept.'

'Good.' He started to walk away.

Glenn raised his beer to him. 'Cheers. You off one of the boats?'

'Yep. Got in last night.' He said over his shoulder as he sauntered across the grass toward the third concrete finger.

Clara watched him intently, the bottle of beer still in her hand, none had been drunk. She noticed Alex looking at her a little bemused, raising his eyebrows questioningly, but she had no time for that. She followed his progress along the walkway. Where was he going? What yacht was he getting on? It wasn't easy, at times he would disappear behind the larger boats, till he reached his own, where he turned and disappeared from view down its side. This time he didn't reappear. She counted the masts and matched that with what she could see of the bows lined up facing the dock. Third yacht from the end, C finger.

Now how to get closer, but first, she had to get rid of her three companions.

She drank generously from the neck of the bottle, watching Megan, waiting for her to look her way. As Megan finished her chat with Glenn, Clara deliberately placed her hand on Alex's forearm looking directly into his face.

'In Havana Alex, a problem like the spilled beer will often end in a fight, but I like what you did, it's much better I think.' She smiled and made sure Megan saw her squeeze his arm, holding on longer than custom would dictate, as was her intention.

'I'm pretty sure it can end in a fight over here as well,' said Alex. 'I don't think it's that much different anywhere.'

'But I like that you held back, it shows...something...I don't know the word.' She laughed, leaning forward into him so that the deep fold of her breasts pressed against his arm.

Megan was watching, and it worked.

'I think we should head off Alex!' Megan said loudly, gathering her string bag from under the table. 'It's been a lovely day sail thankyou Glenn, but we didn't get much sleep last night,' she pointed out coyishly, as she pushed back her chair. 'We should do that again Glenn.' She remarked, shook his hand and without looking at Alex began to walk toward the side gate.

Alex finished his beer in an ungainly gulp, watching his wife's receding figure.

'Ah, thanks Glenn. Do you need a hand to get the boat out? I can wait,' he asked.

'No mate. I've done it enough times by myself. Clara is here if the wind gets up and makes it difficult. Have a good night.' He waved Alex away. 'Bye Megan,' he called.

Megan turned and waved briefly, then signalled for Alex to join her.

'Been a good day,' Alex said to Clara. 'Talk tomorrow about what else you want to do while you're here, but I don't have your number.'

'I don't have a phone,' she said. 'I'll ring you from the hostel.'

'Fair enough, talk to you then.' He nodded and turned, following Megan out.

Glenn had watched the whole exchange and smiled knowingly at her.

'Well, that broke up the party pretty quick. But I think that was your intention Clara. So, I think there is more to your story than you let on.'

'Yes, but I think its best you don't know.'

'You don't want to stay for something to eat?' he offered hopefully; eyebrows raised.

Clara looked down at the sausage rolls and playfully waved them away in disgust.

'I don't think so. I don't want to spoil what has been a very good day.' She laughed. 'Thank you again, but it is time for me to be gone as well.' She shook his hand as she stood, she liked Glenn, he was perceptive, while Megan could be easily manipulated with jealousy. And Alex, she wasn't sure how she felt about him yet, she liked what she saw but for the moment she had a job to do. She looked toward the yachts lined up, once again noting their positions on C finger, then turned away leaving Glenn to finish the two cold sausage rolls by himself...if he was game.

# CHAPTER 13

Yachties had been moving back and forward between their boats and the shower block for the last half hour. They carried small toilet bags and towels over their shoulders, calling good evenings and offhand comments between them as they passed through the security gate or met on the walkway. The nighttime gate was automatic and shut behind each one, but Clara noticed that people kept it open as a courtesy if they saw someone coming. She looked at her watch; it was after nine. The bar had shut an hour ago, and the last of the drunks had staggered home. The club lights had just turned off; it was nearly time. There were still too many people around for Clara to move yet, so she hunkered down behind the shower block out of sight and listened to the idle chatter and hiss of showers emanating from the patterned breeze blocks set high in the wall.

Half an hour later, a sprinkling of rain set in. Clara shivered but she took it as a blessing. This would keep the boaties inside and the darkness would do the rest. Movement had all but ceased. She watched intently for just the right moment. In the distance, a figure climbed down from a large motorboat and sauntered toward the shore, a black rubbish bag in hand. She raced around the back of the block and slid into the light next to the woman's entrance. Damn, the boatie was coming quicker than she thought.

'I'll see you back at the boat,' Clara called out loudly to no-one, and headed down the path toward the security gate, hoping she had timed it right.

The rubbish man beat her to the gate and opened it to step through while she was still twenty paces away. She pretended to fumble in her pocket as if looking for her key, quickening her pace. He almost let the gate spring closed but hesitated when she smiled broadly and skipped the last few metres, calling thankyou to him in a heavily accented Cuban voice. Who could resist that, she thought, not adverse to using her background to her advantage. He mumbled some platitude, but she didn't hear it, she was through and already making her way along the dock as the gate shut behind her in a metal rattle.

She walked along B finger until the boatie was out of sight, then quickly reversed back to C finger and began a silent watchful walk toward the third yacht from the end on the right.

It was there, three of the boats near the end had lights on, but only one was a yacht with a centre consul cockpit. She walked straight passed it, then sharply dropped down and crept back along its berth till she was crouched below the windows out of line of sight.

She breathed out slowly and studied the yacht's length and shape. Over fifty foot long, a high centre cock pit, three blue barrels of ropes tied to the back rail. Attached to the cabin was the word Amel in an oval plate, that must be the make. She was sure it was the same one she had seen in Havana. The life ring attached to the rigging near her said *Cosmos.* So that was what it was called now. Voices emanated from inside, muffled in part but enough for her to hear what was being said if she could get close enough. At first two, maybe three men were discussing the dinner, in between the clatter of cutlery on plates. The skipper, his voice distinctive, complained of a lack of something to drink. She knew that voice, she was at the right boat. Glasses and a bottle were retrieved, when suddenly the light flickered, and a figure appeared in the cockpit. Clara crouched lower and leaned in against the boat. Light rain was still falling and masked any sound of her movement. An arm stretched out above her and tipped the contents of a glass into the water next to her. The figure retreated back inside.

'What time are we heading out tomorrow?' one of the voices asked.

'Don't make it early,' pleaded another.

'No problem with that,' replied the Skipper. 'We don't need the tide, south easterlies predicted. We've got plenty of time to rendezvous with the ship. Adam rang from Tunkumba earlier, it's all ready for us at the camp whenever we arrive. He's hiring a truck tomorrow.'

'Is he coming down here before we go?'

'No, he'll stay there till we arrive, I told you that earlier.'

'Just asking.'

'Well, sharpen up will ya, and I want you to check the floor lockers again for water ingress before we go tomorrow.'

'But I did it when we got in, before the Customs bloke had a look.'

'Well fucking do it again Troy. No point trying to find a leak out there before we take delivery, it's too late then.'

'Jesus, ease up Vaughn. You're fucking putting us on edge.'

'You should be on fucking edge. You know what will happen if we stuff this up, don't you. Kiss goodbye to your Pommy girlfriend waiting for you in Panama. You, me, Adam, we'll all be fucked. There'll be nowhere to hide, they'll find us, wont they Mendez?'

'Yeh, you've told us that a thousand times,' came Troy's voice. 'Look Vaughn, Mendez and I are with you, we know our jobs, we just don't need to be reminded of it all the time.'

There was a silence, a creaking of movement as one of the men shuffled in his place.

'Troy, when you and Mendez came aboard in Panama, I was told I could trust you. In the sailing, I do, I trust you. You have to trust me now.' His voice less aggressive, more conciliatory. 'Just do what I say, we make the transfer, and we'll all be rich, O.K.? This is big. Mendez knows that don't you? You're watching over us too, aren't you? Making sure we don't slip up.'

'That is not true Vaughn, I'm part of the syndicate, just like you.' It was Mendez's voice that responded for the first time. It was thick and heavy, in an accent not unfamiliar to Clara.

'Yeh right,' scoffed Vaughn's voice. 'Well, at least you've proved you can sail. But until it's over, I'm the skipper, I'm in charge. After this, you can take your money and clear out, go live in Panama with Troy if you want, but till then, just do what I say.'

'You're the boss Vaughn,' said Mendez.

Clara concentrated on Mendez's accent, it was certainly Spanish, a little less precise, slower, more liquid in pronunciation than pure Spanish. He spoke like the street vendors from Venezuela or Columbia. She realised he was south American just like her and would likewise spot her accent a mile away. She couldn't resist it; she had to see what they looked like.

Behind her was darkness, no lights, no silhouette, if she was careful. Slowly she raised herself up from the crouch till she could see through the side window. Vaughn, the Skipper was easy to recognise, he was larger than the other two, and sat at the table with his back to her, One of the two facing her was big in the shoulders, with dark hair and olive skin, that must be Mendez. The youngest of the trio, slim, with unruly blond hair, early twenties she guessed, must be Troy. She memorised their faces, sure she would know them again, then sank back below the sill, confident she had not been seen.

'We know,' said Troy's voice. 'Now are you finished? You want a rum? I've still got some of that Fijian stuff.'

'Only one,' said Vaughn. 'We've got work tomorrow before we leave, like checking the storage spaces.'

'Oh fuck, you never give up do you?' complained Troy with a laugh. A bottle clinked against a glass.

Clara had heard enough. She was cold, wet and could confirm that she had the right yacht and the right man. They had been discussing a drug pick up, which came as no surprise, that was

Vaughn's stock in trade, it was why he was in Havana three months ago. She started to crawl away from the yacht, keeping in close to the side and the shadows, hoping there were no more rubbish bag walkers out there. The muffled voices receded behind her as she got to the main walkway and stood up straight, heading for the security gate as if she was a yachtie on a late-night trip to the toilet block.

She stopped at the gate and looked back at where *Cosmos* was berthed. Clara had no idea how to progress from here. Cuba had given her instructions that went little further than finding and identifying the Skipper. But there was no doubt that it was her responsibility to bring him to justice. How she was to do that was left up to her.

She was tired, she shook her head and turned away. The adrenaline was wearing off. All she wanted was to get warm and dry, and crawl into bed...alone. It was a long walk in the dark back to the Hostel.

# CHAPTER 14

### Friday

Alex turned the lights on and collapsed on the couch, sifting through the news clippings Megan had showed him that morning, letting the seed of thought work its way to the front. It was dark and drizzling light rain on the verandah. Although there was no wind, he was glad they had finished their sail today before it had set in. Megan was showering, scrubbing the salt from her hair and skin from their day on the water. Alex hoped it would also expel some of her coldness toward him. Clara, shit! She didn't have to make it so obvious that she was flirting.

Megan appeared from the steaming bathroom, wrapped in a dressing gown, brushing savagely at her hair. Alex opened up with all the enthusiasm he could muster.

'Megan, this is great. I can do a new *Cold Case* episode on this; it has all the right elements. A missing body found in the dunes, sleepy coastal town, the possibility of skull duggery, in the past.'

'Skull duggery? Nobody uses that phrase anymore.'

'True. But the promise of mystery with a dead body is like pheromones to a stud ram. Audiences lap it up; they can't help it. Look at the reviews we got on *Somerton Man,* and we still don't know who he is, but we uncovered a few possibilities. That didn't harm the ratings at all. If we can make a success of that formula once, we can do it again. Besides, this place has got history. Remember the bombing in the early eighties. Not such an innocent fishing village after all. But I don't want to bring that one up, I'm not doing a program on that, it's way too close to the bone, but this is something different, it's not personal, not as close to me. And Dittman has something to do with it, I'm sure.'

Alex stood up and walked around the room, deep in thought.

'If you go after Tiger with his development, I'll go after him with my investigation. The publicity will force him to suspend his work at Cedar Vale. It will unpack the issue of environmental vandalism, and save the creek, and I'll get my show. What do you think?'

'I think you should get Debbie Marcello on the job, she's at Byron Bay at the moment, I'm sure she won't mind giving up some of her holidays to dig into Tiger Dittman's background for us.'

'Not a bad idea,' mused Alex. Marcello was his background researcher for his production company. 'But she is on her holidays.'

'She works for you Alex and gets paid well for it. After all, it's not the first time you've called on her out of hours.'

Alex stopped pacing, and looked intently at Megen, searching her face for an indication of a double meaning in what she inferred. Megan could suggest infidelity all she liked, but up till now, he had been loyal to her, regardless of what she thought. He had tried to tell her this many times, but mostly she preferred to play the aggrieved wife, always suspect of her husband.

He watched Megan's guileless face for accusation but saw none, he had previously told her that Debbie Marcello was gay, and had no interest in him apart from the professional banter they engaged in.

'No. I'll leave her out of it this time. I'll call only if we get stuck.'

'So, what do we do now then?' Megan asked.

"I need to find out how Dittman knew of the boy in the dunes before it was publicly announced. But... he'll be a hard man to crack. Woods will be easier. I'll pay Clarry Woods a visit up past Dunoonan first. I've still got to find his place; it's an old house or shed on a large block on the way to Kenilworth. Near a nursery apparently. Do you want to come?' he asked.

Megan sat quietly on the couch, looking out at the lights illuminating the beach. She seemed lost in thought.

'Do you want me to come?' she asked.

'Of course.'

'Did you want me to come sailing today, or would you have been happier on your own? '

'Of course I wanted you to come. It was great day wasn't it. You didn't get sick. Look, you got a tan.' Her bathrobe had slipped off her shoulder, revealing the white line where her bikini strap had prevented the sun from darkening her skin. When he pointed to it, she responded by pulling the robe back to cover her. He wished she hadn't, it made her sexy as hell, but that was the furthest thing from her mind.

'When you go off on your tangents, you leave me behind. You know that don't you? You get an investigation going and it's like I don't matter anymore. The only way I can become part of your life is if I Inject myself into the case, visit the sets, come into the office, and then you treat me like I'm some sort of nuisance. I have to bother you because if I don't, it's as if I don't exist until the project is finished.'

Alex stood looking down at her, unsure where this was going. What she said was true to some degree. He had to admit that that was exactly how he treated her during production. It was also how some of his staff looked at her as well, as an annoyance, resenting her interference.

'Take this place for instance. You came up here three years ago for a funeral, but something happened while you were here, something you haven't told me about. You came back a changed man, something deep had shaken you, but you haven't told me what. You keep it away from me, just like your investigations, as if I don't need to know or be a part of it. As if I'm just someone who hangs around on the sidelines.'

Alex sat down in the armchair across from her. He had hoped that they would address their problems while they were up here on holiday, in neutral territory, it just came a bit too sudden tonight, he wasn't ready for it. He had so many things he wanted to say, but none came to mind right now, so he said nothing.

'See,' she said, 'you're doing it now, retreating into your shell, mouthing things to yourself, but you don't actually say them. I can see your lips moving.'

'I'm sorry, it's just...' he didn't finish his ineffectual response, unsure if parts of it, or all of it were true. All of it, he thought.

'Do you remember when you first started Pinnacle Productions, we were a team, we worked well together. I know, I didn't know much about the media industry then, but I do now. But it's like I'm still an outsider. Half your staff treat me like one, and you do too.'

'No, I don't,' he said.

'You do. You keep me at arm's length. Come home late all the time. Never include me in the planning anymore, keep me off the sets, so that when I try to show up, to get involved, you wave me away... as if I was bothering everyone by being there.'

'But you're never around,' Alex countered. 'You're always out to lunch or have appointments of your own to keep with your friends. There's no time to fill you in on what's up to date with the productions, you can't swan in and out and expect to know what's going on.'

'I go to lunch because I'm not part of it Alex. I see my friends because you are never home, always at the office or on set. I drink, because I'm sad at what we've become, and I've got nothing else to do. You pay more attention to your staff than you do to me.'

'I don't have a mistress if that's what you're implying. I've never been unfaithful to you.'

'Well, it certainly feels like it,' she sneered.

In there was a truth that Alex needed to face up to. He didn't have a mistress, he hadn't wandered, but today with Clara on the yacht, was an intimacy that he hadn't had with Megan for a long time. He loved the closeness of her, was flattered by the attention she gave him and the ease with which they seemed to understand each other. As if Megan had read his mind, she asked.

'Are you seeing her tomorrow?'

'Who? Clara?'

'Who do you think?' she snapped. 'That Cuban woman!' Megan bunched her dressing gown around her, then just as quickly, smoothed the wrinkles out across her legs, then went on in a softer tone. 'I'm sorry. I didn't mean to raise my voice.'

'That's alright,' said Alex.

'Well? she enquired.

'I don't know. Maybe.'

'I'm not talking about her, she doesn't matter. What about us? About what I said.'

Alex thought for a few seconds and took in the truth of the matter.

'You are right. I do keep you at arm's length from the production schedules. It is harder to bring you into a production if you're not there from the start,' he conceded.

'That's not an excuse, I'm your wife, your partner. We started this company together.'

'If you are worried about your role in the company...'

'I'm not.' She interrupted. 'I'm worried about us. When we came away on this holiday, I thought it would give us a chance to face a few truths, reset our marriage, come back together again.'

'Funny, that's what I thought too.'

'Then why are we finding it so hard? I'm just as apart from you today as we were on the first day here. I was humiliated today on the yacht; you spent more time with that woman than with me. And when she grabbed your arm this afternoon and shoved her boobs in your face, that was the last straw.'

'I've never been unfaithful to you, I've said that before,' he said, exasperated.

'Sure. But you wanted to, I could see it in your eyes, the way you looked at her. I know you Alex, I know you better than you know yourself. You love the attention.'

'So do you.'

'Don't we all? It's part of human nature Alex.'

'So do we give in to it or work around it. Seems like it's just come to a head now.'

'Don't kid yourself Alex, it's been coming for a long time.'

The fight went out in both of them. They sat staring at each other, separated by a coffee table and a chasm of emptiness. The shared truth helped them step back from the brink, away from words that once said could not be undone and therefore became irrevocable. But he didn't know what to say next. Nor did Megan, her eyes, as beautiful as ever, were awash with accusation, her lips pursed shut.

'Do you want a family?' he asked.

She was quiet for a while.

'Not if we are going to bring a child into our present relationship. No. We're not going to use a child as a lifeline for us.'

'I agree with that,' he murmured. 'It's something that we agree on at least. So where do we go from here? We know what the problem is. How do we fix it?'

'You can start by telling me what really happened three years ago when you came up here to Nerimbah. The whole story, not the abridged version you gave me at home.'

'It's a long story; it started over twenty years ago.'

'We've got all night. I'm not going anywhere, yet. If we are going to make this work, perhaps our first concession is time.'

So, Alex told her.

This time he left nothing out. To Megan's credit, she didn't interject or ask for clarification at any time. She gave no reaction away but sat stone faced as he retold the time he spent with Beau and

Janice Mckenna, spanning more than two decades. Outside, the rain had stopped. There was no sound of vehicles along the front beach road, it was late.

When he finished, she leaned forward and held his gaze as she spoke.

'So, you drowned a man? You killed him on purpose?'

'I'm not proud of it, but I had to, it was self defence.'

'Who else knows this?'

'Only Beau and Janice, and their daughter Elizabeth.'

'If it ever gets out, we lose everything, and you will go to jail.'

'Yes,' he said.

She was silent for a while, then gathered her dressing robe around her and headed toward the bedroom.

She turned and said to him. 'I do want to have a family with you one day. But not tonight.'

So much more could have been said but wasn't. They could have touched but they didn't. Their feelings lay bare, their emotions raw. Megan walked into the bedroom, a gulf still between them. Alex collapsed exhausted into the chair. At least she didn't close the door this time.

# CHAPTER 15

## Saturday

Clara sat at the breakfast table outside the hostel, deep in thought. A plate of croissants and mug of coffee wriggled precariously on the mosaic table top every time she leaned against it. She hadn't touched her breakfast but concentrated on jotting logical arguments in her note pad.

Now that I've found him, what do I do with him, she thought. Like the dog that chases the car, what happens when they catch it? She knew all along that she would face this dilemma. What to do to fulfill her instructions. For starters, she had no jurisdiction here, for all intents and purpose she was officially on a short leash, she had been eased through the Australian hospital system to interview that Fijian boy by Sousa from the Consul, but he made it painfully clear that was where his help ended. He wasn't interested in an Investigator from Havana chasing some far-flung crime that had nothing to with him. Australia had yet to sign a formal extradition treaty with Cuba, and Sousa knew this, so diplomatic avenues to expediate law and justice were limited, and if it was not diplomatic, then he didn't want to know about it. There would be no joy in asking for guidance or help there.

She shook her head and dunked a piece of day-old croissant in her coffee. Around her, guests of the backpackers' lodge were scattered among the round tables and garden chairs in the courtyard soaking in the sun with their morning coffees. The leisurely atmosphere was punctuated by soft peals of laughter and reminiscences of shared entertainment from the previous night. The croissant might be stale, but the coffee was delicious, and the strong bitterness helped her formulate a plan of action.

The sailor she knew as Vaughn was a criminal, a murderer in Cuba and now that she had found him, it was her duty to bring him to justice. But how was she to do that if she had no official standing? Vaughn had to have a surname, and if she made it a priority to find out his full name, she could call on Sousa to find out if he really was an Australian. Extradition of Criminals to Cuba from here went through the British Embassy. What if he wasn't Australian after all, but a different nationality, one that had direct extradition to Cuba. Would Australia want to get rid of him if he wasn't theirs? That could simplify things. First step, find out his surname.

Then there was still the matter of Police Jurisdiction. She had none. She could not arrest him here for a crime committed in Cuba, but if he committed a crime in Australia, then he could be arrested in Australia, only not by her...and he was definitely going to commit a crime here by importing drugs. She knew that. Maybe she just had to find a policeman to do it for her. Agent Hughes of the AFP sprang to mind. If all else failed, she could turn to him.

Warrants for arrest were relatively new in Cuba. There was nothing like that in the corrupt days of Batista's regime, and there was precious little need to show cause during Castros revolutionary period, arrests and executions were too easily performed in the name of justice for the people. Some of those old generals in the Ministry still believed in imprisonment and disappearances without due process, that still happened, much to Clara's disgust, but she was trying her best to drag her Police force into this century. She needed details, photos and a solid list of those onboard. She could get that today.

Feeling satisfied she drained her coffee, gathered her hat and sunglasses and headed for the Marina.

*Cosmos* was gone.

The space where it had been the night before was empty. Puddles of water from the rain still dotted the concrete finger. Clara stood with her hands on her hips surveying the empty berth.

'Shit...*a donde diablos fuiste*?' she said out loud to the empty berth, wondering where they had gone.

'Pardon?' a voice broke in from the yacht next to her. She held her arm up to shield her eyes from the morning sun, just able to discern an elderly man standing in the cockpit of his boat sipping at his tea. 'Are you looking for the *Cosmos*?'

'Yes,' she said,' I was wondering where it had gone?'

'It left early this morning, in the dark, woke me up, his fenders tangled with mine and just about pulled the rail off, so I helped him get out.'

'Do you know where he was going to? Vaughn didn't tell me yesterday,' she asked, pretending a familiarity she didn't have,

'Didn't tell me either, but then I didn't ask.' He chuckled at his own witticism.

'Have you got any idea?'

'Crowther said they were heading north. That's all I can tell you.'

'Crowther?' she queried.

'Vaughn!'

'Oh, that Vaughn Crowther?'

'Who else.'

At least that's one confirmation, she thought, now she has his full name to pass on to the Consulate.

'He didn't say Tunkumba Creek did he?'

'I didn't hear anything about that. He just said he was heading out offshore, and the slight Northerly would be fine by him. You wouldn't want a northerly if you were heading to Tunkumba today, you'd be against the wind all the way. But you never know, he might have been in a hurry.'

She thanked the old man and made for the telephone booth outside the Marina carpark.

The first call she made was to Anton Sousa at the Consulate in Sydney. He didn't strike her as someone who started the day early, and the receptionist was not hopeful. By the sound of her voice, she had her own issues with starting in the office before 9am. To Clara's amazement, Sousa answered the phone.

'It's Investigator Ramirez here Mr Souza. I require some assistance.'

'Oh, it's you,' he said dismissively. 'I was under the impression you had finished your duties as an investigator here and was spending the last few days as a tourist.'

'I'm sorry if I gave you that idea Mr Sousa, but I'm far from finished. I need you to find out the background of an Australian Citizen and open a channel of Official communication to Cuba for me.'

'I do not need to do any such thing, Ms Ramirez.' He dropped her official title, she noticed, that makes it even she thought with a smirk, but she wasn't going to let him get away without doing his job.

'Can I remind you that you are required to render me assistance in the prosecution of my duties while in Australia. I haven't left yet.'

'The instructions I received may have pointed at that, but I assure you, there is a limit to how much valuable time we can afford to spare from Consulate duties. Perhaps if you came to Sydney directly.'

'I can hardly do that Mr Sousa; I'm still in Queensland.'

'You can phone Havana direct, Ms Ramirez. These are not life or death tasks.'

'They are to me. Mr Sousa, my authority comes direct from the Ministry of the Interior. I'm sure when I talk with General Abelardo, I'll be able to explain how helpful the Consulate in Sydney had been, rather than the obstacles you seem to be placing before me.' She bullied him, riding over the top of his quasi-diplomatic office speak with the veiled threat of her own.

The receiver was silent, she wondered if she had pushed too hard. It was always dangerous to take on bureaucrats with grand visions of their own importance. You had to pick the right ones and never bluff the ones with real power. She gripped the receiver tightly...had she picked right?

'What is the message you wish relayed?' Sousa asked, his voice flat.

'The message is to read, *To General Abelardo, Office of the Committee for the Defence of the Revolution, Ministry of the Interior. I have acquired the subject and await further instructions on how best to prosecute the orders required. Await your reply. Investigator Ramirez.* Have you got that?'

'Yes,' said Sousa. 'I have recorded your message.'

'Good,' said Clara. 'Make sure you send that immediately. Now for the name. Vaughn Crowther.' She spelled out his name slowly, 'Age, approximately 40. Want whatever background you can give me, and if he is an Australian Citizen.'

'Is that all?' Sousa asked.

'Yes, for now. I'll contact you in the next day for the information.'

'Anything else?' Sousa asked, a sarcastic note to his voice.

'No,' said Clara. The receiver clicked loudly in her earpiece as Sousa broke the connection. No friend there, she thought, but at least he is working for her, attitude or not. She brought out more change and pushed it into the phone slot. This should be a much easier call as she pushed the numbers and listened to the dial tone.

'Alex?' she inquired as he answered his phone, 'Its Clara.'

'Yeh, I think I'd know that accent anywhere. How are you this morning?'

'I have a question.'

'Of course you do. Fire away.'

'I'm sorry? What do you mean?'

'Let me have it... What do you want to know?'

'Oh. If I wanted to go to a place called Tunkumba Creek today, how would I get there?'

'Tunkumba? he exclaimed. 'Why would you want to go there? It's much better here, more surf, less mosquitos.'

'Alex...I have my reasons...I want to go to Tunkumba Creek, can you help me with how to get there?'

'OK, sure. It's about 150 kilometres north of here on the coastal strip inside Yindibar island. Now that's a place you should see, full of freshwater lakes and hidden valleys, maybe you want to go there instead. Plenty of day trips to the island, you can even get one from here.'

'No, its Tunkumba I want.'

'Well, it's not very big, a small fishing community, a few holiday shacks with miles of sandbanks and mudflats out the front. You'd have to catch a bus or train to Gildston first, then I imagine there's a bus to Tunkumba from there. But I don't know how often or when. You probably have to get out to Dunoonan to begin with, that's where the train line is, there won't be a direct line north from here, it would need to be done in stages. Bit complex, probably take you most of the day.'

'Is there much in Tunkumba? Could I stay there?'

'There's a caravan park, I know that. They usually have cabins to rent, so you'd probably get one if you ring ahead. You really want to go there? Did I mention the mosquitoes?'

'Alex!' she snapped, bringing him back to the point at hand, no matter how incredulous it sounded.

'Alright,' he said. 'I could give you a lift this morning. I'm going out along the Kenilworth road to do an interview, I can drop you off at Dunoonan station on the way to catch the train or bus, which ever leaves first.'

'I can do that. Thank you, Alex.'

'Do you want me to pick you up?'

'Perhaps I'll pack my things and meet you along the front when you are ready. The coffee shop across from the swings in the park.'

'*The Bean Counter*, I know it.'

'I'll be waiting there, watching the beautiful beach, which it seems I am leaving for some hell hole of mosquitoes instead.'

He laughed at this.

'See you in about an hour.' He signed off.

She smiled to herself as she put the receiver back in the cradle. She liked him and looked forward to meeting up with him again today, even though she had reprimanded him like a schoolboy, but then that was part of the fun. Ahead was the walk back to her hostel, and a quick pack up. Tunkumba was where the *Cosmos* was aiming for. It was where Crowther would be, with a boat load of drugs ...and she would be there by the end of today. The investigation was taking a solid turn, if only she knew what to do after that.

# CHAPTER 16

Apart from Clara's phone call, Alex's Saturday had not started that well. It began with a tense stand-off between he and Megan over who needed the car more, and had ended predictably. Alex didn't stand a chance when she reminded him that he had said she should be more involved with the investigation, and here she was, doing just that and Alex was depriving her of the transport needed to properly research Dittman. She had finished with a statement to the effect that if he wanted a car, then go and hire his own fucking one!

Alex's grief had not stopped there. When he canvassed Villi for the loan of his car for the day, Villi was only too happy till he found out what it was for.

'And you're really shaking down Tiger Dittman by going after his right-hand man?' Villi questioned him, holding up his car keys but not yet willing to hand them over. They were standing out the front of Villi's house. The silver Mitsubishi Triton Ute was parked under his two-story house, going nowhere yet as Alex tried to placate him.

'Mate, Tiger Dittman is tied up with some serious business, the body in the dunes, illegal earthmoving, and whatever else I can find on him. Clarry Woods is my way in, I reckon he'll crumble under a bit of pressure.'

'And then you'll have your story?'

'And then I'll have my story!' Alex repeated as confirmation.

'Alex, you don't want to dig too deep man. That Dittman is not to be messed with.'

'Well, neither am I,' said Alex, full of conviction.

'You be careful. Anyone going with you? Megan?'

'Not today, that's why she's got the rental. I'm taking Clara Ramirez with me. She's a Policewoman, will that do?'

'That Cuban woman again. Why are you still hanging around her?' he said angrily.

'I'm not hanging around her; I'm just giving her a lift to Dunoonan.'

'You're not doing it in my car.' Villi made to put the keys back in his pocket.

'Jeez you're a pious bastard. Just give me the keys.' Alex demanded.

'At least tell me that Megan knows what you're doing'. said Villi.

'She's already gone. Now gimme the keys Villi, you owe me.' He didn't budge. 'I'm going to do this, with or without your consent, or car.'

'Shit. Here.' He threw the keys to Alex. 'Get out of my sight. You're wrecking your marriage, and it's dangerous going after that Tiger Dittman. Be careful, you'll get burnt.'

'Look, all I'm doing is going up to Kenilworth to ask Clarry Woods a few questions, and I'm dropping Clara off at Dunoonan on the way, that's all.'

'Yeh, that's what you said last time. Just bring my car back in one piece.' Villi turned away and marched up his front steps. He didn't wave goodbyc.

It had been a while since the Triton had been cleaned out inside, residue of fishing gear and quick bakery lunches swirled around the floor. Alex brushed sand and crumbs off the seat, but when he started it, the engine purred and the odometer showed it hadn't done many kilometres. Fishermen, Alex concluded, messy bastards. He put it into gear and headed to the beachfront for a quick coffee and rendezvous with Clara.

Alex ordered his takeaway coffee and glanced around at the new shop fit out. It had once been a pie and hot bread shop that he frequented regularly on Saturday mornings after a surf when he was younger. It had since been converted into a quasi-rustic coffee shop of designer beans, *The Bean Counter* café. Alex had to admit, it looked good, and had a welcoming presence about it, the modern morning meeting place. No more sitting in the gutter dripping saltwater after a surf, tearing at a loaf of hot bread like a hungry raptor.

His name was called, his coffee retrieved, and Alex crossed the road to the fence surrounding the foreshore park. Clara should be somewhere here, he thought, as he perched his foot on the bottom rail and began to scan the foreshore. God it was beautiful, the gentle push of broken water up the beach, only to retract and repeat the whole process over, and over again. He could watch it all day, in fact, there was never a day when Alex would willingly turn away from the mesmerizing draw of the oceans repetition. From its mellow allure to the screaming wilds of a cyclone, it gripped his soul and entranced him, whatever the mood it was in.

Today, it was a welcome beach, ideal for the families, parents shepherding their children toward a makeshift camp in the sand, unable to hold back the smallest ones from racing ahead to the water's edge. There was no need for frantic warnings, the wash of foam with each wave had no threat to it, only wonder at its cool white embrace. Children reached down and swept their arms back and forth in the foam with squeals of delight. Parents and grandparents smothered their resisting children with suncream as they tried to squirm out of their grasp, but in the end, it didn't matter, enough sunblock made it to the desired areas. Squeals of delight engulfed protective fathers hoisting their children high as they strode into the deep, edging their children to even greater feats of daring. His heart ached to be doing just that.

To his right, couples sipped coffees and chewed on buns at the tables, one pushing a pram back and forth lazily with his foot. A lone woman sat at the far bench, long brown legs stretched out before her, shorts and tight T shirt revealing a generous body, with an unruly mess of auburn hair piled on top. Alex hoped she would turn around so he could see her face. With a start he realised he'd been staring at

Clara. His foot slipped from the rail with a jolt. Shit. He finished his coffee, sighed and threw the empty cup in the bin. If only he could cast aside his thoughts as easily as he could an empty cup.

'Hi Ya!' he called as he strode up to Clara's bench. She turned her head and beamed a smile up at Alex standing next to her. 'Are you ready? Got your bag?' he asked.

'Of course,' she said, as she unwound those long legs to stand up next to him, almost to the same height. For a brief moment, they stood facing each other, smiling in mutual appraisal, till Alex broke the spell.

'Look, I was thinking that maybe I could help you out a little more today. What if I drop you all the way up to Tunkumba Creek this morning, it's only another fifty minutes, maybe an hour's drive onward from where I was going today anyway. It would save a lot of mucking around for you on public transport.'

'That would be very good,' she exclaimed. 'It's not too far out of your way?'

'Not really,' he lied. 'Besides it would be a shame for you to spend a day like this inside buses and trains or waiting on platforms. Might even go for a swim while I'm up there,' he stumbled on.

'Is Megan coming too?' she enquired quietly.

'Nope. She's got the car. She's busy running down some research for an environmental project she's involved with, up the range at Cedar Vale. I should take you up there to look at that too. The interview I'm doing today is tied up with that as well. We're both working either ends of the same project. Anyway, enough of that, come on. Do you mind coming up to the unit while I grab some boardies and a towel.'

Clara said nothing, just hoisted her bag on to the shoulder strap and gestured for Alex to lead on. He was pleased with himself. He only just thought of that plan to take Clara all the way to Tunkumba as he stood looking at her, and it was a plan he was well happy with, a few hours in the car with Lieutenant Clara Ramirez was no real hardship.

They had fast become comfortable with the drive if it wasn't for bits of Villis fishing gear and empty drink cans appearing from under Clara's seat and rolling around her footwell. To be fair to Villi, he wasn't expecting to lend his utility to Alex for the day and would probably have cleaned it first. Villi's Mitsubishi utility was noisy but didn't interfere with their talking. He chatted to her about life growing up on the coast and how it shaped his view of the world, a desire to see more, do more and media production was the best way, but not on the coast. Clara in turn, told him how she left central Cuba to attend university in Havana, where she studied English, History and Criminology. She explained that everyone had to study Cuban history at school, but it wasn't till university that the history took on a more worldly view. Her father had boldly said to her that he was proud to have fought the USA, a powerful enemy, but that enemies can become friends over time and still be powerful. He encouraged her to go to university to find out for herself, but never to forget that she serves her country, and becoming a policewoman may be the best way to do that. Their conversation ebbed and flowed between them, each revelation shortening the gap that may have otherwise separated them.

He bypassed Dunoonan to get on the highway, and fifteen minutes later passed the sign to Kenilworth. He was so engrossed in conversation with Clara that he missed the turn off the highway. Alex quickly readjusted his schedule and accepted that he would drop in to see Clarry Woods on the return journey. Clara's presence had a way of realigning his priorities, and already his primary reason for driving this far north had shifted from work to pleasure. Clarry Woods could wait.

The town of Gildston, 90 kilometres up the highway appeared all too quickly. It was the central hub for the predominantly rural farms around the area but originally got its name for the gold prospecting that opened the valley up to settlement. By quarter past ten, signs to Tunkumba Creek and Yindibar Island loomed large on the right, and Alex concentrated on making the turn. A half hour to go, he settled onto the road toward the coast, it was single lane with more potholes, but less traffic.

'Alex, do you mind if I ask you a personal question? You once said you were involved with the drug scene.'

'That was when I was a lot younger. We do stupid things when we are young, I'm sure you did a few, you have that look about you,' he said, hoping to have turned the question back on her. But she said nothing. He glanced across at her; she seemed to be waiting patiently for him to continue.

'My friend was heavily involved with a local drug gang, more like a syndicate really, led by an American. He got in a bit too deep and took me with him. He was my mate, and I stuck by him when I really should have walked away. I think I was in love with his girlfriend at the time, which may have had something to do with it.'

'Was that Megan?'

'No. Not at all. I met her later in Melbourne. No, this girl was different. But anyway, no regrets. My friend, Beau, had been dealing drugs for this pair of arseholes, but he didn't really understand just how dangerous they were. Neither did I at first, but at least I began to suspect them before he did. They masterminded a bombing in Nerimbah that killed the wrong person, and that changed everything.'

'Your friend did this?'

'God no. But the people he worked for did. Both he and I got caught up in it. The police were looking for him to blame, and his bosses were trying to get rid of him, so I helped him get away, disappear, so none would find him. That's all.'

'You were a good friend then?' Clara remarked.

'Don't know about that. I was also in love with his girlfriend. I never should have let it get that far in the first place. besides, if Beau was arrested or they got rid of him, I thought that I would be next. It was pure selfishness on my behalf, Clara, no more.'

'I don't think so. I think that you would always help your friends.'

'Don't be so sure about that Clara.'

'Would you help me If I needed it?'

'I don't know, are you my friend? That's the first criteria,' he mused, stoking his chin, pretending he was deep in thought, considering her request.

'Well, you are helping me now, so I must be,' she concluded.

Alex drove on in silence, wondering where this flirting cross banter was taking him. He looked at Clara; she was staring straight ahead. It was hard for Alex to know what she was thinking.

'How did you meet your wife?' she asked.

'Is this part of your Police interrogation?'

No,' she laughed, 'I'm just curious. It's a long drive, and how else do I become your friend if I can't find out about your past? I already know you were deep in the drug trade, perhaps I should arrest you,' she chided.

'Good luck with that Lieutenant Ramirez.'

'No, seriously, how did you meet your wife? I'm interested, that's all.'

'Well, it was in Melbourne. I'd just started my Media company, doing mostly ads and TV promotion, it was a start. Anyway, Megan was the client for a small promotion, and she was also the main model, both the client and the talent, a rare combination, doesn't always work well, but in this case, Megan was very good at both. So, I ended up working pretty closely with her on the project, and that didn't stop when the job finished. We liked being with each other both on and off the set. Her business knowledge brought her into partnership in the company, and we flourished. And now we're married.'

'It sounds more like a business arrangement. Are you happy?'

'Jesus, you're a bit forthright aren't you!' He admonished her. But Alex didn't answer the question, perhaps he couldn't. She had crossed a line that stripped away the usual pretence of social chit chat, that you don't question other relationships. Bugger, he wasn't sure he wanted to answer her, so he didn't.

'You said you make TV programs looking at old crimes. So, what are you working on now?' She had switched tack, perhaps realising that she had touched on a raw nerve questioning his relationship with Megan. This was much safer territory.

'I'm looking at a case in Nerimbah where a body has just been found in the dunes after many years disappearance.'

'Was it your friend Beau?'

'God no!' he exploded with laughter. 'Perish the thought. But you're very quick. No, this boy's disappearance is a bit of a mystery. Audiences love mysteries and bodies and sand dunes. There is a famous one in Adelaide called Somerton Man, I did a program on him last year. We still don't know who he is, but this one, we do know his name. I'm going to interview a bloke who knows about it after I've dropped you off at Tunkumba today. So, what about you, Clara? Enough of me, what are you working on'?

'I can't tell you that.'

'Come on, tit for tat, fair play. Maybe I can help you. Why are you so hell bent on going to Tunkumba Creek?'

She didn't answer at first. Alex held his tongue, forcing the silence between them to be the best accusation.

'I'm looking for someone,' she finally said.

'Kami? Villi's cousin from the hospital?'

'No. He is... incidental to the investigation.'

'So have you found the person you are looking for?'

'Yes.'

'And they are in Tunkumba?'

'Not yet.'

She stayed silent, looking resolutely ahead.

'Well?' asked Alex, seeking more.

'You ask too much of me Alex.'

'What?' He complained, incredulous. 'I give you my life story and the best you can give me is a yes, you found the guy you are looking for. I presume it's a guy. Am I right?'

'When I was growing up, my mother told me that you must always keep a mystery in your life, never reveal all.'

'I don't imagine that applies to a Policewoman.'

She sighed. 'Of course not, but in Cuba you learn to keep your thoughts to yourself. It does not do to let everyone know what you are thinking...or doing. Surely you have secrets Alex, all men have secrets.' She smiled at him.

'And women don't?' Alex questioned.' What about you? Apart from this mysterious man you seek, is there someone at home holding on to your secrets?'

'Only my mother and brother Raul.' She said flatly.' But no secrets there.'

'Do they live with you?' he asked.

'It would not be very wise for me to be in the same house as my brother, or mother for that matter. In fact, I don't know where Raul is at the moment, he's somewhere in Havana. He keeps moving around, trying to stay ahead of the authorities.'

'I thought you were the authorities?'

'I am, but I'm with the Directorate of Criminal Investigation. I deal with social not political crimes. There are other Police who work in the Security Division...for crimes against the State. These men are not so easy to work with, they are more secretive, and the people they arrest are dealt with in a more secretive way. They would like to speak with Raul.'

'Is this because he is your brother, or because of what he does?'

'Raul thinks the Revolution has not succeeded, that it does not give freedom for the Cuban people. He believes that the country should be more like America, with private ownership, that that is real freedom. Our country is moving slowly toward this, but he openly criticises the Revolution, and this makes it dangerous for him, you cannot do that. So, I have to look out for him, to protect him as much as I can, but he doesn't want it. He looks at me as if I am the enemy. I might be with the Police, but he is also my brother.'

'That must make a conundrum for you?'

'What is a conundrum?'

'A dilemma, a difficult position for you to be in, on both sides.'

'Yes. It can be. I try to do my best for Raul; I've risked my job once before to keep him out of jail. But he won't stop, and he is always hiding, from the Security Police and from me. He doesn't realise that if I can't find him, I cannot protect him.'

'So, this is not Raul you are looking for here?' Alex questioned.

'Of course not,' she snapped. 'He is still in hiding; he cannot leave Cuba. Nobody can.'

'But you did.'

'Please understand, Alex, the man I am looking for here is part of my Investigation. I was allowed to leave Cuba for one reason only, to find this man. But it is more than that. Raul's freedom hangs on the success of my investigation. I don't know where Raul is hiding in Havana, but the Security Division does. I know how they work; he will stay free as long as I do my job and come home. Otherwise, he goes to prison or disappcars. Is that a big enough secret for you Alex?'

'Shit! And I thought I had secrets.' Alex exclaimed.

'Don't feel bad Alex, I just wanted you to know why I am doing this, this is part of my job, but without you, I wouldn't be here now.

You have helped me so much already, we have shared our secrets, so we must be friends.'

Yes', he said, 'we must be friends.'

Ahead the pine trees were thinning to the tea-tree melaleucas of coastal forest. The road verge had changed to white sand that contrasted sharply with the black of the bitumen. Patches of blue began to appear between the trees, and both Alex and Clara swept the road ahead for more glimpses of the ocean.

'I think we're here,' he said, slowing the car at the intersection. Signs pointed left to the shops and the township, but a small sign pointed right to the beach and boat ramp.

' 'Can we see the water?' Clara asked.

'Sure thing,' Alex replied and swung the car into a dusty parking bay, delineated by a ramshackle white fence and a track through the long grass that clearly led to the water.

Clara was quickly out of the Ute and striding purposefully toward the gap in the fence and the beach beyond. Alex took his time, stood next to the car and stretched, watching Clara weave her way out of sight along the sandy track. Friends, he thought, what does that mean? The last two meetings he had been drawn to Clara's company, but now he found her complexity even more attractive. Where was he going with this? He shook his head in obtuseness before locking the doors and following her to the beachfront.

# CHAPTER 17

Clara squealed with childish delight as she kicked off her sandals and skipped to the edge to douse her feet in the clear water.

'This is just like Cuba,' she yelled back to him. She lifted her arms and twirled on the spot, kicking small flecks of water around her ankles. The sand on the small beach was of the whitest purity, the clarity of the salt water unparalleled, set against an aqua blue sky. Across the water, a kilometre away was the low southern tip of Yindibar island, and on the opposite bank to the entrance, was Pelican Point. Beyond was the open ocean. Here there were no waves, they stood on the shores of a vast inlet ringed by mangroves and scrubby coastal forest. The tide race pushed and pulled at the inland waters. At high tide the water was crystal clear, but at the low, sand banks and mud flats appear as if by magic as the water retreated to the ocean passage, leaving channels and deep holes, until the tide changed and it returned again to cover the whole area in an unbroken sheet of liquid blue.

Alex strode up behind Clara, her joy infectious.

'Look, we have that at home.' She pointed down the beach to where knee high grass trailed off the shore into the water, and mangrove roots stood out like a carpet of soft spikes. 'And it is so clear and shallow.' She squealed and jumped backwards as small fish darted in to peck at her feet. She turned and faced Alex.

'It is so like The Bay of Pigs. My father used to take us there all the time, pretending it was for historical reasons, but I know he just loved swimming there. My mother would sit under an umbrella up on the sand, she never swam, but she did like seeing us have so much fun. I was a good swimmer too. This reminds me so much of it. We should swim.'

She brushed past Alex and strode back up past the tide line where she quickly unbuttoned her shorts and let them fall to her ankles, stepping out of them, revealing a striped bikini bottom. As she pulled up her T shirt Alex drew an involuntary breath, her matching bikini top strained to hold her breasts in the right place as her arms moved around, she quickly readjusted her top, and flicked her sunglasses onto the sand, turning to face him. Alex hadn't moved, and she saw this. A slow smile came to her lips as she strode down past him to the water. She cast him a quick glance and called out 'Chicken!' as she splashed into the shallows.

Alex needed no goading, he stripped off his shirt and threw it up onto the sand, then turned and sprinted into the water, surging past Clara, blatantly splashing her, daring her to follow him in deeper.

Twenty minutes later, they emerged, laughing and still flicking water at each other like flirting teenagers. Alex collected his shirt and handed Clara her sunglasses. She wriggled into her shorts, instantly soaking them in the age-old pattern. She draped her shirt over her shoulder and swished her way across the sand toward the carpark. Alex was happy to follow and watch her swaying bum and broad brown back.

It was a short drive into the town of Tunkumba Creek, it was not very big, only one main road skirted the sea front. Holiday houses and bungalows on the ocean side sported large areas of grass and eucalyptus trees down to the shoreline where the sand and mangroves began. Trailered boats and fishing gear littered most yards. Each house was serviced by a water tank and a garage facing the road. On the inland side of the road were the beginnings of newer houses as wealthy retirees found their sea change and either renovated or built new. In the middle of it all was a bowls club with a small clubhouse advertising Chinese meals every Friday and Saturday nights. The only shop and general store served as the main office for the Caravan Park, with a phone box and petrol pump in attendance. The park boasted an expanse of grass pads for caravans, a lonely toilet block and a half dozen cabins along the back fence.

Alex pulled up at the shop front awning and directed Clara to inside where she would be able to rent one of the cabins. As he waited, Alex quickly changed into his dry board shorts, ruing the fact that he swam in his good Bermudas, he threw the wet shorts into the tray at the back.

Clara came out twirling a key on her finger and pointed to the second cabin along. He parked the Ute next to the door and grabbed Clara's bag while she opened up. Inside, it was clean, white and functional; a small kitchenette, small settee, a bathroom to the left and a double bedroom on the right, towels neatly folded on the end of the bed.

'Say, why don't you have a quick shower, and I'll go get us a couple of beers.'

'Alex, you have such good ideas.' she said.

He left her to start unpacking her bag and headed for the shop. There were half a dozen caravans scattered among the sites, but despite the glorious weather, there were few people about. The park shop had a licence to sell alcohol.

With two long necked local beers in hand, he sauntered back along the gravel path, hopped up the three front steps onto the verandah. and nudged the door open with his foot.

Clara was standing in the centre of the room in a wet towel, tied around under her arms in a knot, her bare legs protruding from the bottom of the white wrap. Beneath the towel her breasts swelled against the wet cloth. Her hair was piled on her head, her lips slightly parted, eyes intense, staring straight at Alex. She didn't move or make a move to retreat.

Alex didn't move either. He offered no apology for intruding. Time slowed down. He breathed heavily in and out and willed his right hand to reach out and slowly undo the knot holding the towel. Alex closed his eyes, opened them again... his hand was still by his side. Clara reached up and tasselled her hair, he knew what she was doing, he could barely breathe.

'Perhaps I'll wait on the verandah,' he said quietly, but his feet wouldn't move. Her eyes held his, daring him as she had in the water earlier. He slowly backed out, eyes still locked on Clara's, then turned and sank into the verandah chair, blowing his lips out in an exaggerated release of breath, realising how hard it was to deny himself something he wanted so much to have...but knew he couldn't.

Behind him he heard Clara move past the door to the bedroom, closing the door behind her. When she reappeared, she was in a fresh open collared shirt and dry shorts, the towel now wrapped around her hair in a giant drying knot.

Clara squeezed down in the chair next to Alex, grabbed the beer and clinked the long neck against his. She took a swig at the beer.

Alex drank deeply from his, put his beer on the tabletop and bit at his bottom lip in confusion. Not today he said in an imaginary apology to himself.

She winked at him and smiled.

It was all OK... for now.

# CHAPTER 18

When Alex left Tunkumba Creek he almost missed the turn back to Gildston and drove to the boat ramp instead.

'Shit. Get a hold of yourself. Nothing happened.' He chided himself... but it could have. Oh god, but it could have. He was no stranger to situations that threw sexual confrontations at him, he was in the media industry after all, it was a hive of possibles and probable's...and today had been a probable. He toyed with the idea of turning around and driving back to the park, almost letting his imagination get the better of him.

. He had always had women around him but was faithful to Megan. It didn't matter that Megan was distant with him at the moment, she was his wife, his partner. It would have been easy to have sex with Clara, or not, either way, she would be out of his life soon, but the memory would go on as a secret. All men have secrets, Clara said, perhaps sex with her may be too big a secret for his soul to bare.

'You're a dickhead,' he admonished himself out loud, and settled into the drive back down the highway to Kenilworth Road to find Clarry Woods. All the way, he had trouble concentrating.

He had been told Woods's house was close to a big nursery, one he just passed, and sure enough, a driveway hidden by a row of trees revealed a bulldozer on a long flatbed trailer and a car and old truck scattered in front of a small timber house. He reversed up, turned in and drove slowly toward the man leaning over the bulldozer tracks. He didn't look up but kept working. Alex stopped the car and walked up behind him, ignoring the bull terrier barking and dancing around protectively.

'Clarry. Clarry Woods?' he called.

'That's me.' Woods turned to face him. He was just as tall as he remembered, maybe in his 50's or 60's, Alex couldn't tell, his skin was like old leather from too many hours outside, his grimy overalls unbuttoned in the hot sun.

'I'm Alex Holmes from...'

'I remember you. Saw you at Cedar Vale.'

'That's right. I was up there. About that...'

'Nothing to do with me,' he interrupted. 'That's Tigers project. I just drive the dozer for him; I do what he pays me for.'

'That's not why I'm here, I'm more interested in something from twenty years ago, the boy in the dunes at Hideaway Beach.'

Woods said nothing, just stared at him.

'You were there with Tiger Dittman the other day when they dug him up.'

'Yeh. So?'

'How come you and Tiger were there?'

'What's this all about?'

'I'm researching for a Cold Case program I'm making. I'm building up the background story to the boy in the dunes they found. Can I ask why you were there the other day?'

That seemed to satisfy Woods enough for the moment.

'Tiger was interested, that's all. He wanted to see where the waves had broken through, if it was in the place where it had before. He used to sell land for that development at Hideaway when it first started years ago, about the time the boy disappeared. The surf had broken through then as well.'

'Is that all?'

'That's all,' he said non-committal.

'I understand you worked on the rock wall for the river mouth about that time.'

'Yeh. That's right.'

'How long were you working there?'

'Five months.'

'Afterwards, you started work permanently for Tiger Dittman?'

'What's that got to do with anything?'

'Were you there when the boy disappeared?' Alex asked.

'Wouldn't know anything about that.'

'Did Tiger know anything about it?'

'You'd have to ask him.'

'Where would I find him then?'

'Cedar Vale's on hold, he's probably up at Tunkumba Creek.'

'I've just come from there. It's only a small place, I'm sure if he was there, I would have seen him.'

'You wouldn't. He wouldn't be in town. We cut a road through the forest to a creek side camp there a couple of weeks ago. Tigers been spending a bit of time there on the weekends. You could go see him there if you're game.'

'What's he doing there?'

'I don't know, fishing. You'd have to ask him. Look, I'm busy, whoever you are, whatever you are looking for, it's got nothing to do with me. I just work for Tiger, that's all. Take up your beef with him. Whatever it is, it's got nothing to do with me.'

Alex said nothing, and continued to stare at Woods, assessing whether he could extract anything more from him. But Woods had clearly had enough. Alex took a card from his wallet and handed it across.

'Here's my card, if there is anything you might want to discuss with me, just call. I'm staying at the Windshore Apartments in Nerimbah for the next week.' He handed his card over. Woods looked briefly at it. *Pinnacle Media: Melbourne*

'Up from down south, are you?'

'I grew up here Clarry, I'm as local as you are.'

'Sure.' He dropped the card in the dirt and turned away.

Alex walked back to the Ute, opened the door and glanced back at Woods. He was already at work again, pushing an iron spike into the tracks of the bulldozer, prising away dried mud and dirt. There was more, there had to be. Woods pretended to be angry, had tried to ignore him and blunt his enquiry, but Alex detected something else in his eyes, fear. He slammed the door and strode back over to Woods.

'So how did you know what year the boy disappeared?' Alex accused him. 'And how did you know it was a boy? The other day the Police had only recovered the bones and a bit of clothing from a body, yet you and Tiger both knew who it was and when.'

Clarry turned to Alex, his face blank, eyes narrowing, the iron spike still in his hand pointed at him. Alex was suddenly aware of the remoteness of this place. The distance from the road, the thicket of trees that ringed the property, blocking it from view. He didn't look around but held Clarry's stare. It was a tactic that had worked before, show no fear and definitely don't flinch. Demands for the truth gave him the moral high ground, it put the accused on the defensive. It nearly always worked with the innocent. But when it didn't, when he had faced a real criminal, that's when he needed a Plan B, a means of escape. Alex didn't have a plan B because instinct told him that Clarry was not a criminal. The look on his face when they uncovered the boy in the sand dunes last week told him Clarry had empathy, he was genuinely sad. The spike that was aimed directly at Alex was lowered and dropped to Clarry's side.

Alex repeated the question. This time with a softness to his voice, seeking a way through his barrier, seeking an admission.

Clarry stood silent. The dog had stopped barking and roamed just beyond the bulldozer sniffing at the dirt Woods had prised loose. In the distance car traffic echoed against the wall of trees, but it was the bird calls that he heard the most. Clarry looked around as if seeing it all for the first time, or the last. He breathed deeply and sighed in resignation. Alex waited patiently for Clarry's disclosure.

"I didn't think it was right.' Clarry said.

'What wasn't right?' Alex prompted, his voice a soft gentle query.

'How we covered up the boy after we found him.'

'When was this Clarry?' Alex was starting a timeline in his head.

'Back in mid-eighties, when the waves first broke through in the storm, and Tiger was ordered to fill in the gap in the dunes. The Council were on to him about that.'

'This was at Hideaway beach?'

'Yeh. That's right. I was pushing sand from the middle dunes to plug the gap when I uncovered some clothing. I stopped and pointed it out to Tiger.'

'This was the boy. His body?'

'It must have been, I didn't really look too hard, there was a bright blue jacket and some jeans, I first thought it was just some clothes, but there was more there, you could tell. There was a body. I pointed this out to Tiger. He had a quick look, it was raining hard, and the waves were starting to come back in with the high tide. He jumped down into the pit and had a closer look, pulled at it a bit, then told me to push the lot into the gap and bury it.'

'Shit. And you did?'

'Tiger said we were in enough trouble already and this would only make it worse. I should pretend I didn't see it and bury it all. I didn't want to, I said we should tell someone about it, but Tiger forced me.'

'No one forced you to do anything Clarry.'

'Bullshit! You don't know what it's like, blokes like you. I was already in trouble with Wallace; I nearly lost my contract on the rock wall for leveling the dunes for Tiger in the first place. I was behind with me repayments on the dozer and the truck, wife was fucking some fisherman every time I turned my back. If I reported the body, then the whole job would stop, it'd be shut down, Tiger wouldn't pay me, and I'd lose everything.' He stopped and looked around again before coming to the point of no return. 'Tiger said that if I ignored it and kept quiet, I'd have a job with him for life.'

Alex knew the next question was the make or break of his Cold Case.

'Did Tiger know who the boy was?'

'I don't know, I think he did. He was a bit surprised at first, but after he had a look at it, he acted like he wasn't interested. Ordered me to fill it in.'

'Do you think Tiger did it? Is that why you didn't report it?'

'No. He never would have done that. He didn't act like he'd done it, more like it was an annoyance.' Alex tucked that observation away for later. Tiger obviously knew the boy and had subverted Clarry into covering the body up. That made Tiger Dittman the number one culprit in his books.

'And you protested?'

'Course I did. I told you. I told him we have to report it...'

'But you didn't!'

Clarry was slumped against the trailer, dejected.

'I know I should have. I've known it all my life. Someone's kid had gone, and I knew where he was, where he'd been all these years. Some parents been looking for him all this time and not knowing.'

'Mr Woods have you got any children yourself?'

'Nah. Wife left me long ago.'

'Maybe you've got a chance to redeem yourself, go to the police now.'

Clarry straightened up and faced Alex directly.

'You wouldn't fucking know,' he snarled, and threw the iron spike on the ground. 'Maxi! Come here,' he called to the dog and headed for his front door.

'Clarry, it will all come out eventually,' Alex called after him. 'And you need me to be able to tell your side of the story, not Tigers.'

Woods clumped heavily up the stairs to the verandah, the screen door banging shut behind him.

Alex stood in the yard, staring after him. He now had solid leads for his cold case. Clarry was seeking redemption, but Tiger was a block to his conscience. As long as Tiger held sway over Clarry, he could deny anything that was said this afternoon. Alex mentally checked off all that Clarry had told him, he would make a transcript as soon as he could, but he needed more, he needed proof. It would all eventually catch up to them; time was now just a stalling factor. It was Tiger Dittman that Alex was hunting now. He knew where to find him, and Clara as well.

# CHAPTER 19

### Saturday

Clara finished her beer as she watched Alex drive away in the utility, crunching over the gravel drive past the few caravans, until he turned at the gate and was lost from sight behind the shop. Pity, she thought, as she reached for a cigarette and lit it. She knew she had been deliberately provocative, had waited in her towel longer than necessary, hoping the coincidence of his return would coincide with her still drying off, and it did. She wanted him, the sex would have been good, but married men had to make the first move, otherwise they played the victim, and would place the cause of their infidelity squarely on her shoulders. Certainly, she would provide the place and time, she had done that more than once before, but it was up to them to move upon it. He wanted her, she saw it in his eyes, the subconscious wrestle, it nearly happened, but in the end, he backed away. His choice. No matter, she thought, there will be another day, another time, she was sure of that. For now, she had a job to do. She stubbed out her cigarette and stepped off the verandah, heading for the esplanade, time to walk the town.

It's what she liked about Tunkumba Creek; it was so much like home. The beachfront houses, all a little ramshackle, ringed the clear waters of the shoreline, no waves. The feeling of comfortable life all around. Ahead a woman was mounding the fallen palm leaves on her front yard with a rake, her large straw hat flopping in time with her strokes. Clara stopped in front of her and smiled.

'It looks like you are fighting a losing battle there,' she remarked.

'All year round.' The woman replied, stopping to lean on her rake. She was approaching sixty, Clara thought, a diminutive figure in sun protective leggings and long sleeve shirt, but her eyes smiled as she spoke. 'The leaves build up when we're not here, and it's the first thing I have to do when I come.'

'You don't live here?' Clara asked.

'Only on weekends, and holidays. We live down the coast usually. By the sound of your accent, you don't live here either.'

'I'm here for work...and some holiday too.' Clara replied.

'Just like my husband. He pretends to work when he comes up here but goes sailing instead. He's out there somewhere now with the neighbour.'

'So, he has a yacht?'

'I wouldn't call it a yacht, it's a trailer sailor, a sailing boat that can be towed by car and launched from the boat ramp. It's twenty foot long, with a swing keel that retracts up into the hull. Perfect for around here. It's too shallow to have a full keeled boat here.'

'So, yachts can't come in here?'

'Well, they can, at high tide, they can get into Tunkumba Creek if they stick to the channel, but they won't get out when the tide drops. Its deep enough if they stay in the holes at low tide, but the sandbanks are too shallow for a full keeled yacht to get out then. When it gets to be a big blow, a few of the yachts hide out up the creek, around the corner from the ramp. You can't see it from here, but it's a good anchorage in a storm. There's no other place here that's deep enough or protected. Pelican Bay over there to the south is too shallow, only for motorboats, it's all mudflats and mosquitoes... and the odd crocodile or two,' the woman smiled slyly.

'You have crocodiles here?' Clara asked incredulously.

'There's been some sightings, one in Pelican Bay and the other over at Yindiba Island. My son fishes for barramundi in the creek, and if barra can live here, then so can crocs.'

'What is a barramundi?'

'It's quite a big fish, great eating, usually likes the rivers and estuary waters up north. Same as the crocs.'

'We have crocodiles as well, mostly small ones, they are in creeks around Bahia de Cienfuegos, the bay near where I used to live.'

'And where is that?'

'Cuba.'

'I thought you were Spanish.' The woman observed.

'That is the language, it's similar to Cuban, but we have our own way of speaking it.'

'Well, we have our own crocs too, and they are large. You don't want to meet one.'

'We swam at the beach earlier, was that safe?'

'Oh, most probably, they like the dark muddy riverbanks usually. It's the stingrays you have to watch out for here.'

'I think there are many things in Australia I have to watch out for.'

'All the tourists say that.'

'I might go and see what the creek looks like.'

'Well, just watch where you step when you walk in the shallows.'

She gave Clara a wave as she went back to her raking. Clara worked her way down to the water's edge and spent a long time following it around to the creek entrance. The shallows were clear, a mix of sand and mud, with small outcrops of rock and mangrove trees standing forlornly just offshore. She passed the spot where she and Alex had swum that morning and kept meandering the shoreline until she found the boat ramp.

The ramp was a rough concrete pad that disappeared steeply into the water. Parked under a tree in the sandy turn around was a four-wheel drive with a long boat trailer attached. The sun was still hot at this time of day, and cicadas rattled their wings to give off that piercing whine that split the still air. The water looked inviting, but the warnings unsettled her, and she found herself looking hard at the bottom as if a stingray or crocodile would materialise, but neither animal did.

Beyond the ramp, the creek entrance was quite wide, but the dropping tide had revealed large areas of sand bank. The central channel was a deeper blue. Upstream, the water was changing to a dirtier colour as the outgoing tide was drawing the silt from the mangroves down toward the mouth and eventually into the estuary. The creek bent to the right inland and disappeared out of sight among the mangroves and overhanging trees. That must be where the yachts could anchor in a storm. Across from the mouth was the northern bank of Pelican Bay. She couldn't see much of it from there, but Alex had explained where it was to her, and pointed out the entrance to whole estuary, guarded either side by breaking surf. Against the dark green of Yindiba island in the distance, a sailing boat moved steadily toward the creek.

She turned to head back into town, unsure if what she had heard from the *Cosmos* was true. The creek entrance looked very narrow for an ocean-going yacht; they would have to time the tide right to get in. They couldn't anchor offshore to unload the drugs, it would be in plain sight of everyone, and even she could see that bringing a yacht into that entrance would be difficult. But it was the only anchorage in the whole area unless you stayed over at Yindiba Island, and that was too far away from the mainland. There was no clear solution to her quandary, only mosquitoes taunting her as she slowly made her way back to the shop, her sandals slapping on the hot bitumen.

Clara wiped the cold can of soda water across her brow before opening it and taking a healthy slug. The shop was a true general store, the aisles held a myriad of canned food, biscuits and household needs, while the corner was stacked with beach chairs and sand spades for children. A hot box of pies sat at one end of the counter while the other served as the post office and reception for the caravan park. The large fridge inside the door held everything from lemonades, milk and beer to flat packs of sausages and cold meat. Clara stood trying on a pair of sunglasses at a tall rotating stand, looking into the small mirror to see how they fitted. She paid no notice when a truck pulled up outside.

The truck door slammed shut, a small bell ringing from above the screen door signalled that the driver had entered the shop.

By instinct, she didn't turn around to look but moved slightly to the left where she could see his reflection in the small vanity mirror on the stand. She adjusted the pair of sunglasses, pretending to make them fit, all the time studying the man at the counter buying his cigarettes. He looked vaguely familiar.

He turned, and leaned against the counter, blatantly checking her out, but all he could see of her face was the glasses in the mirror. And then she recognised him. He had been a crewman on the *Harmony* in Havana the night of the shooting. She was sure of it. Vaughn Crowther had called out to him to let the lines go, and she barked at him not to. Adam, that's what he was called. That night she had looked directly at him, and he at her.

She ducked away from the mirror and walked down the aisle, keeping her back to him.

The doorbell tinkled again, and outside the truck started up with a throaty roar. Clara moved to the end of the aisle and stepped out from behind the shelves. The truck was still there, and Adam was staring straight at her through the glass of the front window. He kept looking at her as the truck did a U turn, kicking up dust on the far side of the bitumen as it roared off down the road.

'*Mierda*!' she admonished herself. Had he seen her? Did he recognise her? Not likely she thought. But it is here, this is the place. She wasn't wrong after all. If Adam is here, then the *Cosmos* will come here, and so will Vaughn Crowther. She slotted into Policewoman mode. Adam was tall, sandy haired, off-white sweatshirt, green shorts and thongs, she'd recognise him again. The truck was a four-ton cab with a large box on the back. Japanese make, registration beginning with OHG. She didn't get the rest, but it was from a hire company called *Rent a Load.* Brown mud around the wheels, splashes of it up the side.

She walked out the door, glancing down to where the truck had disappeared around the bend in the road. Nothing.

'Love. Are you going to pay for those?' the owner called, pointing at the sunglasses still on her head, price tag attached. Clara turned and went back inside where she returned them to the stand, nodded at the woman and went back out the door. A hundred metres away the truck had returned and was stopped on the side of the road facing her, the engine idling.

Inside the shop was no means of escape, more like entrapment. She was better off outside. No other way but to bluff it out, act natural, and walk away while she tried to sort out her next move. He was there because she was sure that she had been recognised, or he wasn't sure and wanted to look again, no doubt about it.

She began a slow walk back along the road in the other direction, feigning interest in the houses that skirted the roadway, till she was opposite the place she had stopped earlier. In the front yard was parked the four-wheel drive from the boat ramp with a sailing boat on the trailer behind, dripping water, fresh from its haul out. Glancing surreptitiously back, she noticed the truck had moved a short way in her direction. It was parked outside the Bowls Club now. Smoke curled out from the driver's side window. He was waiting.

He might not be totally sure if it was her, or why she was here, and that was something she could play on. In his place, she reasoned, if he positively identified her then she posed a threat to their drug operation, but how much of a threat, he wouldn't know, or even if she was alone or not, but he would need to find out. Behind her, the sun was nearly at the tree line, in twenty minutes it would be getting dark, and then Adam would have to make some move,

However, she was a policewoman, and not without her own resources. Ultimately, she could deal with him, but Crowther was her main goal, and she couldn't afford to scare him off. I need help, I need transport, she thought.

She stepped boldly into the yard and knocked at the door. The woman she had spoken to earlier opened up to her, a little startled at the intrusion on dusk.

'Hello, do you remember me from this afternoon?' Clara said, both as a welcome and a query at the same time.

'Of course,' the woman said. 'What can I do for you?' She stood in the doorway, blocking any entrance, her stance wary of unannounced callers at this time of the evening.

'The phone box at the store doesn't work, and I need to make contact with a friend. It's not urgent, but I'd like to be able to ring him tonight. It's about transport tomorrow. Can I use your phone?'

'You don't have a mobile?' she queried.

'No. I wasn't issued with one when I left Cuba.'

'Issued?' she questioned, lifting her voice at the use of that word.

'Oh! I'm sorry, I usually have one for work but not for holidays,' she smiled politely.

That seemed to satisfy her, and she stepped back inside, waving her in.

'Come in, I'll get Mike,' she relented, closing the door after her.

Clara stepped straight through a long galley kitchen that opened into a broad lounge area facing glass doors and the estuary, Yindibah island across the water was picking up the last rays of sunlight in the treetops.

The room was cleanly furnished, with a warm glow from the standing lamp in the corner, lighting an inviting lounge and bookcase against the wall. There was no TV. An elderly man appeared from the bedroom beyond, tucking in a fresh shirt, his damp hair plastered across his forehead and droplets of water falling from his beard.

'Hello,' he said, 'I'm Mike.' He offered his hand without a pause, as if finding strangers in his house was an everyday occurrence.

'I'm Clara,' she said.

'How do you know Kay?' he asked.

'We haven't formally met,' the woman behind Clara spoke, 'but we chatted this afternoon. We don't have a land line, only a mobile. Can you get yours Mike?'

'It's just in the bedroom charging up.' he retreated through the door behind him.

Clara searched in her pocket for Alex's card. The Consulate number was back with her bag in the caravan park. If she couldn't raise Alex first, she would have to try Sousa at the Consulate later.

Outside, a truck engine slowed, it's heavy breaks squealing to a stop near-by. Clara looked sharply toward the kitchen door, the roadway entrance, he would come in from there if he was going to. Kay stood looking at her quizzically while Mike stepped back into the lounge, holding up a flip cell phone with a long recharging cord still attached.

'Not a lot of charge in it, but enough for you,' he said.

Clara glanced between Kay, Mike and the kitchen door. These were good people; they didn't deserve to be mixed up in anything she was bringing to them. She was running out of time. Behind her, the sliding door to the front lawn was ajar, beyond was the evening dark of the estuary waters. She made a quick decision, a phone call would take too long and implicate them in her actions, so she thanked them for their trouble and darted out the door before they were able to respond.

She moved swiftly across the grass down to the water's edge and pushed into the mangroves, crouching in the shallows, sure she couldn't be seen from the house. She only had to wait a minute before a dark figure detached itself from the side of Kay's house, silhouetted by the lamps in the kitchen and lounge. The figure stopped at the glass doors, Adam the truck driver was standing there looking in, his back to her.

Clara took the opportunity to silently slide away through the shallows, gingerly placing her feet in the water without splashing. Stingrays the least of her worries she thought.

A yell of surprise came from the house; Clara watched the figure break away from the doors and race back around the side into the dark. A few moments later, a truck engine started and moved away from the front, disappearing with no lights on. Loud voices of outrage floated across the still night air, outside wall lamps were turned on either side of Kay and Mikes. Amid all the confusion and raising of alarm, Clara kept heading away, skirting the front yards that ended in the saltwater shallows, home of the stingrays.

When she felt it was safe enough, she tip-toed past a vacant beach house, out on to the front road. She looked back the way she had come, lights flickered between front yard trees and letterboxes. Ahead the caravan park shop was lit up like a beacon. But there was no truck to be seen. She moved swiftly along the road verge, weaving in and out driveways, staying in the shadows until she climbed the fence to the caravan park and lightly skipped across to her cabin, staying out of the glow cast by holiday makers cooking outdoor BBQs at their vans.

Her cabin was in darkness when she jumped the steps up to the verandah, reaching into her back pocket for the key. That was when the light burst out of the dark, flooding the verandah and stranding her in full view at the door, key in hand.

# CHAPTER 20

Clara stood stock still, like a deer caught in the headlights, unable to move from the confusion of darkness suddenly exploded by light.

'Clara?' Alex called from behind the headlights of Villi's Ute.

'Alex, you scare me.' She expelled. 'Turn your lights off please.'

'Why? What's up? I thought you might like to see how to get in.'

'Just turn the lights off Alex,' she repeated, a touch of anxiety in her voice. This was not how he expected to be greeted. But he saw how serious she was, so he reached in through the open window and twisted the car lights to off. It immediately plunged them back into the half-light of dim shadows.

'What's that all about?' he asked.

'How long have you been waiting?'

'Not long.'

'Have you seen a truck here, in the park?'

'No, why?'

> 'Can we leave here? Drive back to Nerimbah? Tonight? Now?' she insisted.

'Sure,' he said. 'But what...'

'I'll tell you on the way. I'll just get my things. But we must hurry, and no lights.'

Alex felt his way on to the verandah and through the door. Clara pulled the curtains back to take advantage of as much ambient light as she could.

'Don't turn the light on.' she ordered as she skirted around the cabin collecting clothing and scooping up her toiletries from the bathroom. With it all stuffed in her bag she stood before Alex who had waited inside the door without making comment.

'Thank you,' she said, and leaned forward kissing his cheek in a brief embrace. He was conscious of her body against his, but this was not the embrace he had been hoping for. It was involuntary and heart felt, but there was an element of relief in it, not desire. Despite this, he still felt a thrill at her touch, the warmth of her full body, but he resisted a second squeeze. She broke contact and swept past him. On the verandah she swivelled her head from side to side, before settling on the front gate.

'Can you see a truck out there at all?' she asked.

Alex saw nothing out of the ordinary for a caravan park, let alone a truck at the front gate.

'All good,' he said. 'Come on.' He pulled the keys from his pocket and headed for the Ute.

She bundled her bag into the back seat and quickly settled into the front. 'No lights please. I can't let the truck see me.'

'Is it a big truck, like one with a long trailer?'

'No. Small. A container on the back. The only truck that's been here today. Can we leave without you putting on the lights?'

'I don't know what's got you spooked Clara, but if you want to be inconspicuous, driving down the road without lights on is not the way to do it. If you're looking for a truck, or don't want it to see you, then lights are your best friend. They can't see in our front seat if my lights are on.'

'They would see us from behind.'

'They would see from behind if my lights were on or not Clara. But from the front, my lights would blind them, without them its highly suspicious. I presume you don't want to be seen, so let's see what I can do about getting you out of here, OK? Trust me,' he said, feeling more confident than he had a right to be. He didn't wait for her reply but put Villi's Mitsubishi in gear and slowly wound his way to the front gate...no lights. At the main road, he scanned both ways, no vehicles in sight.

'Squish down in the seat,' he told Clara. 'Don't peak till we are out of here.' He flicked on the lights and swung onto the road, heading for the turn to Gildston. After he turned the corner away from the beachfront road, he told Clara she could sit up.

He picked up speed on the long straight heading out of town. In his rearview mirror, distant headlights suddenly appeared, but he was fast outrunning them. If it was the truck, it was no match for Villi's utility.

'Did you see them? Was it there?' she asked.

'Not that I could see.'

Clara twisted around to look at the darkness behind them, then turned back to the warm orange glow of the dashboard and the cocoon of the bright headlights tunnelling their view ahead.

Alex looked across at her. Inside he was wound up with the shared tension, but it wouldn't do to show that. Ahead was the open road to home, and whatever threat the truck was, it had been left behind. He stole a glance between the road ahead and Clara's tense form.

'Was it only this morning that we drove up this way?' He observed with a slight mocking humour to his voice. 'I've driven it three times today; this is my fourth. I can't wait to find out why. This had better be good Clara.'

'But why are you here?' she asked. 'You came back.'

'No,' he said. 'You first.' He nodded at her before returning his eyes to the road. 'You don't get out of it that easy. Did you find your man, the one you were after? Was he in the truck?'

Clara paused before answering, as if arranging the parcels of information in the order that she wanted to feed them to him.

'To answer you, no. The man I'm looking for is not here...yet. But he will be. I found that out today.'

'When is he coming?' Alex prompted her.

'Soon...I don't know exactly, but within a few days, he is coming in a yacht.'

'Who was in the truck that you are trying to avoid?'

'He works for the man I'm waiting for.'

If she was looking for a guy who is arriving in Tunkumba in a few days, he wondered, why are we going in the other direction? What's with the guy in the truck? It wasn't making sense to Alex, he was missing something, a reason for this hunt, and a reason to flee.

'Come on Clara,' he said. 'Don't make me keep asking questions, give me the background story, I need to see a reason, a motive for all this secrecy.'

Clara broke the silence a minute later.

'When we swam this afternoon, did you see the scar on my shoulder? A bullet went through it. The man I'm looking for shot me there, and left me for dead in the harbour, in Havana.'

'Wow,' said Alex.

'This was three months ago. He was on yacht. I was to search it for drugs, and he shot me and the Customs officer as well before he escaped. I lived, the Customs Major died. That is why I am here, to find Vaughn Crowther the captain of that yacht.' She paused before continuing. 'The man in the truck today was on that boat, the *Harmony*, in Havana when it happened. His name is Adam, and he might have recognised me today. That's why I had to get out.'

Alex took it all in, swirled it around, and still found something missing. Why does she have to leave if they are the ones being hunted?

Clara continued, as if reading his thoughts. 'The yacht is called *Cosmos* now, and these men are dangerous, they have a lot to lose if they are caught. That Adam, the man in the truck, I think he may have recognised me, and if he knows I'm with the Police, that is enough to want to get rid of me... because I am a threat to their operation.'

'Their operation?' he queried her.

'They are bringing a shipment of drugs into Tunkumba Creek. I overheard them back at the marina in Nerimbah. That is why Crowther, the captain is bringing the *Cosmos* here. Adam is getting the place ready for the transfer; it's why he has a truck I think.'

'But you are with the police, you were with the AFP at the hospital, with that Federal policeman. Can't you just arrest them, get your man that way?'

'Alex, I have no jurisdiction here. There is no extradition with Cuba. I'm on my own here.'

'And this bloke Crowther, the captain, he shot you, and you want revenge?'

'No Alex, I want justice,' she said.

Rows of pine trees lit up then disappeared in the glow of the headlights either side of the road. Alex focused on driving, involuntarily speeding up, as if hounds were on their heels. The tyres hummed and the radio crackled in and out of station, but Alex wasn't really paying attention, his mind was trying to comprehend all the implications.

'You know,' he said, nodding his head out the window to his side, 'that here we grow plantations of European pine trees for timber, while in southern Turkey, they grow forests of Australian gum trees for timber. Fancy that.'

She didn't say anything to his innocuous observation, it was so far out of left field that it deserved to be ignored, but it gave him a chance to digest all that she had told him.

'You really are in the shit, aren't you; messing with these drug traffickers.'

'You have met the one I'm after already. At the yacht club, Vaughn Crowther, he knocked over your beers and came to the table.'

'Was that him? Shit. Big bloke, with a temper. Where is he now?'

'I think at sea, getting the drugs before coming here. I think it will be very soon, within the next few days. Now you know who I've been looking for.'

'What are you going to do when he gets here? What justice do you want?'

'I don't know. I have a lot to think about.' She answered lamely. 'Now it's your turn. Why did you come back today?'

'Look, I was up here trying to find my own bloke for an interview, Tiger Dittman. He's at the centre of a story I'm following, one I want to use in my program, the one I was telling you about, a body found in the dunes. Well, it turns out Dittman was supposed to be at Tunkumba Creek today, at a camp on the creek.'

'And did you find him?'

'No. But I did find the camp though. The track to it started just outside of town, we passed it earlier, a bit hard to find in the forest, but I followed it to the creek. There were a couple of tents in a clearing, but no Tiger Dittman, just some bloke, a bit pissed off that I had showed up.'

'Alex why was this Dittman at the camp?'

'Apparently, Tiger had graded the track in, it was new, sure enough. The man I interviewed this afternoon told me Dittman has visited the camp a couple of times to go fishing. I left my card with him in case Dittman showed up. I really need to talk to him.'

'Was there a car at the camp?'

'No.'

'Well how did he get there? Where was his vehicle? Could it have been a truck.'

'The spot was certainly big enough to take one.'

The main turn south was ahead, and Alex slowed down to take the on ramp before he hit the highway at Gildston, then he pushed the Mitsubishi up to 110 kph. Neither of them spoke for the next five minutes. Alex stared straight ahead, not yet daring to voice his next thought. It was tenuous, but he had to explore it.

'Clara...'he finally began, 'Clara, are we investigating the same thing? Well, not the exact same, but crossing over each other if you know what I mean.'

'I know what you mean Alex,'

'Is the truck that your mate Adam is driving, the vehicle that services the camp, that my mate, Tiger Dittman built the road to?"

'Coincidence does not prove a connection; it only points to the need for further investigation.'

'Is the camp the transfer place?'

'It is possible, but you must be careful of drawing the wrong conclusions, it is easy to do as an amateur.'

'An amateur! Thanks!' Alex said in disgust. 'I saved your biscuit today, and you rank me as an amateur?

'I didn't mean it that way. Please don't get me wrong.'

'I think there is a connection between Tiger Dittman, my shifty businessman and your Vaughn Crowther, a drug trafficker, and you dismiss it out of hand.'

'I have not dismissed it, but you should not make such a big thing of it.' Her voice took on a note of condescension to it. 'It is too easy to go off following false leads if you do not have the experience.'

'And I suppose you do,' he asked stupidly.

'There is only one police investigator in this car, you should remember that.'

'I've done this sort of investigation before.'

'But not like I have,' she said sharply.' I know how to follow proper procedure. Men get so wound up with their feelings, too much placed on coincidence and their silly intuition. Police work is not about feelings.'

'Is it because I'm a man?'

'Don't be so stupid, Alex. That has nothing to do with it.'

'I bet it does. You told me how hard it was as a woman to become a police officer in Cuba,' he accused her. In his anger he rushed on. 'I bet you pushed aside a few men to get what you wanted.'

'Well, I didn't have to push you aside did I, you stepped out of the way all by yourself today.'

'Oh fuck...that's cruel., Alex blurted, noting the sarcastic switch to her voice. 'I am married, you know,' he said taking the moral high ground.

'So typical. You use that as an excuse. Men always do.' Her Latin sneer contemptuous.

This burned Alex even more, he was furious, stung by her comments. The conversation had switched and turned, and neither of them had backed down. He knew exactly what she was referring to. It hurt because she was right, he had reverted to the age-old moral vindication. He knew he was acting petulant, but being called out for something as intimate as declining sex, had not yet turned around to examining his deeper feelings about why not. Overshadowing this was the bland argument about sexism and archetypical actions of men. What a crock of shit, he thought, she started it, and he got sucked into it. Until now, he had been in awe of her, she was smart, ambitious and desirable, but she admonished him for holding back on sex, and rather than see it as honourable considering his marital status, he was castigated for it.

He turned away from her and concentrated on his driving. Bugger it, he thought, I'm not helping her anymore, she can do her own thing from here on in. It had been a long day and he wanted no more part of it, or her for that matter. They said nothing more for the remainder of the drive, lost in their own musings and hurt.

In his head he prepared what he would say to her as a parting shot, his lips moving as he wrestled with the wording, hoping to hurt her with a jibe about gender wars and revenge being a shitty motive for her police work. He wasn't going to help her any more.

He slowed onto the front esplanade of Nerimbah and turned down past the river to the Hostel. As he drew up outside, Clara looked at him and made to get out. He turned to her, his speech ready to recite, when she beat him to it.

She reached across and placed her hand on his forearm, a gesture of reconciliation.

'Alex, please understand that I have a job to do, I am under some pressure, and do not always say and do the right things. I haven't thanked you for getting me out of Tunkumba Creek today.'

Alex just nodded. All thoughts of his sanctimonious diatribe went out the window. He hadn't bargained on her own remorse.

'I loved our swim together and would like to do that again. Can I talk to you tomorrow after I have called the Consulate?'

'Of course,' he said, hating himself for weakening so soon. He sighed in resignation and smiled at her. 'It looks like you may not get much sleep here tonight.' He nodded toward the flashing neon lights and thumping music beating its way out from the Hostel bar. 'I don't know if you'll get a bed in there. Do you want to crash on the couch at my unit tonight?' He winced, regretting the offer as soon as he had said it.

'I don't think that would be a good idea,' she responded, grabbing her bag and sliding out the door, closing it after her. She leaned in the window with a parting shot. 'Even with Megan in the apartment, I don't know if you could sidestep me for second time.' She winked at him and turned away.

Shit. How does she do that to him? Damn if she's not right, he blurted to himself. She's been right too often. He turned Villi's Ute around and headed back to Windshore apartments, wondering how he was going to explain this day to Megan.

# CHAPTER 21

### Sunday

The light streamed into the front windows of the bedroom. It was Sunday, that special day, a licence to sleep in, lie under the covers, make French toast and read papers on a verandah drinking coffee. It wasn't a workday, it was a day when you strolled down to the corner shop and brought fresh orange juice, damn the expense. It was a day when you snuggled up to your loved one. Alex snuggled into Megan's back and reached around to draw her closer. Megan wriggled and stretched. He had no idea when she had come to bed, nor when she had pulled the covers up over them both, but in the morning light, it felt delicious waking up with her in his arms. She rolled over to face him.

'Guess what I found out yesterday?' she whispered.

'I don't know,' he said. 'Tell me.' He expected a grand idea.

Megan reversed out of his arms, almost jumping out of bed with her enthusiasm.

'I'll be right back.'

He had been surprised when he returned last night, Megan was curled up on the couch, tapping away on his laptop, sheets of Government information and reports scattered across the coffee table. When he suggested they go out for a bite to eat, she just pointed to the fridge and told him to warm up the takeaway Pizza she had left for him.

He watched her while he ate at the kitchen bench. She was engrossed with her work and wouldn't be drawn into any explanation of what she was doing. She was too busy, she said. Alex was tired so he left Megan to it in the loungeroom, showered and turned on a Rugby League match on the bedroom TV. Brisbane was playing his Melbourne side; it was a close game. He collapsed on the covers, staring at the screen till he dozed off before full time and hadn't found out who had won. He slept all night without waking till dawn.

She returned with a sheaf of papers in her hand, waving them at him as she settled cross legged on her side of the bed.

'We've got him.' She stated.

'Who?'

'Dittman and his lap dog ...Clarry Woods, is that him?

'Yep. I saw him yesterday.'

'Well, he's just minor fish, but if he does what Dittman says, he's just as liable for prosecution. Doesn't matter that he's an employee, he's still culpable.'

'So, what have you got?'

'Preservation of Breeding Habitats. He hasn't applied for an application to waver the tampering with animal breeding places.' Even though she held the government information in her hand, she didn't refer to it, it was one her strengths, the almost encyclopaedic memory for information that was pertinent to her work. It was what made her so valuable in the company, and what made her so unpopular with the other employees, she was always right.

'It's not the fact that a platypus is found in the creek at Cedar Vale, that's not enough, the animals can be shown that they are capable of adapting, or moving to another part of the creek, but It's the tampering with the animal breeding places that we can get him on.'

'Go on,' said Alex, impressed with the direction of her argument. She pointed to one of the pages in her hand and waved it at him. She didn't refer to it at all as she recited the appropriate passage.

'The loss of vegetation destabilizes platypus burrows and reduces instream shelter, habitat and food for benthic fauna.'

'So why can't the platypus just move downstream or go somewhere else to eat and have sex?'

'Are you on Dittman's side?' she accused him.

'No, I'm just playing the devil's advocate, giving his response as to why he can push on with the development. You're the one who said they were not endangered. Surely there is plenty of room for those little guys to dig burrows in other parts of the creek, just as long as there are no burrows where he puts the causeway across. His argument will be that the creek is big enough for both of them, its not like he's blocking the creek permanently. The little furry creatures can easily move to another part of the creek if it's too noisy and live in harmony with the local hippies if they want.'

'Don't be facetious. It doesn't become you.'

'Look, I'm sorry, I was just seeing it as Dittman would. What's benthic flora anyway? Is it the ferns that I bullshitted to Dittman about?'

'No. It's all the stuff on the bottom of the creek that platypus need to live off and breed, all the bi- organisms that get pushed up by their bills when they feed. You know when you see underwater footage of platypus snuffling their bills back and forward across the bottom, and lots of sediment and bits fly everywhere, dirtying up the water, well that's benthic flora. The platypus needs that. And if you push gravel into the waterways, it changes the speed and currents of that water affecting the benthic flora. A causeway speeds up or slows the water flow, strips away the benthic layer, or covers it with gravel and voila...the platypus can't feed properly, and it affects their breeding cycle.'

'And I suppose, you can't do anything that affects the breeding of a protected species?'

'Exactly.'

'You clever girl.' He reached for her, eager to show her how clever he and she could be together on a Sunday morning in bed, but she rolled off the covers out of reach and stood facing him in her T shirt.

'Come on, stop thinking about sex,' she scolded him. 'We don't stand a chance with that argument. He'd knock us out of the park.' She turned on her heels and marched out of the bedroom. From the kitchen he heard the sounds of the jug being filled and the clatter of cups on the counter. Resigned to following her lead, he staggered to the en-suite, showered and joined her at the bench. She stood sipping at a cup of hot fragrant tea.

'Alright. I'll take the bait. Why won't your breeding habitat stop Dittman. It sounded all right to me. It's a good argument.'

'It is, I know, but it's not enough.'

'Heh, I stopped him with a bullshit argument about an endangered fern, little pregnant platypus should do the job,' he quipped.

'They aren't endangered. They are not even a protected species in Queensland; they are classed as common. Dittman would win. If the platypus doesn't like what's going on with the causeway, they can go live somewhere else, according to the environmental department, pregnant ones or not.' She stood smiling at him.

'Come on,' Alex said, perplexed. 'What gives? You don't smile when someone proves you wrong. I know you,' he chided, 'you're never enthusiastic over something that proves to be a bust.'

'Your right, I am a clever girl.' She smiled and moved her hips flirtatiously. 'That regulation alone is not enough, but if the creek is declared a Special Wildlife Reserve, then it is. I can get an interim conservation order slapped on the creek habitat, and the best thing is, the platypus doesn't even have to live on that part of the creek where Dittman is pushing his causeway across, as long as they are in the creek somewhere near, and we have the proof.'

'Shit, that makes it easier,' said Alex, not knowing what she was on about now.

'Bonny's taking me to buy a Nikon camera, one with GPS that stamps location on the photos. She knows where there is another platypus hidden away downstream. If we get the photos today and match that to a map, we can present Dittman with the proposal for declaration of a Special Wildlife Reserve, and nothing is allowed to alter the landscape until its ratified.'

'Hold up there a little. Isn't that government? Its Sunday, government departments don't work on the weekend, or that fast for that matter. How do you propose getting that together in a day?'

'It's only a proposal. All the forms are on the net. All the information will be right, it just won't be a signed document from a government department... yet. it will just look like one without a signature. Tomorrow, he might think twice about getting his bulldozer in action up at Cedar Vale. If we need to, we can threaten him with two years jail for breaking an interim conservation order.'

'It's all bluff, isn't it. He will notice no signature or date stamp you know. He might be a dick, but he's not stupid.'

'Not if we work a slight of hand, use a bit of feminine wiles on him and wave it fast enough under his nose that he won't stop to look at the squiggle we present as a signature, especially if he's distracted.'

He smiled and hugged her. 'I'll come and visit you in jail for fraud, falsifying Government Documents.'

'It's only to delay him, long enough to get the real ones signed.'

'Excellent,' he said. 'I hope it works.' He kissed her deeply and she responded just as heartfelt. He moved his hand along her back, beginning to scrunch up her T shirt. but she broke off and leaned back.

'Down boy. Plenty of time for that later. Bonny will be here soon; I need a shower.' She poured the remnants of her tea down the sink and headed for the bathroom.

'What happened to you yesterday?' she called from the shower. Alex didn't respond at first, he was glancing through some of the highlighted pages she had been working on. It might just work, if Tiger Dittman was distracted, not his usual self, under pressure and not able to focus on the problem at hand, then he might make a mistake. Alex was planning to interview him this morning, which would give him something different to think about, it would help both he and Megans objectives.

'I got an interview with Clarry Woods out at his place,' he said loudly over the sound of the shower. 'Woods took a bit of coercion, but he cracked in the end. Guilty as hell and pointed the finger squarely at Dittman. Dittman is either culpable of hiding a dead body from authorities, or he is culpable of putting it there in the first place. So, I took a run up to Tunkumba Creek to find him.'

The shower stopped and Megan appeared in the bathroom doorway, a towel wrapped around her, knotted over her breasts.

'And?' she enquired.

Alex stood staring at her, he'd been here before, the dripping hair, a wet towel, the desire.

She sidestepped into the bedroom and called out behind her. 'Did you find him?'

'I um... got up there but he wasn't around.' By the time he got to the bedroom door, she was already squirming into a pair of khaki shorts.

'Pity,' she said.

'Pity,' Alex echoed, meaning something different. He stood watching her. 'I ran into Clara up there and brought her back down here last night.' He knew when he said it that he had made a mistake.

Megan froze. 'Oh!' she said haughtily, part way through selecting a white long sleeve shirt from the rack. She slowly slipped her arms into the sleeves before buttoning it up all the way to her throat. Mentioning Clara was stupid. It didn't have any bearing on their discussion, but he wanted to be able to talk freely with Megan without her jumping to innuendo all the time.

'I'm seeing Dittman this morning, find out what he knows about the kid in the dunes. Plenty, I think. Between you and me, we should put him off enough that pushing a causeway through your creek will be the last thing on his mind.'

She walked up and faced him, not quite eye to eye, but it didn't matter, her intent was what counted.

'I hope so Alex, I really hope he has a lot to think about...and I hope you do too.' she said and moved around him to get her sandals and grab bag from near the door. 'I'm going downstairs to get a coffee and wait for Bonny there. Don't forget to return Villi's car.' She walked out, closing the door. Alex noted that he hadn't been invited to join her.

# CHAPTER 22

Tiger Pitmans house could only be described as grand. Its façade emulated an Italian Villa, one of many similar in appearance along the street. The pebble driveway ended next to two large columns straddling the double entrance doors. The garage door was up, a neat empty space, only one car present, a white Mercedes sport. Alex grabbed the lions head doorknocker and belted it against the striker with an urgency that demanded attention.

Gloria Dittman, tall, blond hair, green eyed. He could see she had striking features that had been softened with age till her face bore the current redness and slight bloating from too much good living.

'Yeh? What do you want?' she demanded, standing in the opened doorway.

'Hi. You must be Gloria. I'm looking for Tiger Dittman if he's home,' Alex asked.

'Home? Hardly. He's not here.'

'Do you know when he'll be back?' Alex leaned out a little to look past Gloria.

A house always gave away clues. Too neat, too messy, ordered or overstuffed with non-essentials, it always told him something about the person. He took the opportunity to learn what he could of Pitman. There was no artwork or furniture in the hall entrance. Contemporary but bland. The large white hallway tiles opened to a white leather lounge facing a huge TV cabinet that encompassed half the wall, the other half was glass, looking through to a back deck overshadowed by a stainless-steel BBQ and outdoor kitchen, an old gym set leaning against it. For Tiger, bigger was obviously better. Alex straightened.

'What do you want to see Tiger about?' She repeated.

She was bare foot, in a patterned dressing gown, and although it was still early morning, there was no doubt she was having difficulty standing straight without holding on to the door frame.

'When he gets back in, can you give him my card. It's got my number on it, if Tiger can give me a call.'

Gloria glanced down at the card, and nodded, then without any further discussion, closed the door.

Within ten minutes, the mobile rang as he pulled up in Villi's driveway. He turned the motor off and answered the flip phone.

'Mr Holmes? Terrance Dittman here.' Alex recognized his gravelled voice.

'Mr Dittman. Thank you for calling back so promptly. Your wife must have passed on the message that I dropped by.'

'I'd appreciate it if you kept my wife out of anything we have to say. What do you want Mr Holmes?'

'Terrance. Can I call you Terrance, or do you prefer Tiger?'

'Neither to you. I don't like journalists.'

'Lucky I'm not a journalist. I run a media company,' he replied.

'Same thing as far as I'm concerned.'

'I understand, point taken. I was wanting to ask you a few questions.' He hurried on before Dittman could reply. 'I'm developing a TV program about the boy Crinns they found in the dunes the other day. If it becomes a cold case, it will make an interesting story. I was talking with Clarry Woods yesterday, and he indicated that you may have known him. Would that be true Mr Dittman?'

'You talked with Clarry yesterday?'

'Yes, That's right.'

'What did he say?'

'He indicated that you both knew that the body of Barry Crinns was there before the Police recovered it last week.'

'Clarry is full of shit. I don't know where you are getting your information from Holmes, but if it's from Clarry, then I wouldn't believe a word of it.'

'But Clarry was adamant that his memory was correct, you were both present when he was ordered by you to fill in the gap in the sand dunes in the 1980's. You were there weren't you?' Alex kept pressing.

'So? What if I was there?'

'Well, according to Clarry Woods, you uncovered a body while working on the site but failed to report it.'

'You've got to be kidding me! I know nothing about that,' he denied.

'I'm not kidding Mr Dittman. I've got one witness already, and a transcript of that interview.' Alex didn't have a transcript of what Woods had said, but he would soon. Dittman didn't need to know that.

Tiger was silent. There was the faintest breathing over the phone. Alex waited patiently, he had served up a serious accusation, any answer could not be given or taken lightly.

'Would it be possible to meet today, Mr Pitman? In person, not over the phone. Then we can discuss this fully and you can tell me your side of the story, not just what I've heard from Clarry Woods.' Come on Tiger, Alex willed him, this is your best chance. Your side of the story. He could play one off one against the other.

Tiger came back after the prolonged silence, strong and confident.

'Can't today, got meetings all day. I'll be free later. Tell you what, meet me at Hideaway beach tonight at six thirty, at the breakthrough, where the Police recovered the body. I want to show you something they didn't see, I'll talk with you then.'

'That would be fine. If you decide to meet up earlier, I'm staying in Unit 6 Windshore Apartments, you can call me anytime today. I'm putting together a Cold Case episode about the Crinns boy, any input you have will be much appreciated, and I'm sure your side of the story is in your best interests Tiger.'

'Six thirty.' Pitman said as he broke the connection.

Alex closed his flip phone and looked up at Villi standing at the car door surveying him. Alex wound the window down.

'You had breakfast?' he asked Villi.

'Of course, I don't lounge around on holidays like you lot from Melbourne. Narina and I are going to watch Xavier at football carnival today. What about you?'

'I've just been after Tiger Dittman, to find out what he really knows about Barry Crinns, the boy in the dunes. He knows something, Clarry Woods confirmed it yesterday,' he said.

'You talk to him face to face?'

'He wouldn't be drawn into it over the phone. He's meeting me tonight to tell me about it. I went to his place this morning, but he wasn't there, his wife Gloria was though, pissed, or halfway there. It was ten o'clock in the morning and I bet she's giving the gin bottle a nudge.'

'If she wants to have a drink in the morning that's her own business, not yours.' The reproach in Villis voice stung Alex.

'She had trouble standing up straight,' he offered, as if her inebriation justified his moral judgment.

'So do I sometimes. Means nothing.' Villi pushed off the door frame, totted a little on his damaged leg, then stood straight and still as he directed his next question at Alex. 'Are you sure you want to keep heading down this path? What are you getting out of this? Is this for you, to prove something to yourself, or to Megan, with your TV show? I though you told me you were here for a holiday, not work, give yourself a chance to get you and Megan back on track. You can't do both. What's it going to be?'

Villi had a point. What was he doing this for? He was reaching a stage he often thought of as the 'Go' or 'No-Go' point, where he has lined up all the elements and would either commit or back away to start again elsewhere. Like the Houston space centre before a rocket goes up, 'Go' or 'No-Go'. Damn, he thought, I need to reach my Go or No-Go point. He smiled at Villi.

'Can I keep the car for one more day?' he asked.

'Yeh...go on.'

'Thanks for that Villi. I needed that. Got plenty to think about. I'll let you know tonight if it's worth it.'

'Have a holiday Alex, go for a surf and stop running around the countryside. Treat yourself, and Megan. She's a good woman you know.'

'Yeh, I know,' he said.

Villi pointed at his car calling out in farewell. 'And you don't have to wash it when you bring it back, just don't scratch it.'

Alex waved to him and turned the motor over. It also occurred to him that in that famous astronaut movie were the words later uttered alarmingly from space, 'Houston, we have a problem.'

He reversed out on to the road and headed back to his apartment. Alex emerged from the underground carpark, looked across at the surf, it was running at about three feet. Across the road, the waves peeled effortlessly onto the shore, clean, only a slight breeze to hold up their progress. Funny, he thought, how we still judge wave heights in feet not metres, old habits die hard. Damn if Villi wasn't right, he did need a surf, he'd been wound up for the last few days, juggling his time, trying to give his cold case investigation some sort of direction, dealing with his emotions every time he was around either Megan or Clara. It was time to focus. He'll give the meeting with Tiger tonight a go, and decide what to do after that, decide If the story is a 'Go or No-Go' proposition. Maybe he should stop fluffing around and devote his sole attention to Megan. Maybe he should escape to the surf to bury his head in the sand. No surfboard today, bodysurf only.

The first wave was way too big for him. He knew it as he stroked into it. Always start with a small one to limber up the muscles, get the body ready for the contortions of the larger waves, but hubris again had its part to play in surfing disasters. Without thinking, he took his first wave, the largest in a set, one that was to break in shallow water nowhere near deep enough to cushion his drop. In fact, a straight front on drop would probably break his neck. This beach was well known for spinal injuries. By reflex, Alex twisted his body left as he free fell from the lip, flinging his arm out ahead and taking the wave side on in a twist so that his body rolled rather than bent over itself with the force of the water behind him. He was slammed into a foot of water at the bottom, his body lifted in the bounce and rolled mercilessly over twice in a maelstrom of sand and foam until it released him, and he struggled spluttering to his feet. It hadn't end smoothly, but least he could stand up straight after it.

Not to be daunted by his first wave, he pushed his way out past the break and vowed to choose a less damaging wave next time, something smaller, with more form to it, proving his prowess and dexterity with judicious wave choice. The set came, don't catch the biggest one... don't catch the biggest one...he did. He couldn't help it. The result was the same as the last, but at least he caught sight of the tube as it curled over the top of him before slamming him into the sand, that was his one reward for the pain. He stood waist deep in the foam, straightening his back, shaking the water from his body, when it came to him. Why was Tiger Dittman at that fishing camp when nothing about him said fisherman? There were no fishing rods in the garage, no fishing paraphernalia. He might be wrong, but Tiger projected white collar businessman, not muddy riverbank fisherman. And if that was a proper fishing camp he walked into in Tunkumba, then he was the Prime Minister of Australia. There were fishing rods there he realised, but none were rigged up. It was all for show.

At that point, he realised why he was here. This wasn't going to be the holiday he thought it would be. This story was like paddling into the biggest wave of the set, he couldn't help himself, he had to ride it, all the way to the bottom even of it ended up crushing him. The surf...the story... both could be relentless, drive him forward, drag him under, or offer up the gold nuggets of reward for the risks. His next three waves he body surfed with the skill of a seasoned performer, he'd found his rhythm and his drive.

The slow drip of water from Alex's boardshorts made a puddle on the lino floor of the newsagency as he stood in front of the stacked newspapers and lottery dispensers on the display counter. The large print headline on the paper was what drew his attention. *Australian girl arrested for smuggling drugs into Bali*; blurred photo accompanied.

'Sign of the times.' The newsagent remarked, surveying Alex with mild comradery as he drew his attention to the anomaly of the headline. 'In my day, people only smuggled drugs out of Indonesia, not into it.'

'They must be running out of them or something.' Alex quipped. Then he noticed a small story at the bottom of the page. It probably wouldn't have made the front page if not for the slight relationship to the attention-grabbing headline. *Last of the crew from the Pong Su deported*. Alex brought the paper, a notebook and pens, tucked it all under his damp arm and headed for home.

Inside the unit the sunbathed living room tiles were already warm and reflected light into the furthest corners of the room. Alex could hardly slow down, he showered and changed, casting his wet boardshorts and towel into the bath to be hung up later. Coffee was made and spilled in haste as Alex eagerly arranged the laptop, paper and pens on the bench.

The Bali story he ignored, sensational as it was, it was the *Pong Su* he wanted to read about. He remembered the incident clearly.

In 2003, the freighter *Pong Su* was busted for heroin smuggling off the Victorian coast, and though this was not remarkable, it was how they were busted, the link to North Korea and the unfolding of the Federal Police investigation that was the best part. It had ended with upturned inflatables, dead bodies and manhunts, packages of heroin floating in the surf, even an SAS ship raid. The story recapped the original incident, the truth was so bizarre that you couldn't make this stuff up he thought. Alex scanned the article for the details he sought. The last of the ship's crew, apart from the main perpetrators of the trafficking, were recently deported. Although the ship was registered in Tuvalu in the Pacific, the crew were sent back to North Korea not the Pacific Island. It was the Pacific connection he was looking for. If the AFP discovered that the ship had stopped at or near a Pacific island, they weren't saying. Nor was it discussed about how the drugs were to be smuggled into Australia, only that it all went wrong, the traditional transfer offshore to a yacht or motor boat didn't eventuate, so they had to come in close to shore and use inflatable dinghies instead. The article hinted at further investigation when more international evidence comes to light. For the moment, the primary criminals are in jail, the ship impounded, the crew sent home yesterday, and there are still 20 kilos of heroin not recovered floating around out there. He knew from experience how easy that could be. What a coincidence.

Clara was right, coincidences are not Police work. But then, he was not a policeman, and he placed a lot of stock in coincidence and instinct, it had worked for him before. Tiger Dittman knew more about a young boy gone missing twenty years ago than he was letting on, both then and now. The *Pong Su* incident and Pacific island connection bore too many similarities to Claras investigation of the *Cosmos*, and somehow Tiger Pitman was involved in both. His investigation of Dittman was running in parallel with Clara's investigation of Vaughn Crowther. Megan was also gunning for

Tiger and had a legal avenue to his past. Their investigations did cross over, no matter what Clara said in the car, he was sure of it.

Alex opened his laptop and started his notes and a transcript of Clarry Woods interview.

# Chapter 23

Clara armed herself with her notebook and the phone card she had brought from the reception desk and squeezed into the booth outside the hostel. The booth was warm with the Sunday morning sun. She was well rested, but nervous, determined. She smoothed out her contacts page on the top of the phone box and made her first call.

Assistant Consul Anton Sousa picked up. Remarkable for a Sunday thought Clara, he might be a sanctimonious little shit, but a hard working one at least. After identifying herself she asked about her inquiries from the last phone conversation.

'Where are you at present?' Sousa asked indolently.

'Nerimbah. But I have been away following leads, no concern of yours. Now I'm back, so perhaps we can get on with it.' She bullied him. Sousa waited for a long pause before he responded.

'To answer your inquiry about the nationality of a Mr Vaughn Crowther; he is an Australian citizen with an Australian passport.'

Another moments silence. Clara prompted him to go on.

'Anything more?'

'I wasn't aware you asked for more than that. I've delivered.'

She left that arrogant bastards answer swing in the breeze and pushed on.

'Have you heard back from the Ministry in Havana about my instructions on how to proceed in prosecuting this investigation?'

There was no answer, only silence at the other end, again.

'Mr Sousa, are you still there? What did they say?' She hated to sound desperate for his response, but it had been eating at her all night. What now?

'Miss Ramirez, if you are not able to finish your job, go home. Stop bothering me. Your time in Australia is over.'

'You didn't talk to the Ministry, did you? You haven't called them.' She accused him.

'Remember who you are talking to, your investigation is over. Do yourself a favour, go home.' Sousa hung up.

Clara leaned back against the cabinet glass. Fuck. Was she being left to fail deliberately? Why not do as he suggested, accept it, go home. She had been seen in Tunkumba, she could have spooked them, they could be packing up and getting out, their whole operation off, and she would never see Vaughn Crowther again. Maybe they will still go ahead with the drugs, and Crowther will be there in a day or two, but who knows about that apart from her and Alex. She could tip off Agent Hughes from the Australian Federal Police, get them involved. They would place the yacht under surveillance and arrest them all, but then she would never get close to Crowther again. If he is arrested for drug smuggling, he would face Australian justice and never be brought to account for the crimes he committed in Cuba. She would fail in her task, and she couldn't afford that, nor could her brother. No, Clara could not involve the Australian Police yet, she will have to find another way.

Her watch said 9.15 am, that would put it at about 7pm in Havana, well past the end of the day, but fanatics don't sleep, and there is always someone at the Ministry of the Interior. She fumbled with her notes and began the long sequence of numbers that would connect her with General Abelardo's office.

'I have not heard from you in some time Ramirez.'

'I have been busy. I've found the Australian.'

'You have dealt with the person in question?'

'That is what I am confused with general. You tasked me with finding him and bring him to justice. I was hoping for instructions on how to do that. I have found him but he is an Australian citizen, and at present, out of my reach.'

'Then get within reach. I made it perfectly clear Ramirez; you must bring justice to this man for the crimes he committed here.'

'How do I do that? I have no jurisdiction.'

'I did not tell you to bring him to justice, but to bring-justice-to-him. Cuba does not want some lengthy court case amid extradition charges. Just do your job and prosecute this case of the murder of Major Colomè.'

'But what of my own shooting, he tried to murder me too.'

'Then you have double the reason to see this through.'

'But how,' she pleaded.

'You're a smart woman Ramirez, I'm sure you know what to do. After all, Colonel Perez endorsed you as the lead investigator with temporary rank and privileges. Did Perez make a mistake in appointing you?' Already he was distancing himself from any hint of failure, Perez stood to be blamed as well.

'No sir. Both you and he can have faith in my investigation.'

'Then finish the job!' he said angrily. 'The continued welfare of your brother and the privileges that your mother enjoys is reliant on it.'

'There is another problem General. The man in question is about to commit a crime on Australian soil, and the Australian Federal Police may arrest him.'

'You had better make sure that you get to him first.'

'I might not have that option. But then he would be serving a lengthy jail time in Australia, if I can make that happen, would that be justice enough?'

'It is not up for debate. Prosecute the justice Cuba demands, as best you see fit, and come home. Those are your orders.' The phone line immediately cut.

She knew what he wanted of her. There was to be only one successful outcome of this case, anything less would be a failure. He threw it back on her, *as best you see fit*, was entirely on her shoulders. But there was no doubt it meant death for Vaughn Crowther, in whatever way she saw fit. Failure to prosecute that form of justice meant that her family would suffer and Perez and she will end their days in the police force on Isla Juventud serving the revolution by giving speeding tickets to donkey carts. She needed Perez on her side; he put her up to it after all.

Firstly, she tried Perez's cell phone, but there was no answer. Not even a ring tone.

She immediately rang Perez's office at the Ministry, where she was told he had left for the Main Police station headquarters at the Harbour over two hours ago. She followed it up with a call to the harbour headquarters where the duty Sergeant chided her for having a long holiday while the rest of the force worked hard, but he did tell her that Perez hadn't been seen there all day. If he was neither at the Ministry office or the headquarters, then he was at home... or there was another place he frequented.

Clara rang the headquarters back, asking to be put through to *Sergeant de Primero* Paulo Vasquales. The Sergeant was older than her, and had a chip about her more rapid promotion, however, Clara felt it was founded more on the fact that she a was a woman than any professional jealousy. He wasn't a total sleaze, but he held that deep seated machismo that many Cuban men saw as their right.

When Vasquales answered, Clara immediately cut to the point, told him where she was ringing from, not giving Vasquales any time to pepper the conversation with sexual inuendo. It didn't work.

'Clara Ramirez,' he drawled. 'I thought you were over at the Ministry, perched in the laps of those dogs, having a break from real police work. Instead, you're on holiday in Australia. How did you get out of the country? Special privileges from the Ministry? What did you do to get that?'

'I'm working a case; I need something from you.'

'What do I get in return?'

'You don't know what I want yet'.

'I could suggest something,' he tried as an attempt at sleaze humour.

'I need a number. Colonel Perez's home phone number. I know you have it.'

'He won't be there yet; he only just left here.'

'We both know that's a lie Vasquales, he hasn't been at either headquarters all day, the duty sergeant told me. Just give me his home number, I'll ring him there.'

The phone was quiet, no response.

'He's not at home, is he!' Clara guessed. 'I bet if I rang his home, his wife would be wondering where he was too. And we wouldn't want that, would we?'

'I don't know what you're talking about.'

'Come on, you and Perez are old buddies, that's why you get all the cushy jobs.'

'*Vete a la mierda* Ramirez.' He abused her, his machismo dented, but it was true, the two men had been on the same beat when they were young cops just starting out. Perez had a quick promotion, while Vasquales stayed in the cushy area of the old town precinct where the tourists hung out, an easy beat, lots of easy tourists, lots of easy bribes.

'I'm not after you Vasquales, I need to talk to Perez now. Not tomorrow. I know where he is, with his mistress. I need that number.'

'Can't do it Ramirez.'

'I think you can.' She thought a moment, before trying a new direction. 'It's true, I was at the Ministry of the Interior before I left. I got to look through lots of Security Division files. Does your wife know what's on your file?'

'You wouldn't dare.'

'You bet I would. Now what's the phone number of Perez's mistress?'

After a minute's silence, just as Clara thought she had gone too far, he came back on the line and read out the seven digit number.

'You didn't get the number from me, alright.'

'Alright,' she said. 'And thanks, Vasquales. By the way, I haven't seen your file, but now I can guess what might be in it,' she remarked lightly.

'*Cono*.' Was all he said as he closed the connection.

She promptly dialled the number Vasquales had given her. At first, Perez's mistress refused to acknowledge that Colonel Caridad Perez was in her apartment, claiming not to know who he was and that Clara had the wrong number. But when Clara told her to mention her name to the Colonel, demanding an immediate response or she would be calling his home, his voice came over the receiver.

'How did you get this number?'

She ignored his question, she had the number now, and there was no going back, he was with his mistress, not his wife, and Clara was bound to his future with that shared knowledge.

'Colonel Perez, I need your help.'

'You have been given all the help you need to complete your investigation and reach a successful conclusion.'

'I never had a conclusion, as you call it. This is not an ordinary case of bringing a fugitive to justice under Cuban law. There is no law here for Cuba in Australia, we don't even have an extradition treaty with them, I have no jurisdiction here, you knew that when you assigned me the job. The Consulate have hung me out to dry, and the Ministry have given me only one course of action. I did my job, I found the man who murdered Major Colomè, and when I call for final instructions, there are none, except thinly veiled threats. You tasked me this case, now what do I do to finish it?'

'I think that's obvious, don't you? You must have figured it out by now what the Minister wants.'

'I can't do that. It goes against everything I believe in as a policewoman. They can't ask me to do that.'

'They can and they did.'

'And if I can't?'

'You know what they will do if you don't prosecute this case...not just to you but to your family. They will bear the brunt of your failure as well.'

'And so will you,' she quickly added.

'Don't threaten me Ramirez.'

She was shaking, Perez didn't have any answers, only one course of action was left open to her.

'Colonel, the Ministry pointed out that you selected me for this case, you gave me special powers and expenses, what do you think will happen if I fail to do what they want...we both will suffer, not to mention your family...and the woman you are with now.'

After a long pause on the phone, he came back to her.

'What do you want from me Ramirez?'

'I need a gun to prosecute my orders. I have nothing else here to work with. The General has all but ordered me.'

'If you use a gun, you risk arrest if you are caught, you will be alone in this. I won't be able to help you.'

'You're not helping me much now. I'm already alone, I have no choice. I'm sure you've been in the same position as I am now. Don't go all moral on me Colonel. So do I get a gun or don't I?'

'Ring me back in one hour.'

She sat in the shade, on the edge of the hostel fence, lighting cigarette after cigarette, trying to calm her nerves, oblivious of the traffic going by. The phone box was only metres away, it may as well be the other side of the moon, the way she felt. Dead on the hour, she rang back. Clara had to will herself to make the call, knowing that she was stepping further away from her moral core.

'You have a contact. It is in a place called Caboolture. He spelt it out for her. 'You will meet him at 4pm on the railway station platform. He may be able to help you.'

'Does he have a name? What will he look like?'

'I've never met him.'

'How will I know who it is then?'

'He'll know you. Don't ever ring this number again.'

The phone went silent.

The train pulled into the station at 4pm, disgorging a multitude of passengers, some old, some young, but nearly all immediately left the platform. A small phalanx of teenagers stood around, heads bent in to each other talking as she walked off the carriage. They laughed and cajoled each other till one of them noticed Clara standing alone further down the platform, watching them. He nudged one of his friends and spoke into his ear which resulted in a deep throated chuckle. The suggestion rippled through the group, till they all looked in Clara's direction, offering their own opinions. She stared them down, until they lost interest and turned away, pushing and jostling each other as they ambled off.

Clara stood alone on the vacant platform, her 4pm rendezvous nowhere to be seen. Across the tracks on the opposite side, a middle-aged dark-haired man stood appraising her, his hands deep in the pockets of his long pants, a small carry bag at his feet.

He nodded at her then moved away toward the exit. Clara quickly crossed the overhead walk bridge and clattered down the stairs, keeping him in sight as he walked toward the cafe across the road. By the time she made it to the small table on the footpath, he was seated and just finishing an order for a cold beer. Without breaking eye contact she pulled out the opposite chair and sat down across from him.

His white open sports shirt exaggerated his tanned complexion, dark eyes black hair, medium build. Clara guessed he was in his late fifties, fit and exuding an aura of relaxed competence. He looked at her and tapped his finger on the table. Clearly, she thought, she had to go first.

'You have ordered anything for me?' she asked.

'No. You can get your own.' His voice revealed something more, a slight South American intonation.

'I understand you are meeting me at the request of Colonel Perez?' she smiled as she spoke.

'Colonel Perez. Who's that?' he queried.

Clara was little bemused.

'I'm to meet a man here. With a specific request.' She offered, pulling back from her initial friendliness.

'I might be him, if you tell me your request.'

'*Mierda*, I'm sick of playing these games. Do I look like someone who picks up strange men at railway stations? You must be my contact. Am I right?'

'You haven't been long in Australia, have you. Let's start with who you are first.' he offered. 'Then I'll tell you if I'm your contact.'

'You are my contact,' Clara said defiantly.

'I'm very careful with whom I share my confidences. I've learned that the hard way. Why should I help you?'

'You wouldn't be here if you weren't. You were sent.'

'As were you. I know your kind.'

'And what kind is that?' She challenged him.

'You are from Government...Cuban by the sound of you. Probably from the Ministry of Interior, Security Division, they are the only ones allowed to leave Cuba, outside of Russia and a dozen paltry republics, nothing like coming here. Yes. I think you are from MININT.' He referred to the shortened version of the Ministry. 'Are you here for me?' He looked directly into her eyes, challenging her for the truth.

Clara was taken aback. He was so close to the mark, she needed to be careful, unnerved to be revealed so easily, yet she still had trouble placing him.

'No. I am not here for you. And I'm not from MININT. It is something else I am after.'

'I can smell officialdom from a mile off. So why are you here Miss Official woman?'

Both their suspicions were turning the meeting against her; she needed to change the direction if she was going to get what she came for. It was time to get to the point.

'I'm a policewoman, an Investigator,' she said earnestly. 'I have no jurisdiction here, but I need your help. I was assured you could provide what it is I want. Can you do that?' She reiterated.

'That depends.'

'On what?'

'On whether I want to. Madam, I am a free man; I live here now, I make my own decisions. I left Cuba with the Mariel Boatlift in 1980 and spent the next fifteen years in Miami. I'd had enough of Cuba, and I've had enough of whinging Marielitos in Florida. I'm not a threat to anyone anymore. This place.' He waved his arms expansively about him. 'Australia, it is so much better than either of them...and those MININT pigs cannot touch me here. I decide if I want to help you, no one tells me to.'

'Fuck you,' Clara blurted out in disgust. 'You're no good to me.' She pushed back her chair and made to leave.

'Now we are getting somewhere,' he chuckled, breaking the tension. 'Sit down.'

Clara returned to her seat.

'What's your name?' hc asked.

'Clara. What's yours?'

'That's for me only at the moment. Tell me why I should give you what you want?'

'I need it to prosecute a case I am on.'

'Not good enough. No case is worth using that here, where you have no official standing. I will not give it to you so that you can do the work of the 'so called' Revolutionary Government. Fuck the Revolution. I won't help you do that.' He almost spat the last words, leaned back in his chair and gulped at his drink. His detest of Castros regime was palpable.

Clara could think of nothing more, she had tired of his games, leading her around in circles, each time probing more, deflecting her questions. She leaned forward, staring him in the eyes, all that was left was the truth.

'I was shot and left for dead in Havana harbour by the man that I have followed here. I want revenge, will that do?'

'Now that... I understand,' he said. 'Retribution for a wrong that was done to you? Revenge? That is a good enough reason.'

'So, you'll help me?' she asked, clarifying his response.

'I can. But it is not such an easy request in a country that has no 'firepower', shall we say. Not as easy as in Miami, everyone there had one, and used them. But here it is a different matter, we barely even use the word, let alone carry one. It's why I like this place so much. No one can shoot you in the back.'

He sat watching her for a few moments, quiet, assessing her, before reaching down into the small bag at his feet.

'Here, let me give you a present. Then you can let me kiss you like you are the long-lost Niece that we can pretend you are.' He placed a small, gift-wrapped box on the table, and leaned across to peck her on the cheek.

'See. That was easy,' he said as he folded himself back into the chair. 'Government officials are never honest, they cannot be trusted, any of them. But police, now they are different...they come from the people, both the good and the bad, they can't escape that.' He rose to leave.

'Why won't you tell me your name.' She had to ask.

'That I can't do,' he said. 'It is safer for both of us. But I know who you are, Clara Ramirez.' He stood and walked away without turning back. It struck Clara that in his past life, he was probably once a policeman... like her father.

It was a small calibre Baretta; the serial number had been ground off. It would be reliable and deadly, but only if she was very close. It was no match for the service Makarov she left in Havana, but it would have to do. She released and checked the magazine, a full load. There was nothing more in the box, no extra bullets, no holder. A simple raw firearm. She checked the safety and slipped the gun into the back of her jeans, flipping her shirt over the top to cover it. She stood and flushed the toilet behind her, opened the cubicle and dumped the box and wrapping paper in the bin as she left. Outside, the sun was beginning to set over Caboolture and the range of hills beyond, it was getting dark as she joined the commuters filling the platform. The next train taking her north to Nerimbah would come in ten minutes.

# CHAPTER 24

Parts of blue and white police tape still hung from the she oaks drooping their heavily barked limbs over the dunes at Hideaway Beach. The sand still bore the scars of the Police excavation of Barry Crinns' body, the hole made by the shovels in the soft sand made a natural amphitheatre for the local kids who had come to the spot to drink and smoke in some bizarre platitude to the loss of a fellow teenager. This had all the hallmarks of future legends of ghostly apparitions and yearly gatherings in the dunes to mark the passing of something held dear to them all...youth.

At 6.30 pm, the setting sun had cast the last of its long shadows. Alex was accustomed to Melbourne's twilight, and hadn't figured on it getting dark so quickly here, otherwise he would have pushed for an earlier meeting time while they still had light. At the top of the dunes, he could see the white of the surf breaking below, and the long spread of foam as it came ashore on the open beach. The ocean was turning black. Behind him, through the trees, a cars headlights flickered as it pulled into the parking space near where he had left Villi's twin cab. He heard a door open, and close.

Clarry Woods appeared through the trees, climbing the dune, a torch in hand.

'I was expecting Tiger,' said Alex cautiously, a little unsettled by Woods appearance.

'Tiger couldn't make it, but he said I could show you. You'd be interested in this. You got a torch? he asked.

'No,' Alex replied,' I didn't think I'd need one.'

'Well, take this.' He handed over his. 'I've got another in the car. What you'll want is in the next dune hollow, not this one where the cops have been.' He pointed over the next brow. 'I'll be right back.' He turned and disappeared back down the dune, a dim figure only slightly darker than the light around him.

Alex moved across the brow of the dune and found himself in the hollow of the next dish, protected from the south easterly wind that swept the beach. He was out of sight from the road, and the houses 100 meters away to the south, and stood listening to the crashing surf and the wind as it swayed the grass and she-oaks around him.

'Turn your torch on,' Clarry yelled from the dark.

Alex looked at his torch and found the switch, illuminating the depression. The torch was immediately smashed out of his hand. Alex stood looking at his numb fingers, not quite sure what had happened. He didn't hear the first shot, but he heard the next and Alex felt a sharp sting at his right shoulder. Now he knew what it was, he turned in the direction of the shot, saw the dark figure of Woods in the distance and dropped to the ground.

He was breathing heavily; he had been set up; Woods had a rifle and had shot him. The wound was a graze, no hole, his fingers came away, a bit of blood and lost skin. Why the fuck was he trying to shoot him?

Don't think, move. He couldn't stay here, Woods would find him. If he ran over the brow of the dune toward the sea, he would be silhouetted against the night sky, making him an easy target. Ahead was a gap in the dunes, leading into the tree line. He scrambled toward it and slid across the sand into the next hollow, rolling onto his back. Could he stall him, give himself some more time?

'You don't have to do this Clarry,' he yelled out.

'You know too much.' Came the distant reply.

'I'll tell them Tiger put you up to it.' Alex pleaded out loud, skirting sideways across the sand.

'I got no choice Holmes. I'm fucked either way.' Woods' voice carried to him from the depression he'd just left. Shit, he was close.

Alex kept crawling sideways across the dunes, keeping a brow between himself and where he thought Woods would be.

A torchlight arced out from the first depression and swept across the tops of the dunes directly behind Alex, lighting up the shrubs and hollows Alex had skirted around. He stayed silent now, and so did Woods, both knew how this was supposed to play out, how it would end. Alex would disappear, his body would be buried in the dunes, lost, and found twenty years later by a dog walker, just like the Crinns boy.

Alex didn't hear the squeaky steps of Woods in the sand as he topped the brow, but his sudden hacking cough gave him away. It was enough for Alex to jump to his feet and launch himself over the top of the dune toward the sea, rolling down its steep face till he hit the bottom and scrambled to his feet. Above him, the torch swept the dune tops to the north and the south of Alex. Maybe he hadn't heard where he had gone, but Clarry was making sure he was being herded onto the beach and not back toward the carpark. He crouched over, clutching at his stinging shoulder, only a graze but enough for him to feel the wet patch of blood through his shirt.

He stumbled along the base of the dunes, trying to stay under the torch arc, but it caught up to him when he made a run for the walkway. Another shot hit the fence post ahead of him. He peeled away into the dark and made for the waterline instead. Escape in the waves, Clarry wouldn't expect that, hide in the swirling foam. By now, Clarry was on the hard sand, sweeping the beach back and forward, the shape of a rifle held to his shoulder in the reflected glow of his torch. The beam caught Alex as he was waist deep, striding deeper. He barely heard the shot this time, but it didn't matter, he dived under a wave, disorientated with the dark, but harder to hit now. From the breaking wave line, he heard nothing but the crashing of the water around him as he struggled to get his breath, looking ashore at the dark figure shin deep in the wash. A flash of orange light, exploding gases, Clarry was shooting straight at him. There was no option, he turned back toward the ocean and struck out swimming deeper, ducking under breaking waves when he saw them, and getting pounded by sudden impacts when he didn't. Beyond the break line, he lost sight of land and could only gauge where he was by the light house to the north. It took all his will to stay afloat as the wind tried to fill his mouth with salt water at every breath. Alex struggled to know which way was up, let alone back to shore. He began to panic.

He was pummelled, his lungs filled with water, coughing and gasping for air. It took all his will not to thrash against the inevitable, but turn his face away from the wind, protect his mouth and accept that as long as he can breathe, he will float. Forcing himself to stay calm he turned his head away from the wind, keeping the chop out of his mouth.

The lighthouse ahead was getting closer, that was land, but it wasn't necessarily safer, not as long as Clarry walked the water's edge. Every now and then he picked up the lighthouse as it swept its beam out to sea. The current had taken him a long way, he was being swept northward, but the headland was rocks, and he could hear the waves smashing against it. He was getting closer to them, enough to feel the bounce back from swells against the cliff face. He wanted to swim to shore, but the cliff face was too dangerous here, waves hit vertical rock faces, he would be smashed with nowhere to get ashore. If he could stay afloat for another hour, he might come around the north side of the cliff face where there was a wave cut platform, a shelf that he had used at night once before to retrieve his friend from the ocean during a storm. That they survived it then had been a close-run thing, it will be a close-run thing now too, if he can stay afloat that long.

Alex fought hard to keep away from the cliffs, he swept his arms back and forth to keep his head out of the water and hold position, conserve energy and let the current do its work. For the moment he had some control and was optimistic that he could make the rock shelf around the headland.

He first thought that the bump against his legs was a rock, until he realised how far out he was. The bump turned into a caress, a large body caressing his leg as it swept past.

'Fuck! Fuck! He screamed to nobody. He immediately tried to lift his legs as far up under his body as they would go, to make himself as small as possible, splashing down with his hands trying to lift his body out of the water.

'Fuck! Stop!' he cried to himself, spinning in a circle, trying to see what it was in the dark. His arms thrashed at the water till Alex imposed some will on them, stopping them from flailing the surface.

'Fuck it.' he screamed in defiance. Against his instinct, he stretched his legs out below him, sweeping his arms slowly back and forth, returning his body to a sense of rhythm to help him stay afloat. Nothing can be done to prevent a shark from doing what it wanted...if it wanted him, he had no say in it. Fate! To go down fighting meant to stay afloat for as long as he could, sweeping his limbs, reducing the panic when every nerve of his body screamed at him to swim for shore and be smashed on the rocks, maybe that was preferable. He stared resolutely ahead. His arms swept back and forth, he closed his eyes and concentrated on sweeping in rhythm, staying afloat, trying to ignore his fear. For how long he did this, he had no idea.

He was cold, his body started to cramp up from the exertion and the need for fresh water. The ocean around him had its own rhythm, it ebbed and flowed like the tides, like the fish migrations and the birds. It was its own life force and Alex was visiting it tonight, so the less you broke the rhythm, the more you were part of it. His eyes closed again as he felt the wind slow and the chop ease from attacking his breathing. He slipped quietly below the surface to see what was below, surely there was less movement there, much quieter. Water filled his mouth and nose, breaking his rhythm, jerking him awake. When he hit the surface he vomited, the salt water he'd ingested sprayed out in an arc in front of him, he gasped for air and sucked in what he could greedily. When he finally settled back, he'd noticed that the turbulence of the open water was less, the wind not as strong, and even though the surf was pounding at the rock shelf, he was around the corner of the headland, out of the wind, and below the lighthouse where he had been to rescue Beau three years before. He knew this place, even in the dark, the sea was pulling him closer.

The first swell of the set took hold and lifted him higher than he expected, so high that he saw the flashing green navigation beacon on the rock wall for the first time. The next swell broke on his head from behind, driving him down to the rocky bottom before he surfaced and was swept against the edge of the rock shelf. Lift your legs, over the shelf, before they get smashed by the next wave. The third wave came, it gathered him up, sweeping him across the platform in a ball, pushing him into loose rocks, his elbows, his legs, rolling with it, allowing himself to be deposited like a sack of flotsam. The water receded and the next wave was not nearly so full, it massaged his lower body but left him where he lay.

Alex tried to get up, his mouth so dry he could barely swallow, his elbow wasn't working the way it was supposed to. As he tried to rise, his arm gave way and he collapsed hard, stunning himself and opening up his scalp, blood pulsing out down into his eyes, but he was alive... fuck you Clarry Woods, fuck you shark. Alex rolled onto his back, watching the lighthouse above sweep its light out to sea. He might just stay where he was for the moment and close his eyes to have a little rest till the pain in his head went away.

# CHAPTER 25

It had been a long day, Clara's nerves had been on edge, but the rhythmic clatter of the train from Caboolture had gently wound her down and gave her time to think. Her path in this case had been set, she understood where it would lead, and it could end in her arrest for murder unless she found another way out.

Clara found herself standing in front of Alex's apartment door, it was late, but she wanted to get her options sorted before tomorrow. She needed Alex to get her to Tunkumba as soon as possible, then she would cut him loose before facing Crowther. There was no place in her plans for him, and although Alex thought he was up to the task, he was an amateur.

The door to Alex's unit was slightly ajar. Clara didn't think that strange at first, until she knocked and got no answer.

'Alex?' She called out, edging the door open with her foot. Clara leaned in and called out again.

'Alex are you there?' From inside the unit came a rustle of movement. 'Hello. Is that you Megan?'

She walked slowly down the hallway till it opened out into the kitchen and lounge. Cushions were scattered across the room, a table lamp broken on the floor, and Megan was slumped on the tiles, next to the couch, her legs tangled with the coffee table. She wasn't moving.

Clara started forward but was hit in the side, knocking the breath from her. She pirouetted away from the kitchen to fall against the small dining table, pushing it over to arrest her fall, she spun around to face her attacker. He launched at her again, holding a laptop high as he tried to bring it down on her head. Clara dropped into a defensive pose, taking the down-swinging laptop on her shoulder, it hurt, but rather that, than her head. She pushed up with her legs, shoulder charging him, pushing him off balance. Chest to chest with him, she forced him back into the kitchen, her arms trying to tackle him. He dropped the laptop and beat at her back and side with clenched fists. The blows stunned her, he was powerful, older than her, but much stronger. She tried to stay in close and pin his arms to his side to nullify his strength as they taught her at the academy, but he quickly stopped his punching and used his leverage to lift her up and force her back up against the kitchen bench. His breath stank, his shirt salt wet. Her back was arched against the bench, bending her as if she would break, the Baretta pressed hard into her lower spine, but she couldn't reach it. She released one arm and stabbed her fingers into his eye, he grunted in pain, and that was when he hit her. His fist drove into her cheek bone, splitting the skin, throwing her backwards, lifting her up off her feet, but it was the unfamiliar experience of losing consciousness that scared her the most. One moment she was in the kitchen, the next she was on the tiles on the other side of the bench. She opened her eyes to see the man scooping up scattered pages off the settee, stuffing them into a small backpack. He turned, searching for more, and saw Clara watching him. She tried to sit up.

'Stay down,' he growled.

'*Vete pa la puñeta*,' she spat and tried to raise herself.

He grabbed the fallen laptop off the floor, shifting it into both hands to hit her with it like he did the first time. Clara was able to reach behind her for the Baretta, it snagged on her underwear and didn't come cleanly from the back of her jeans, but she had enough time to swing it up and point it at him. He hesitated; she racked the pistol and slid the safety off. He stepped forward, the laptop raised to swing down at her, she pulled the trigger.

Her arm was shaking, and the shot was off centre, it hit his abdomen instead. His downward swinging computer connected with Claras outstretched arms, knocking the gun from her grasp, flinging it across the room.

'You bitch,' he howled, clutching at his side where the bullet had entered, bright red blood beginning to ooze between his fingers. Clara tried to get to her feet, but he stepped forward, swung his leg back, and kicked her. Her head snapped back, and for the second time, Clara lost consciousness.

Her eyes seemed to be glued shut; she couldn't open them. There was someone moving in the apartment, a hand swept across her face, warm, liquid, it wiped at her eyes and her right lid opened. Above her, a large man was kneeling over her, a bloody tea towel in his hand. Clara swiped at him, but he said for her to keep still.

'I'm not the one who hit you lady. I'm trying to get rid of the blood, don't struggle,' he said, his voice deep and reassuring.

Clara reached up with her hand and felt at the split skin of her cheek, she was nauseous and wanted to throw up with the pain. Her other eye opened, she began to pull the room into focus, Megan was sitting on the couch, her head leaning into a pillow, her clothes ripped, a blue and red welt visible below her hair line.

'Has he gone?' Clara struggled into a sitting position against the concrete stucco wall, not yet ready to try standing.

'Yes.' The man replied. He was leaning over the sink, rinsing the blood from the towel. 'I'm Villi.'

'What happened?' she asked.

'You tell me!' He muttered as he strode over to Megan with a fresh towel. She watched on as he knelt next to her and applied the cold compress to the blue and red welt on her forehead, pushing her hair back behind her ears with a gentleness that belied his size.

'I know you,' Clara said, recognising him from the hospital. 'You're Villi, Alex's friend. We've met before.' He was big, heavy set, not unlike some of her Cuban friends, but his features slightly different. He didn't turn to face her but kept applying pressure to Megans head while cradling it with his other hand.

'And you're the Cuban cop. What are you doing here?' he asked, without looking at her.

She ignored the question, rose unsteadily to her feet and waded through the mess to stand opposite them both. Around her the detritus of the fight was strewn across the floor, cushions and lamps upended. But the laptop was gone, and only a few scattered papers lay across the tiles. While both Megan and Villi were busy, Clara quickly retrieved her Baretta from the floor. She scouted around for the empty shell, kicked at the cushions and bobbed down to get it from under the chair. She returned to the couch and looked down at Megan.

'Is she alright?'

'I don't know,' Villi replied, 'I found her on the floor, like you, out cold. But she seems to be OK. Hell of a bruise.' He turned and looked up at Clara. 'Sit down,' he said. 'You look ready to fall down.'

'I'm alright,' she countered, and weaved her way around the fallen furniture to look into the other rooms. They were untouched.

'I'll call the police,' Villi called.

Clara shook her head and returned to the lounge room.

'Please don't do that. It would not be good for me.'

'You've been attacked and robbed, Megan needs attention.' Villi rumbled. He reached into his pocket and pulled out his cell phone.

'Megan, when he assaulted you, did he...' Clara tried to find the appropriate words, but Megan cut in.

'No!' She ran her hands over her long T shirt, feeling down her body, and pressed on her upper thighs. 'No.' She reiterated. 'He hit me when I opened the door and pushed me over the lounge. I tried to get away, but he hit me again and I don't remember anything after that,' she mumbled.

Clara reached across and placed her hand over Villi's.

'Please, don't ring the police. I can't be involved,' she said, one hand absently touching the illegal pistol in her jeans, the other pushing Villis phone down. 'Megan, I saw him taking your laptop. What did he get?'

She looked around, 'My purse, the laptop... phone. Alex's notes, all our papers. He took everything.'

'Not your purse, it's still there, in the bedroom, it hasn't been touched.' Clara noted.

'You must have interrupted him,' said Villi. 'I'll ring the police and get an ambulance to check you both out.'

'You can't Mr Villi. It's complicated for me.'

'Why not?' he demanded.

'I shot him, during the fight.'

'Good, said Villi,' he won't get far then.'

'I'm not supposed to have a gun. It is not legal. The Police will arrest me. I have no official notice to be here or have a firearm.'

'Shit! I thought you were with the police' Villi exclaimed.

'Not here, only in Cuba. That federal policeman I was with, he's nothing, and here, I am nothing. There is a long story to this. Alex knows it. Where is he? He was not here?'

Megan shook her head. 'He was gone when I came home.' She got up and shuffled awkwardly to the bathroom.

Clara looked at Villi, raising a bruised eyebrow in question.

'I came looking for my car.' Explained Villi, 'Alex was supposed to have it back by now, and he's not answering his phone.'

'So where is he?'

'I don't know. He had a meeting with Dittman tonight. He should be back by now.'

Clara flopped into the lounge chair and wiped at the trickle of blood walking its way down her cheek. She surveyed the room, and in her best authoritative voice took command of the situation.

'Mr Villi, I don't think this was an ordinary robbery. That man didn't come for money, even though he had time to take it...and he didn't. He stole their laptop instead. Either Megan or Alex was targeted, maybe both, and what is worse, I have wounded him. We can't stay here, and we can't call the Police.'

'So you say.' Villi looked at her, his voice hostile.

'Please. No Police.' Clara implored.

Megan appeared from the bathroom, wearing jeans now, but still unsteady on her feet. She winced as she put a fresh towel to her head.

'If she hadn't come, it could have been worse.' Megan pointed out.

Villi looked from one of the women to the other, before closing his phone and returning it to his pocket.

'We'll you can't stay here Megan. You can come home with me to my house. Narina will know what to do. You can have Xavier's room; he'll sleep on the couch.'

Clara nodded her thanks to him, but he said nothing in return, nor acknowledged her.

'Collect your things, Megan. Ill ring Nerina to come and get us.'

Clara noted that she was not included in the plans. Nor did Villi enquire why she was here in the first place. He fussed around Megan, until she was ready with her bag.

'I don't know where Alex is, but I need to leave him a note about where I've gone,' said Megan.

"I'll write it,' offered Clara.

'No. I'll do it,' Villi interjected. 'Alex is my friend, he'll know where to come.' He turned his back on Clara, looking for a sheet of paper, the implication clearly conveyed, stay away. She wasn't sure why Villi was so openly hostile to her, but she could guess. Villi was busy protecting Megan from the wicked Cuban mistress, even though she'd just saved her ass. It was not the first time she had been cast as a vile seductress and won't be the last, she thought. She straightened her shirt and addressed them both.

'Alex knows where I'm staying. Please let him know I need to talk to him as soon as I can.'

'I think he'll have more pressing things on his mind,' Villi remarked as he picked up Megans bag and slipped his arm under Megan's for her to lean on. Clara turned and headed for the door.

'I'll tell him.' Megan's voice called after her.

She smiled to herself despite holding onto her ribs and wincing with each step as she took to the stairs. It was late, and a long walk back to the hostel where a hot shower and bed were begging. It would have been nice if Villi had offered her a lift.

# CHAPTER 26

### Monday

Lights winked green and red at Alex, alternating in annoyance. His lids were not quite open fully as the rock wall came into focus, followed by those pesky flashing navigation lights, but they didn't move, he was thankful of that. He rolled his head to the other side and watched the first pale yellow light of day appear. Spray was blowing across the wave tops in golden arcs and the clouds beyond skittered across the horizon. He reached up and prodded at the loose flap of skin crusted to his forehead, that part of him was dry but he was still wet around his legs, the tide had dropped and left him halfway up the small sandy beach, his legs still lying in a shallow pool.

In the distance a dog barked and appeared running back and forth in the shallows till it discovered Alex and bounded in closer for a sniff. Alex didn't blink; he let the dog make the first move. It barked, ducked its head up and down, then turned and ran back to its owner before coming back again. Alex leaned on his good elbow as the elderly woman in her yellow spray jacket stopped in front of him.

'Come here,' she ordered. The red setter promptly sprinted off again to circle the two of them before bounding after a sea gull.

'I know he's stupid, but I love him,' she said in dutiful resignation. 'You've had a fall I see.' Leaning over to get a better view of his wound. 'You're a bit of a mess all round really, aren't you' she stated as a matter of fact.

'I got caught...a wave,' Alex struggled to explain, as he got to his feet. His voice distant, almost unrecognizable.

'I'm sure you will need that looked at...do you want me to call someone? Skipper, get out of the way, leave the man alone.' Skipper the dutiful red setter was busy trying to shove his nose into Alex's crotch.

'I'll be right,' he croaked. 'My car is just over there.' He pointed to the other side of the headland.

'You shouldn't be driving like that,' she remarked.

'I'll be right.' Alex had had enough of this mothering and brushed past her heading to the track to the top car park. It was steep and rocky, but the shortest route. From there he would follow the road down to where he left Villis car, and hopefully no Clarry Woods, murdering prick.

At the top of the headland, he stumbled across to the tap and drank greedily, sluicing water across his face and washing away the dried blood. He could see Villis car down below, where he left it last night. His spirits rose immediately. Alex patted his shorts for the keys and was overjoyed to find them, deep in the folds of his front pocket. At least he could drive. He rescued the keys, held up the remote, pressed it once, twice, three times...nothing. School for the gifted, Alex admonished himself sarcastically, the electronic key was hardly going to work after a dunking for the night in salt water.

'Shit,' he remarked. The driver's window was smashed in; rough cubes of glass littered the dirt and were scattered across the front seat. The door was unlocked, his wallet and phone gone. Alex swept the glass on to the floor and tried the manual key. The engine fired, thank God for old technology. He spun the wheels in reverse and left the carpark in a cloud of dust. Fuck he was tired...tired and angry!

His anger hadn't lessened any when he surveyed the mess in the apartment. He hadn't expected this. A quick search revealed no Megan. He called out for her, as if she was hiding where he couldn't see her. This was not good, the table and lamp were on its side, and everywhere was the evidence of a struggle. Villis note on the bench explained that she was safe, but it hardly pacified him, there were blood spots on the wall and tiles. He grabbed some fresh clothes and cast a quick eye over the place before slamming the door after him.

'Villi...Megan,' he shouted as he bounded up the steps to the two-story home. The door opened before he even got there, and Villi ushered him inside with assurances that Megan was sleeping and all was OK for the moment. He led Alex through the sunroom and stopped at the first door, opening it softly for Alex to go in.

She was nestled under a sheet with her back to him, her hair spilled out across the pillow. He leaned over her and gently caressed her head. She jerked awake and groaned in pain, rolling on her back, that was when he saw the size of the bruise on her forehead, glowing with vivid colour.

'Shit, I'm sorry Meg,' he whispered, 'I didn't mean to wake you.'

She murmured an acquiescence, before reaching up with her hand for him to take. He squeezed her fingers, passing his fear and reassurance that he was here for her through his touch.

'Where the fuck were you last night?' she moaned through swollen lips.

'I don't know...I was held up.' He croaked a lame replied. 'But I'm here now. What happened?' He squeezed her fingers and stroked at her hair.

'I was attacked. We were robbed.'

'Who did it?'

'That bulldozer driver, the one with Dittman.'

'Clarry Woods? That fucker.' Alex admonished.

'He hit me when he came in, I thought it was you at the door,'

'I'm so sorry. Arsehole. He came after me last night too.'

'You look a mess,' she said, casting her eye over the split skin above his eyebrow.

'You can talk,' he chortled. 'We're a pair of swollen heads. Is it sore?'

'What do you think? Of course, its sore, my heads thumping'.

He reached out to touch her bruise.

'Don't,' she pushed his hand away. 'Are there any pain killers?'

'I'll get some.' He noticed a strip of capsules and water on the desk next to the bed, tore off two and gave them to her. She sat up gingerly against the bed head and swallowed the tablets. The bedroom was a typical teenagers haunt, covered in cast off clothes and accumulated bits of an adolescent life. Xavier must have slept elsewhere.

'I like what you've done to the place,' he quipped.

'No jokes. I'm sorry, I'm just sore,' she said. 'I'm going to lie back down. Tell me later.' Megan ordered as she slid back down into the sheets, rolled back on her side and pulled the covers up. Alex watched over her until he detected the rhythmic movement of her body at sleep before he backed out of the room, leaving her for the moment.

In the kitchen, Villi and Nerina sat at the kitchen table nursing cups of steaming tea, they broke off from quite discussion as Alex entered. Villi gestured for him to sit, but Alex detoured to the sink for two glasses of water, greedily downing one after the other, before he collapsed in a spare chair.

'Do you have any coffee?' he asked.

'I'll get you some. You need something for that cut.' Nerina rose and retrieved a plaster dressing from a kitchen draw, fussing over applying it to Alex's cut, before she started the coffee.

Alex turned to Villi. 'It was Clarry Woods.'

'I know,' said Villi. 'Megan told me last night. Woods broke in around eight o'clock, bashed Megan, and robbed her.'

'Mate, why haven't you gone to the Police?

'I wanted to... but Megan said no.'

'Why is that?' Alex was incredulous.

'Because last night your Cuban girlfriend shot Woods, that's why.'

'Clara? What was she doing there?'

'I didn't ask. But she said she shot Woods, and Megan didn't want me to call the cops.'

'Shit. Is he dead?'

'No. But she reckons she wounded him badly. Seems like she disturbed Woods during the robbery, and in the fight, she shot him but Woods got away. So, if you get the cops involved, your Cuban friend is in big trouble, her gun is illegal.'

Alex shook his head as he tried to take in last night's events. He was tired and his brain was fog bound with exhaustion.

'Woods tried to kill me last night,' Alex said slowly. Both Villi and Nerina's eyes widened with his revelation. 'I was supposed to meet up with Dittman at Hideaway Beach, but that fucker Woods showed up and shot at me with a rifle.'

'Is that what happened to your head?' Nerina interrupted.

'No. That was my own fault,' he said, reaching up to touch the broken skin. "But he did graze my shoulder.' He pulled at the collar of his shirt to reveal the scored skin. 'He nearly got me. I had to swim for it to get away, spent half the night treading water...nearly drowned. Came in round the headland near the rock wall. That's where I tripped and hit my head. I only woke up this morning. He must have come after Megan when he thought he'd got rid of me.' Alex raked his fingers through his hair, crusted salt falling on the table. Nerina placed a mug of coffee in front of him and took her seat protectively next to Villi.

'This isn't right. Alex,' she said. 'That Clarry Woods needs to be locked up. He hurt your Megan, hit her, and who knows what could have happened if that Clara hadn't shown up.'

'Why the fuck did he bash her?'

'Robbed her. Megan said he took the laptop, and all your notes.'

'Now that makes sense. He came to get rid of all the evidence we've got against Dittman, all the links, the transcript of his first interview, everything so far. Its Dittman's doing. Dittman's behind it, I know.'

'Alex, I'm happy to go to the cops with you, right now.' said Villi.

'And you reckon Woods is wounded, shot?'

'That's what your Cuban friend said.'

'What's she doing with a fucking gun? As if we don't have enough going on.'

'But it looks like she saved Megan's life.' Nerina pointed out.

'Where is she?' Alex asked.

'I don't know.' Villi informed him. 'I didn't bring her home here with me,'

'She'll be at the hostel,' said Alex. 'That's where her stuff is. I think I need to see her first, find out about this gun business before we do anything more.'

'You need to go to the police,' reiterated Villi.

'Yeh...yeh, I know, but I've got to see Clara first, get her story straight, before I go after Dittman and get my laptop back. Nerina, can you stay here and look after Megan? I gave her some painkillers, I think she's gone back to sleep.'

'I'll look after your wife, but who's going to look after you?' She looked pointedly at him. 'I've seen what you've done to our car already. You should not be driving. Villi will drive.'

'I'll pay for a new window.' Alex responded, getting up wearily from the kitchen table.

'Don't worry about that now. Villi is going with you too,' she said. She looked at Villi. 'Well, what are you waiting for? A personal invitation?' she admonished him, pointing at the door.

The Hostel receptionist called down the hall in her best Spanish accent for Clara to come to the front desk.

When she appeared, it was on the tail end of a bunch of noisy backpackers armed with water bottles and daypacks, piling out the door into the minivan emblazoned with the name of a local fruit farm. It was lucrative paid work, but the real reward was the Visa extensions and more holiday time.

Clara limped into view, a cut on her cheek covered in Elastoplast.

'We should move away from the desk,' Alex suggested, grabbing at Claras elbow, marching her outside to the terrace where they could talk in private, Villi followed.

'What the fuck are you doing with a gun?' he hissed.

'That's my business, Alex. You know why I'm here; I told you in the car.'

'But a gun. Villi said you shot Woods.' Alex probed.

'He tried to hit me with the laptop,' she said defensively, her voice flat.

'You didn't tell me you had a gun.'

'You never asked.'

'Where did you get it?'

'I'm not telling you that.'

'Have you still got it?'

'Yes.'

'Well, that just makes things more complicated doesn't it.' Alex surmised angrily.

'I think it was lucky for Megan that I showed up. I came looking for you by the way.'

'I don't think it was that lucky. Not for Woods anyway.'

Clara lifted her shirt to show him the bruise that wrapped itself around her ribs just above the kidney, the injury was a deep purple in colour. She dropped her shirt and faced Alex expectantly.

'I'm sorry. I'm glad you showed up when you did. I owe you.' he acquiesced.

'Then get me to Tunkumba. Today. Please Alex. If the police become involved there will be problems, that gun is not legal, they will arrest me, even for shooting in self-defence, you know that. I need to get to Tunkumba. I have to finish what I was sent here for, and you know why I must do it Alex.'

'Yeh, I know, it's for your family,' Alex cut in. 'Well, I need to find Clarry Woods, injured or not. He tried to kill Megan, he tried to kill me. Dittman put him up to it, and I need his confession. Maybe it's not such a bad thing after all. I want to go after Woods, and you having a gun would be handy.'

Villi grabbed his elbow and spun Alex around to face him.

'This is getting stupid now, you have to go to the police.' Villi protested, trying to get Alex's attention. 'This is a job for them, not you,' extoled Villi.

'It's fucking personal now Villi, he hurt Megan, tried to kill me. I want that prick to suffer first. Did you stop to think why he tried to kill us Villi? That's pretty fucking desperate if you ask me.' Alex exploded. 'Shit Villi, I've got to find out, there's something in my notes, something Woods said that incriminates them both, and now they've got it. If I go to the police now, and they arrest him, I'll never know. All my evidence points to Dittman and Woods killing that boy in the dunes, but Woods has the laptop, everything. If he destroys it, we've got nothing. I've got nothing against them except my word, and everything that's happened so far counts for nothing. I got to get it all back first. I can't go to the cops until then, otherwise, what happened last night will be just hearsay, Dittman could do a runner...and Clara could go to jail.'

'This job is for the Police!' Villi was adamant.

'I am the police,' said Clara.

'Fuck off woman. You're nothing but trouble,' Villi snapped in anger.

Clara bristled and stepped forward into Villi's space, and he didn't back up.

'I am a Cuban Investigator, *gilipollas*,' she spat.

'In Cuba you might be, but you're nothing here.' He turned to Alex, imploring him. 'Cut her loose and go to the police. Let them handle Woods.'

Alex stood looking at both of them, his eyes flicking from one to the other, weighing up their arguments against his obligations. Finally, he turned to Villi.

'I can't mate. Besides, there was something Woods said last night, before he shot at me, that he had no choice. I just want him to admit to what he's done, blame it all on Dittman, and I'll have witnesses now. Dittman gave him the orders. He's the one at the top. He's the one I want in the end.'

'Alex, think about this...it's not good, going after a man with a gun.' Villi stammered, knowing he'd lost the argument.

'I've done it before,' said Carla. 'It takes two, one to distract, while the other comes in on the...how do you say...the reverse side.'

'Does it work?' Alex asked.

'I'm still here, aren't I? I've told you once before, there is no room for amateurs, so you will do as I say.'

'Villi, I need your car one last time,' he pleaded.

'Fuck off Alex, you said that yesterday. I'm not giving it to you just so you can help her.'

'I owe her! And it's not just for her. I promise I'll go to the police after I've seen Woods.'

Villi stood dejected, his shoulders slumped in resignation.

'I have to come with you,' he said.

'No mate. This is not your problem.'

'I'm coming. Nerina would never forgive me if I let you go alone.'

'He won't be alone,' objected Clara.

'He needs a mate watching his back. Not you.' Villi turned away and pulled out his phone.

Alex turned to Clara.

'Get your gear. You help me and I'll help you. I'll get you to Tunkumba one way or other,' he whispered.

She mouthed thankyou and disappeared back inside, heading down the hallway. Villi finished over the phone with Nerina and turned to Alex, reassuring him that Megan was fine and sitting up talking in the kitchen.

'I want to get at Dittman first and foremost.'

'Let's go before I change my mind,' said Villi.

'We're waiting for Clara,' Alex replied.

'Why doesn't that surprise me.' Villi pulled the keys from his pocket and strode toward the exit. 'I'll wait in the car.'

# CHAPTER 27

Villi pulled into the driveway at Dittman's home. The gate was open, and the garage door was up. Only one of the cars was in the bay, Gloria Dittman's Mercedes sport, the boot open. She appeared at the door, struggling with a large suitcase, barely able to stay upright. Alex and Villi got out and walked up the drive. Clara waited at the car.

'Morning, Gloria, is Tiger home?'

She stopped dragging at the bag and turned to face Alex. Her cheeks were puffed and eyes red. She had been crying and was drunk again.

'Who are you?' she asked.

'I came around yesterday, but Tiger wasn't here. He didn't show for our meeting last night either. Is he here now?'

'No. Does it look like it?' She turned back to her bag, dragged it across the concrete and lifted it into the boot of the Mercedes. She leaned against the car and wiped at her eyes, exhausted.

'Are you going somewhere?' Alex asked, stepping closer.

'What do you think. I'm leaving.'

'So is Tiger going with you?'

'That bastard can go to hell. He pissed off this morning. Gone to Tunkumba to meet a boat. Get paid, he said. Paid for what! More money? He's got none. That's all he ever thinks about.'

'What did he do there that he's getting paid for?'

'How would I know!'

'Gloria, did Clarry Woods come around last night?' He ventured.

'Yeh...Tiger met him out front. Comes back in holding a bag, smiling that self-satisfied smirk he gets when he thinks he's won.' She sniffed. 'All those years of that smirk.' Her mouth twisted into a snarl. 'And all the time he knew!'

'He knew what?' Alex tried to draw it out of her.

'He knew my son had been dead all this time and he never told me.'

Alex looked at Villi, who seemed just as surprised as he.

'Mrs Dittman...do you mean that Barry Crinns, the boy they found in the dunes was your son?' She slumped against the back of the car and nodded.

'And you've just found out? No wonder. I'm so sorry Gloria. Have the police been around to see you.'

'They don't know he was my son. Nobody does, except Tiger.'

Alex stood expectantly in front of her, reaching out to touch her arm in sympathy. She straightened, and shook herself, as if shaking off the effects of the alcohol, wanting to unburden herself of everything she carried. She looked at Alex and then at Villi as if noticing him for the first time.

'Hello William,' she said.

'Hello Gloria. I think you should come inside. You shouldn't be driving anywhere. Come on.' Villi offered her his hand. Alex waved for Clara to join them as Villi led Gloria gently back into the house.

He deposited her into an easy chair, where she turned and looked out the front sliding doors to the canal beyond, seemingly lost in thought, while Villi searched the kitchen to make her some coffee.

'Gloria,' Alex began, sitting down on the couch opposite her. 'I have to tell you that I've been investigating Tiger over the disappearance of your son twenty years ago. I found evidence that he knew the body they found was your son.'

She looked at Alex, then Villi in turn. 'Barry was my son from my first marriage. Well, we weren't really married, in a church, or formally, we were just together in those days, but when I left Sydney, Barry stayed with his father, took his name.' Gloria swivelled in the chair, at first looking out at the canal waters before returning to Alex. 'I didn't see Barry for years, till he showed up here, I tried to take him in, but all he wanted was money. Greedy little shit. He tried to get money from Tiger, to shut up about me being his mother, and deserting him.'

Alex glanced up at Villi, and then across to Clara who had sidled into the kitchen.

'I know what you're thinking, I didn't desert him.' Her eyes swung to each of them in turn. 'Nobody here even knew he was my son, or that I even had one, and Tiger didn't want the scandal. We were about to get married and didn't need that.' She pushed and pulled at her wedding bands as she spoke.

'So, what did you do?' Alex asked in a quiet voice.

'Tiger sent him on his way, said he took him as far as Hideaway Beach, gave him some money, he'd make his own way south from there. And that was the last I'd seen of him...thought he'd left for good.'

Alex glanced at Villi and Clara to confirm that they were listening.

'And now his body has been found in the dunes, nearly twenty years on...at Hideaway Beach, and Tiger was the last person to see him.' Alex stated quietly.

'No.' She said adamantly, 'No. I know what you're thinking. Tiger wouldn't have done that. I know him. He's a selfish bastard, but not a murderer.'

Alex had a different opinion on that one.

'Who are you?' she asked, noticing Clara for the first time.

'She's investigating something that Tigers involved in at the moment as well, at Tunkumba.' Explained Alex, waving at Clara to stay out of it.

'Another of his fucking schemes,' Gloria said.

'Why are you so sure he didn't do it?' Alex brought her back to stay on topic.

'I know him, he wouldn't. Someone else did it, I'm sure of that. But when they found Barrys body last week, Tiger knew it was him and he knew all along Barry was buried there and he never told me.'

'I have to tell you that it's pretty strong evidence pointing to your husband.'

'He didn't do it.' She reiterated.

Alex recognised that she was starting to shut down on her confessions, so he quickly changed tack.

'You said Clarry Woods dropped off a bag here last night. Is it still here?' he asked innocently.

'No. Tiger took it with him this morning.'

'Are you sure about that? It's important.'

'I know what I saw.'

'And Tiger is at Tunkumba now?'

She nodded. 'He left this morning.'

'And what about you? Where were you going?'

'Back to Sydney. I can't stay here with him, not after this.'

'Does he know you're leaving?'

'Hope not. It will be a good fucking surprise for him when he gets back.' She laughed bitterly.

'Maybe best you don't drive at the moment Gloria, till you sober up,' said Villi, leaning across to touch her arm in emphasis.

'Piss off,' she spat, shook off his hand and turned to look out at the canal behind them. The room was silent, in the distance, a clock ticked away an echo of time passing from the hallway. Gloria said no more, they had been dismissed.

Alex looked at Villi, eyebrows raised.

'Thank you for talking to us Gloria, we'll let ourselves out.'

She didn't reply or acknowledge them at all. Alex rose and the three of them left, closing the front door after them. Villi marched across to the Mercedes, took the keys out of the raised boot and threw them over the fence. When they were nestled back in Villis car, Alex turned to Villi.

> 'Now for Clarry Woods and Tiger Dittman. Are you coming?'

Villi seemed to be lost in thought and took a few moments before he nodded in reply, before starting the engine and reversing out onto the street.

# CHAPTER 28

Clara moved past the rusty letterbox at the front of Clarry Woods' driveway, keeping to the left on the grass. Ahead, the gravel led to the house where his twin cab was parked. Further past the drive, was his truck and low loader with the bulldozer aboard. She looked back to Alex and waved him to stay where he was while she skirted the open ground in the trees, keeping in the shadows. But it didn't fool the dog. At first, it was laying down next to the car, but the moment it detected Clara, it jumped to its feet and began to bark, dancing around the car excitedly, but not leaving the safety of the house and car.

When she drew level with the twin cab, she waved for Alex to start walking up the driveway.

The three of them had debated earlier who would be the catcher and who would be the distraction. She had won, her reasoning being that Woods would be put off wondering what Alex was doing there, back from the dead, and hesitate, while Clara had shot him and he would definitely have a grudge against her for that. Villi would stay by his own car.

Woods' utility was nose in to the house. She could see the back of his head, he was looking down at something in his lap, the dog was bounding around barking, protecting its owner's property. Clara pointed for Alex to keep walking up the drive, feet crunching on the gravel. To walk like that took some cojones, thought Clara. Woods would be watching Alex in the side mirror. She bent double and raced across the grass to the opposite corner of the utility and worked her way quietly along the side till she was below the passenger window. She felt for the Baretta in the back of her jeans but didn't draw it. Breathing hard, she put her hand on the door and raised her head slowly to sneak a look inside.

Woods was in the front seat, his head lolled forward on his chest, eyes staring sightless at the floor, his body leaning into the seatbelt. Redish brown blood covered the seat and had spilled over into the foot well. Woods still had one hand on his abdominal wound where Clara had shot him the night before. Clara stood up and walked around the front of the car, gesturing for Alex to approach. She reached in the open window to feel for a pulse.

'He's dead.' She announced.

Alex stopped and without taking his eyes off the driver's side door, reached down to pacify the dog. He held his hand out, waiting for the dog to smell him before he joined her at the window looking in.

'The bullet must have nicked an artery, or something deep, he couldn't stop the flow. The blood all ran out of him.' she surmised, talking quietly, clearly, police like.

Alex said nothing, he looked shocked. That was not unusual, the uniforms in Havana were often struck dumb by death or near-death experiences the first time, their minds refusing to find anything to say. Alex reached out to open the door.

'Don't,' she said.' Do not touch any metal.' She pointed to the front the seat next to Woods.

For a half minute, Alex just stood looking at Woods, as if what Clara had said did not compute, then he silently leaned in through the open window past Woods' body and retrieved his wallet and phone without touching anything else.

'They're mine,' said Alex, looking down at Woods in the car. 'Fuck. He didn't need to die.'

'I know, but he attacked me. I was defending myself.'

'I wasn't blaming you, it's just...'

'He had a choice. It wasn't like he was forced to. I don't stand in judgement; I just work with what's right or wrong...and what he did was wrong. If he hadn't done what he did, he wouldn't be here now, like this. As simple as that.' Clara had used this on many occasions, pacifying new recruits who were racked with remorse. Sometimes, she even believed it herself. She could never get used to death, she could only lock it away for the time being, until it reappeared again when she closed her eyes and tried to sleep at night.

'What do we do now?'

'We leave him'.

'You can't do that.'

'My case has nothing to do with him, I have to get to Tunkumba, the boat is coming today, your Dittman is there for it, that's where I need to be. You promised. I saved Megan from this man remember.' She turned and walked down the drive, back to where Villi was waiting by the car.

'Christ you're a callous bitch.' Alex mumbled.

Clara stopped and turned. 'I heard that Alex,' she called. 'Don't judge me, you're the one who wanted to come after him. How did you think it was going to end? Besides, Dittman is in Tunkumba, where would you rather be? There or here waiting for the Police to come?' she said to him, waiting.

Maxi had stopped barking and stood quietly at Alex's feet. Alex told him to stay and the dog lay down in the dirt and stared up at his master motionless in the front seat while Alex followed behind her down the drive, out the front gate.

# CHAPTER 29

Alex rested his head against the passenger side window, dozing in and out, while Villi drove. The wind noise from the missing driver's side window didn't promote lengthy conversation which was fine by Alex, he had plenty to think about and could do with the rest. Meanwhile, Villi asked for and received an abridged version of why Clara wanted to get to Tunkumba. Alex noticed that she left out the part about the threat to her family back in Cuba. For all intents and purposes, she explained how they were investigating a major drug smuggling operation, and while Alex was after Dittman, the motivation for her involvement was based on a high level of revenge.

'The pair of you are making this up as you go,' exclaimed Villi. 'This could get nasty. How many blokes on the *Cosmos*?'

'I had three, two crew and the Captain, Vaughn Crowther.' Clara replied.

'And there are how many already there?' he asked.

'Adam, and another man at the fishing camp.'

'And Dittman.' Added Alex.

'That makes six against three. Have you thought about this?' Villi questioned, glancing across at Alex and flicking his eyes into the rear-view mirror to include Clara.

'I'm only after one in particular,' she said. 'Crowther, the Captain.'

'Well, he's part of a whole bunch of them. And Alex, you only want Dittman, so what are you going to do, cut him out of the herd like a stockman on a horse?' Villis sarcasm bit deep into Alex. 'Come on. Get real Alex. How are you going to do this?'

'I'm working on it,' he mumbled a reply.

Villi guffawed in disbelief. 'What about you Miss Policewoman?'

'Do not worry about me, I work alone. Drop me at the track to the fishing camp, I'll make my own way.'

'Bullshit.' exploded Villi. 'So, follow this, alright. These blokes are doing a big drug deal off this yacht, *Cosmos*, in Tunkumba Creek, putting it ashore at the fishing camp in the forest. That's the place where Tiger Dittman and Clarry Woods used a dozer to cut a road through to, is that right?'

'Yes, so far.' Alex confirmed.

'If what Gloria Dittman says is true, the yacht is coming today and Dittman left early to meet it. Well, the yacht can only get in the creek at high tide.'

'That would be right. The camp is up around the bend from the entrance, difficult for a yacht I would think.'

'I've been in there in a boat. There are markers at the entrance to the creek, and part way along, they stop at the boat ramp, then there is nothing to guide you around the bend. The channel is very narrow, sand banks either side jut out a long way, you could only get in or out of that creek at high tide, even then it's easy to run aground. It would take local knowledge.'

'Dittman!' They both said at once.

'That's why Dittman is there. He's the local knowledge.' Alex guessed.

Villi went on laying out his thoughts.

'It won't be high tide till about 8pm this evening.' He looked at his watch. 'The morning high has just ebbed, and is beginning to drop now, so *Cosmos* is either already there, or it will come in tonight, when the high is back in again. Vaughn won't want to be there during the low when he can't get out, and none of those other blokes will want to be there either.'

'What are you saying Villi?' asked Clara from the back seat.

'If they came in this morning, at dawn, then they will have already unloaded, and left so that they don't get stuck there all day, and you would be too late, it would be all over, you've missed them, we may as well go home. Dittman might still be around, but Crowther would be long gone.'

Alex had nothing to say. If what Villi said was true, then Clara had failed in getting Vaughn Crowther, and he would have to find another way of getting at Dittman.

'But they probably wouldn't unload during daylight. Too risky if anyone sees them. They could stay there during the day and unload and leave on the full tide tonight.' Alex surmised.

'But what if they come tonight instead?' asked Clara. 'Under cover of darkness would be better for a drug transfer.'

Alex jumped in. 'Then we have a chance. We can catch them in the act.'

'What are you going to do with them then Alex? Or you Clara. You both are hell bent on catching these guys, but what will you do with them, a citizen's arrest?'

'What I do with Crowther is my business Villi.'

'Yeh? What about you Alex? Since when did you turn into a drug vigilante, capturing cartel syndicates with the threat of exposing them on television? That's sure to scare them into turning themselves in.'

'I'm not after the drugs, I'm only after Dittman.' Alex protested.

'Well, whether you pair like it or not, you're taking them all on, dickhead. You walk down that road like you did at Clarry Woods' place, and they will shoot you.' Villi remonstrated with him. 'These guys are drug running big time. They will be watching the roads and the approaches to the camp site like hawks, all on edge, protecting their drugs and their escape route, and they will be armed. You can be so dumb sometimes.'

Alex knew he was right. He hadn't thought it through enough, it was why Villi was as successful as he was, people underestimated him. A big, tall fun Fijian, a loyal back up man, but he had a mind as sharp as they come. In all the confusion of the last few days, he forgot that Villis analytical approach had also been at work and was dealing in restraint, rather than the headlong rush that he was prone to.

'How do you know there are not more of them?' Villi stated. 'Have you thought of that?'

Alex hadn't, his silence said it all. Clara said nothing from the back seat. What a mess, he thought. It all seemed so easy, a grand plan to deliver justice to Dittman that Villi blew apart in a few minutes of rational forethought.

'The one place they won't be watching is the water,' said Villi with a surety to his voice. 'So, we come at them from the estuary instead. See, Crowther is a sailor,' explained Villi, 'his home is his boat; he won't abandon that for anything. At the first hint of trouble, Crowther will go for his boat, you watch. He'll do anything to protect it, to protect his home. Once the drugs are off, he'll be gone. Dittman, on the other hand, he'll go for his car. First sign of trouble, Dittman will drive home, big house, big ego, a lot to protect there, that's where he'll go. Find Dittman's car, you find him.'

Villi turned off from the highway at Goldston and pulled into a service station. He stopped the car in the parking lot and turned to Alex.

'If you want to get at Dittman, then we have to come at him by the creek, that's the only way I reckon. Any other way and you'll be spotted, and that will be the end of it. They'll have a sentry guarding the track. Trust me.' He leaned around to address Clara. 'You too Miss Policewoman. That captain won't leave his boat, he'll stay on it the whole time, let the others do the unloading. He won't be watching what's coming down the channel in the dark. Stick to the yacht and you'll get your sailor. Leave the distraction to me.'

Alex found it difficult to argue with Villis logic, but before he could venture his next question, Villi opened his car door.

'I have to make a couple of calls,' he said as he pulled out his phone and wandered off toward the picnic tables.

Alex turned around to Clara.

'Well, what do you think?' he asked her. 'What do you make of Villis plan?'

'I don't know yet. It makes sense. He is suddenly very helpful.' she ventured.

'Well, he's thinking better than I am at the moment,' remarked Alex. 'All morning he's been at me to ring the Police, to leave Dittman to them. And now he's changed his tune, he's even warmed to you. I don't want to pre-empt anything, but we might be better to stick together, safety in numbers, we run with Villis plan, and we both get what we want.'

Villi returned and leaned in the open window. 'I've got a boat.'

# CHAPTER 30

The *Clo-Anne* was a twenty-five-foot fibreglass crabbing boat, with a small wheelhouse forward and most of the deck behind under cover of an awning stretched over stainless-steel pipe. Villi talked with the owner, Roy Masters inside the wheelhouse while Alex walked around the back deck trying not to tangle his feet in the numerous ropes and deck gear scattered around the gunnels. Clara leaned against the large icebox in the middle of the deck, her long legs stuck out in the sun, watching the two men inside going through the boat operations.

Alex stuck his head in and was amazed at the array of electrical gear inside the wheelhouse, chart plotters, bottom sounders, weather displays and radios littered the console. The boat was far more sophisticated than he imagined, dual steering wheels allowed for the skipper to control the boat from out at the winch as well as inside at the instruments. To the left a rudimentary cooktop sat on a bar fridge, a battered jug nestled on the gas rings. Next to it, a small sink with open plumbing was screwed into the wall, numerous cups, sauces and bottles lined the rack above. This was what Alex expected, and he wasn't disappointed, nothing glamourous there, it was a work boat, after all.

'There's milk and coffee, some food in the fridge,' said Masters, a grizzly sixty-year-old. 'If you decide to stay out overnight, there's room in the bunk for only one of you.' He pointed to a single unmade coffin bunk that half disappeared under the fiberglass cabin. 'I usually go out alone, so I haven't made provision for extra crew. Someone else can sleep in the skipper's chair, if you lay it back, its pretty good, and one of you will have to stand up. Anyway,' he glanced at Clara on the back deck, 'I'm sure you can be inventive,'

Villi started the engines; a deep throated rumble accompanied the vibration through the deck. Masters called his goodbye and clambered up onto the wharf and to let go the ropes.

'And don't prang it. I want it back in one piece.' Masters called out.

Villi leaned his head out the door.

'Like you did to mine?' he yelled in reply. 'You owe me.'

Masters flicked the mooring line to Alex and waved his goodbye before picking his way back along the old timber wharf to Villis car. Carlos Creek was the on the southern edge of Pelican Bay, the large estuary that was also home to Tunkumba creek, eight kilometres to the north. There was no town at Carlos Inlet, it was just a haven for a few of the fishermen who would use the old timber wharf to tie up to. Alex coiled the mooring lines before joining Villi in the wheelhouse. Ahead the bay glistened brightly in the midday sun, flicking and reflecting off the tabletop bay. Few clouds in the sky interfered with the light, offering a clear run all the way to Tunkumba. He looked back to Clara leaning against the ice box and gave her a thumbs up. Villi had come good with the boat, borrowed from a friend, and it seemed like their plan was coming together. Clara responded with a nod.

Villi was a picture of concentration, his eyes roamed back and forth ahead, settling on the few sticks that stood out of the water as markers for the channel out into the bay. The shallowness of the sandbanks either side of the boat were defined by the undulating bow waves stacking up and braking in the shallows. Beneath them, Alex could see the bottom, clean and clear, the movement of the tide had formed rhythmic patterns in the sand.

'Tides on the turn, on its way in, but not very deep here yet, not a lot to work with.' Villi remarked, without turning his head. His hand hovered across the throttles ready to power down in case they touched. Gradually the colours began to change, from the light opalescence of the shallow channel to a turquoise green of deeper water. Villi opened the throttles further, and the boat began to surge forward at speed, leaving the inlet behind. The motors took on a greater roar, and the hull split the surface of the bay, casting the water aside in an arrogant display of power.

He headed to the back deck, where Clara stood under the awning, holding onto the metal frame above her. The wind from the boat speed was blowing her hair away from her face, and flattening her T-shirt against her, defining her upper body. She was smiling broadly. Alex looked past her at the wake. He always loved this moment, when a boat came alive, whether under motor or sail, it was what it was meant for. He grinned at Clara, bending his knees and swaying with the motion. He was jerked to the side with the sudden movement of the boat and grabbing her arm to steady himself.

'Sorry,' he said.

'Don't be. She replied, grinning back at him.

'Don't you love this?' he yelled, above the droning roar of the motors and the wind, looking to her left and right, taking in the emerald greens of the bay. Birds on the sandbanks took flight from the noise coming their way, their wings reaching for purchase as they spiralled away toward the trees on the mainland. Theirs was the only boat on the water, leaving behind a broad band of white foam running arrow straight northwards.

'Reminds me of the Caribbean,' he yelled, leaning in, his lips to her ear to make himself heard. 'Have you been there?' he asked.

She looked at him, and Alex detected pity in her eyes.

'Sorry, forgot. Cuba...' Alex mimed a smack to his forehead as a mark of his stupidity. 'Got taken away with the moment.' he yelled to her. She looked at him. Yes, he was definitely taken with the moment, still holding her arm, swaying against her with the movement of the boat. Dittman could go fuck himself. He didn't matter, this is what mattered, being on the water, on a day like this. He could have kissed her then. He wanted too, not because it was Clara, but because the moment called for it. The tension of the last few days had been shed by a simple boat ride, a forgotten pleasure, and his body was thankful for the reprieve. Instead, she leaned forward and kissed him. It was a short kiss, probably the kind he would have given her if he got in first. It was an appreciation of place, time and the intimacy of the shared moment, her lips salty and firm. He let go her arm to reach for her, but she swung away from him.

'I was born there you fool.' She stated in answer to his question. 'It's just like this.' She waved her arm around, to take in the colours of the bay, then turned back to him. 'Thank you.' She paused. 'For a few moments there I felt like I was home, in Cuba, not chasing some criminal on the other side of the world.'

Alex nodded his understanding. He wanted that same reprieve, to be free from his work, to forget about Clarry Woods, and Tiger Dittman and the unknown ahead. For once this week, he just wanted to be on holidays, watching the ocean rush past, look for dugongs and whales, and share the moment with someone who wasn't there to harm him.

Beneath them, the drone of the engine vibrations changed pitch, and the boat slowed as it began to negotiate the sandbanks around them. To the right was the ocean entrance to Pelican Bay, the bar, a distinct gap between the southern end of Yindibar island and the white water of breaking waves on the other side of the entrance. The *Cosmos* would come through that today, if it wasn't here already.

The boat rounded the spit and nosed in slowly to Pelican inlet where a sailing cat was just raising anchor. The inlet was wide, bordered by mudflats and sandbanks. There was no channel here, no creek flowing into it, so it was uniformly shallow as the bottom rose up to meet them. The water was murky, mangroves circled the edge, mudding the clarity. Villi had the chart plotter going, checking it against the soundings beneath the keel.

'We're coming up to 1.5 metres,' he called.

'What do we draw?' Alex asked, referring to the depth of the keel in the water.

'About 1.1 metres I think.' he said.

'We should be fine at this point; it's past the bottom of the low. High is 3.8 today, can you let go get the anchor, we'll put about 12 metres out.'

Villi had slowed the boat to crawling pace as he positioned the bows into the

wind. Alex clambered forward to the anchor well in the bow, freed the chain from its shackle and prepared to drop the anchor overboard. The catamaran edged slowly toward them. Alex waved and the skipper swung the stern of his catamaran toward them. It was called *Cat Baloo,* and looked well lived in, an old awning over the steering station, water drums lashed to the deck, and a general appearance of disrepair. The skipper sat behind the starboard wheel, shirtless, brown skinned from years in the sun.

'I thought I should tell you.' He yelled across the closing gap. 'A big tiger shark

swam through here this morning, I shot it in the head with my .303. I dint' kill it, but it's not very happy.' He laughed at his own humour. 'Just in case you wanted a swim,' he added. He increased the revs to gain speed and swept. past them with a jaunty wave.

Alex stood watching the catamaran disappear south round the point. He heard the call to drop the anchor and secured enough chain before returning to the aft deck as Villi shut down the motors.

'Did you hear that bastard?' Alex was incensed. 'He's shooting sharks. Dickhead.'

'So? We fish for them off Havana all the time,' said Clara, obviously not seeing anything wrong with it.

'Theres a difference between fishing for them and shooting them.'

'Either way they are still dead,' said Clara. 'Whether it's a bullet or a hook, it's the same thing. Makes no difference.'

'If you kill it for food, so be it,' reasoned Alex, 'but to just shoot it because it poses a threat is not right.'

'You should hear yourself Alex, shooting at something that poses a threat is wrong? What if that threat is trying to kill you? We do the same with people, is that any worse? You must protect yourself.'

'That's not a fair comparison, and you know it.'

The heady smell of the mangroves wafted across the inlet.
The trees with

their dark green foliage crouched around the edge of the water, ringing them as they sat at anchor. He never found mangroves a welcoming sight. The clear waters gave way to brown around the tall open roots of the tree stumps dug deep in the mud, and slowly disappearing as the tide rose. Villi came out of the cabin with a pair of binoculars, bringing them to his eyes, he swept the near bank in the direction of Tunkumba creek then passed them to Alex.

'If the yacht is already there, we should see the top of the mast from here.'

Villi pointed in the direction of some low mangroves to the northwest, off the boats front quarter. 'That's the area around the bend in the creek, it's out of sight from the main entrance, but we would see a yacht mast if it's in there, but I can't see anything.'

Alex agreed, he saw nothing that looked tall enough to be a mast.

'If it's not here yet, then we wait,' he said, settling down onto a storage crate,

his back against the ice chest, glancing at Clara, wondering what he was going to do about her. Clara stood looking in the direction of Tunkumba Creek, Villi stood in the cabin doorway, the water kettle in his hand.

'When they come, Alex, what do you plan on doing,' he asked.

'Would this boat be big enough to block the channel in Tunkumba Creek, so the yacht can't get past it?'

'I suppose so, it's only a narrow channel, it would be enough that if the yacht tried to barge past, it would run aground on either sandbank.'

'Good. That would be a distraction,' he said.

'Then can you bring us alongside the *Cosmos* in the dark?' Clara asked.

'Easy enough if I don't run aground myself. But I think I'll be right, I can get you next to the yacht where you can jump on do your stuff, then I'll back off and block the channel, would that suit you?'

Clara nodded in agreement. Alex saw her reach behind and feel for the pistol jammed into the top of her jeans under her T shirt, a gesture of reassurance.

'But it doesn't do me much good,' reasoned Alex, 'I don't want to be stuck on that yacht while Dittman is ashore.'

'Easy enough,' said Villi, 'I'll drop you off in the shallows first, before I take the

little miss here up to her yacht. You can wade ashore and go wreak havoc on Tiger. What did you want with him again? I forgot.'

Villis flippancy unsettled Alex a little, but he had a point. What did he want with

Dittman?

'I wonder if Dittman knows Clarry Woods is dead?'

'Don't know if it matters. The police will come knocking eventually, and Dittman will have some explaining to do.'

'No. Not now. If Woods is dead, then there is no one to testify that Dittman ordered Woods to kill me. I need to get back the laptop and the transcript I made of Woods first interview. It's the only thing I've got against Dittman, it pins him to Barry Crinns death, and the reason he tried to get rid of me. Right now, I have nothing. Dittman has it all. I need that laptop back.'

'You just want to get your stuff back. You don't need to go after him, just find the laptop and scarper out of there. If Clara here is on the yacht giving that skipper a hard time, I'm sure that will provide enough distraction for you.'

Alex snarled. 'I want more than the laptop, I want that prick. He tried to have me killed remember, he hurt Megan, robbed us.'

'It was Woods did that.'

'Under Dittman's orders. He's the one to blame.'

'So, are you going to kidnap him? Under the eyes of a bunch of drug

runners...good plan Alex. That should work.' Villis voice was thick with sarcasm. 'Instead, find his car, and you find Dittman.'

'Just get me to shore Villi, and block the entrance so that the yacht can't get

away. That will distract them enough for Clara to deal with the skipper, I'll get Dittman. I don't know how yet, but at least I'll get my evidence back.'

Alex turned away and walked to the back deck, looking out across the bay. Yeh, good plan he thought, what fucking plan? He was winging it, a dangerous thing to do, but he had no other ideas ...yet. He trusted that it would come to him, it always did. But would it be enough this time.

He glanced back at Clara. She knew what she wanted. She had a motive, a single purpose, her family needed her to succeed, it was easy as that. Alex wrestled with his own rationale. He could just walk away, Megans life was not hanging on retrieving Dittman's evidence, and he didn't think revenge was a good enough reason. Maybe helping Clara was the reason he was here. Fuck. How does he get in such binds. Three years ago, he was in the same shit with his best mate, and he just got out of that one with his life. But who is he protecting this time? Maybe he's the one needing protection. He looked back at Clara again, and Villi in the wheelhouse filling the kettle from a water drum. There was no room for self-doubt. There were only three of them, but they had the element of surprise.

He lifted the binoculars toward the Pelican Bay entrance, it had a reputation that was well earned. A channel swept a long way out to sea, with shallow sand banks either side that broke surf in any sort of swell. Not surf that Alex or anyone would want to ride, the waves broke indiscriminately from any direction, and if a boat that made the turn too early, it often ended up with broken windows or gear swept overboard. Charts gave instructions for specific headings, but the moving sands out at sea couldn't read charts and didn't know they were supposed to stay in the same place, and they never did. Coming into the entrance was even more nerve wracking. The charts warn against entering the channel late in the afternoon when the wind is from the Northeast, the spray blinds you from getting a clear sight on the marker ashore on Yindibar island, then lining it up with a reverse bearing on the southern headland 10 miles behind. He did that once by mistake, never again.

When Alex first caught sight of the sail in the distance, he immediately felt for the wind direction. It was late afternoon and a north eastly breeze.

'Sucker,' he said. Then he realised that he had been waiting for a yacht all afternoon, and here was one now.

He called Clara to the rail and handed her the binoculars.

'Well, what do you think?'

'Could be,' she said.

'Right on time,' Villi murmured.

It took 20 minutes for the yacht to make its way into the bay. Out beyond the bar it lowered its sails before entering the channel and motoring toward them. Slowly it materialised, from a bare mast and white blob beneath, it began to take shape, a largish white sloop with a raised centre cockpit.

'Is that it? Is that the one?' Alex asked,

Clara moved the binoculars around, trying to see all of the boat, but it wasn't till it turned side on inside the entrance that she was able to nod.

'All those blue drums at the back, they are the same as the ones I saw at Nerimbah marina, that's Vaughn Crowthers yacht, the *Cosmos*, I'm sure,' she said.

'You might lower the binoculars; it would look very suspicious if they saw you watching them so intently. Do we have fishing lines Villi?'

Without a word he riffled in a deck cupboard, bringing up a handline and threw it to Alex. Clara did as he suggested and put the glasses aside while Alex lowered a line over the side and pretended to fish. On the other side of the main estuary, the yacht was making its way toward the mouth of Tunkumba Creek.

'Would it be high enough for him to get all the way in yet?' Alex asked.

'Maybe. I don't know what he draws. That would be a bit of local knowledge. If I was him, I'd wait a bit before heading in, we are still a couple of hours off the high.

'Look at those black marks, smeared near the bow, I know what that's from.' Alex stated.

Clara turned to him quizzically.

'When a boat does a transfer at sea, often the gunnels and sides are marked by bumping against cargo ships in the open ocean where the swells slam them together during the transfer, leaving scrapings of hull paint against the yacht, usually black or red,' he explained

'How do you know this?' Clara asked?

'I thought you would know, you were with customs in Havana.'

'Only once,' she protested. 'I was just assigned to customs that night when I was shot and left to die. So, no, I don't know anything about the so-called, paint on the hulls.' She responded testily.

Alex didn't go on, opting not to explain about his own experience. He'd been on an open ocean drug transfer once himself and preferred to leave it where it belonged, twenty years in the past.

'Does it look low in the water?' Alex asked Villi, insinuating that the boat was carrying a substantial weight, more than usual.

'How would I know, haven't seen it when it's not.' Villi remarked sharply, the tension beginning to show in them all.

A figure moved forward to the bows of the yacht and began the steps to releasing the anchor. As it moved closer Clara stepped back under the awning out of sight, while Alex bent to the fishing line, pretending interest in what was on the hook. The yacht motored quietly past their inlet. The only sound over the water a low burble of the diesel exhaust. The wind had died off, and the sun was casting the last of its direct rays across the surface, extending the shadow of the land and hiding the shore in a silhouette against an orange twilight.

The yacht slid to stop around the point, just out of sight in the deeper water off the entrance to Tunkumba Creek. He heard the anchor drop and the familiar rattle of the chain running out, till a muffled shout indicated enough, and the estuary went silent. The yacht mast was visible only 100 meters away just beyond the line of mangroves. Alex looked at Clara and Villi in turn. What went next was now in the hands of the shore party. They would have to wait for it to unfold.

Alex retrieved the line and leaned out from the gunnel, as if he would hear more of what was happening by being closer. The distant drone of an outboard told Alex that they had sent their dinghy up the creek, and on its return ten minutes later was probably loaded with one of the shore party to guide them in. He would give anything to see who it was, sure it would be Dittman. Some unintelligible shouts came from behind the mangroves, then the anchor was retrieved, and a deeper motor started up. The mast began to move inland and was lost against the background of the growing dark.

'Shit,' exclaimed Alex. 'They're on the move. We should think about moving too.' The time had come, he popped upright and indicated for Villi to start the motors, while he went forward to retrieve the anchor. Villi stood in the doorway of the wheelhouse.

'Come on Villi, time to move in after them, block the channel.'

'No. Not doing it.' Villi refused.

'What's got into you? Take us in.'

'No.'

'Fuck you. Then I'll go myself.' Alex made to push past Villi who stood resolutely blocking access to the wheelhouse. He was bigger than Alex, much stronger and if he didn't want to move, there was little Alex could do to force him. He looked past Villi at the instrument panel, there was no key in the ignition, no way to start the engine.

'Where are they?' Alex asked, looking for the keys.

'I've hidden them.'

'Fuck Villi, why are you doing this? What's the problem?'

Villi shook his head in defiance. Alex reached out to push at Villis shoulder, to get into the wheelhouse and look for the keys.

'Don't.' snarled Villi. 'You'll only get hurt.'

'Take us in please, William.' Clara tried a different approach.

'You shut up.' Villi exploded. 'You've got nothing to do with this.'

'Give me the keys Villi. You don't have to come, you can stay on the boat, back out as soon as you've dropped us. Don't worry about blocking the creek entrance.' Alex tried to reason.

'You understand nothing Alex.' He burst out. 'I'm not afraid, if that's what you

think. But I'm not getting you killed for nothing. Theres been enough death, Alex. You go after Dittman, and they'll kill you too. I'm not taking you in.'

'That's not your decision Villi,' said Clara. 'Theres more at stake here than just Alex and Tiger Dittman.'

'Not the way I see it.'

'I have to get on that yacht Villi, any way I can, and you are not going to stop me.' Her hand began to reach behind her back where her gun was hidden.

'Don't' he snarled. She stopped.

'She's right Villi,' Alex implored. 'She needs to get on that yacht.'

'I don't care about her, she's not one of us, she's Cuban, she'll get you killed. Get us all killed. I got to protect my family, Alex. You need to protect yours. Why don't you just leave it alone. Why didn't you just leave Dittman alone...you're so hell bent on getting him. Leave it to the police, but no, you keep at it. And now Woods is dead...shot by her.' He pointed at Clara in accusation. 'And if you get Dittman, what then?'

'But it's what I need Villi. What we both need, Dittman's confession, my evidence.'

'There is no evidence that he killed Barry Crinns.'

'Yes, there is, on the laptop, in the papers, the transcript of Woods' interview,

I'll get him to confess.'

'Confess to what?'

'To having Clarry Woods try to kill me. Weve been over this already.'

'Woods is dead, he can deny anything.'

'Well, confess to Barry Crinns. Woods knew he'd done it. Woods was nearly going to confess himself.'

'Will you fucking stop with the vigilante shit.'

'But he killed Crinns.'

'I don't care, and neither should you. I'm not taking you or me to get killed over someone we don't know, or for a stupid TV show. What you're doing is stupid Alex, that's what it is.'

He looked at Clara whose hand was firmly behind her back on the pistol grip. He jabbed a finger at her face.

'You shoot me, you still won't find the keys.' Villi said, then took a quick step across the gap between them, and before Clara could bring her gun to bare, he smashed her across her upper chest with his forearm, savagely lifting her off her feet and over the rail into the water.

Alex dashed to the side, looking down in the dark waters for Clara. She reappeared in the faint glow of twilight, surfaced and looked up at Alex before she turned and struck out for the shore, swimming strongly. She didn't look back.

'Fuck.' said Alex...his loyalties divided. 'What did you do that for? She can't go up against them by herself Villi.'

'I don't care about her, she's a witch, a fucking Cuban voodoo witch. She's been driving a wedge between you and Megan the whole time, its unholy. I'm not getting you shot because of her vendetta.'

Alex was stunned. Villi had turned against him...Villi had betrayed them both.

'You were never going to take us in, were you?' Alex realised.

'No.'

'You planned this the whole time, didn't you. We'd be stranded out here on the boat while the whole operation unfolds in the creek. The drugs get landed and Dittman gets away, Crowther gets away, and the two people who could do something about it, are stuck on a boat in Pelican Bay with you. Was that always your idea Villi?'

Villis face revealed nothing.

'Did you always want the drugs to land Villi? Is this part of it? Are you part of it?' Alex accused him.

'You got to look after your family Alex.' Villi shrugged, resignation in his voice.

'Do they know we are coming?' Alex asked, horrified, realising that maybe Villi was part of the smuggling operation. Was Villi the Fijian connection? 'Did you tell them we are coming? Are they're waiting for us?' accused Alex.

Villi's silence said it all.

'How the fuck could you do that to me...or her?' He looked from Villi to the shadowy figure of Clara hauling herself out of the water and disappearing into the mangroves. At least she had a clear sense of purpose.

With that Alex chose sides, stepped to the rail and dived overboard.

# CHAPTER 31

Alex pushed his stroke, arm over arm in urgency, willing his body to find landfall underfoot as soon as possible. It was only 50 meters to the bank and he didn't want to think what might be in the water, in the dark. Fucking sharks and now crocodiles, why couldn't Villi have just stuck with the plan. He started to touch bottom, muddy and soft, a mix of sand and sticky silt. By now it was nearly dark.

He found his feet and began to wade ashore, but with each step, he sunk deeper in the silt, the mangroves presented their own problems. The mud took his first shoe, sucked it from his foot, leaving it deep in the mud before he even got to shore. He briefly thought of trying to retrieve it, but waded on in, resigning himself to having only one shoe, till the second one never came up, his foot slipping easily from the heel in even less water. The mud sucked at his legs, shins buried deep so that each step was a drain of energy, arms swinging side to side to gain momentum and maintain his balance. Now he was barefoot he suffered. Mangrove shoots stuck up from the mud like punji stakes. He pushed his feet around them, but he couldn't dodge them all, he gasped in pain when his foot arch bent over the top of one, and he stumbled, pushing his arms up to the elbows in mud in a vain attempt to stay upright.

Ahead of him the mangrove trees were a wall of defence, their open-air root systems tripped and tangled him till his arms and legs ached, his skin scored, and smelling of rotten vegetation. With some relief he burst from the mangroves onto the more secure ground of fallen cabbage tree fonds, still sharp, but firmer underfoot. He scampered across the few meters of solid ground that made up the narrow point till he got to the mangrove line that bordered Tunkumba Creek on the other side. It was less thick here, but small rocks under his bare foot slowed him down.

'Clara,' he whispered urgently, searching for her, past the cabbage palms, and contorting his body through the mangrove trees till he could see clearly across the creek. The yacht lay at anchor only 20 meters away, in the middle of the channel. A small deck light illuminated the cockpit, one of the crew was passing bags up onto the deck from a hatchway, where another was shifting them along the deck to the stern rail where they were being stacked. An inflatable dinghy was motoring between the yacht and shore. On the bank, dim light revealed a small truck, parked up near the drop off, its back doors open. A tent and deck chairs littered the campsite, just as he remembered it.

As the inflatable touched shore, the tall imposing figure of Vaughn Crowther jumped over the side and clambered up the bank. He conferred with the two men waiting for him there. Like a general inspecting his troops he strode around the camp, looking in the back of the truck and checking in the surrounds. A call from the shore party revealed a figure appearing out of the dark, coming down the track from the road entrance. And there he was, Tiger Dittman, the track sentry. After a quick discussion with Crowther, Dittman headed back into the darkness, returning to his vigil. Villi had been right about that; there was a sentry guarding the track in from the road. Alex wondered if Villi had told them they would be coming by land. So far, none of them one had taken any notice of the channel behind them or the opposite bank where he was hiding. Alex was drawn to a soft sound in the water, a kind of swish that formed ripples on the surface. Then he saw her. Clara was breast stroking toward the bow of the yacht, her head bobbing slowly up and down with the stroke. She reached the anchor chain, and held on to it, treading water in the shadows.

He immediately slipped into the water, gingerly pushing his feet ahead to avoid any nasty surprises. Fuck, if it's not sharks and crocodiles its fucking stingrays, but if she made it OK, then so could he. He was quickly afloat and emulated Claras movements to cover the distance between the shore and the yacht. She was so engrossed in what was happening ashore that when Alex came up beside her, she muffled a cry of fright.

'What are you doing here?' she hissed.

'Shhhh,' he directed her, holding on to the chain. 'That's Crowther isn't it?' he whispered.

She nodded.

Who's on the yacht?'

'Troy and Mendez, I think their names are.'

'Only two. He's coming back.' Alex observed Crowther climbing back into the dinghy, where he started the motor and headed back to the yacht, the small outboard pushing the water before it in a bow wave. They both floated back around the bow out of sight.

'I need to get on board,' she whispered.

'I need to get to shore,' he replied. He looked at her, hair plastered across her face, bedraggled and muddy, but eyes fierce, determined. Alex reached out and gripped her arm, as if to touch her was to draw upon himself some of the courage she exuded, the fight in her soul that would transfer to him. She returned the gesture, maybe she was looking for the same. Fuck it, he thought, we've come this far, time to see it through. He turned away and began his swim to the shore.

This time, the bottom was sand, no flailing arms for balance or sucking steps in the mud, he could float close into the bank and use his toes on the sandy bottom to edge his way into the shadows of an overhanging gum tree about twenty meters east of the camp. The bank had washed away, exposing the root system, giving him a hand hold and cover to climb up. He pulled at the roots, and slid himself over the grassy edge, and crouched behind the trunk.

Dittman was alone somewhere down the track to the road, away from the camp. He could skirt the camp and come up to Dittman from behind, without having to face any of the smugglers. He wondered where Dittman's car was. It certainly wasn't at the camp. That's where his laptop would be, he just had to muscle Dittman into giving it up, but the courage he originally had for a direct confrontation was faltering. Maybe he could break into Dittman's car without having to see him at all, that would be better. Crucifying Dittman could wait. Find the car, find the evidence. Alex took a deep breath. Finding the car became Alex's new mantra. He could do that.

From behind the tall gum, Alex slipped across the gap to the first of the underbrush, ducking beneath the spindly leaves, trying to place his feet on the sand and not fallen branches that would let off a crack like a gunshot and draw attention to himself. He was reasonably successful at the subterfuge. Another few minutes and he would be well past the camp and could start to angle back toward the track. To his left a thick shrub looked like good cover, until it moved. Alex froze. The bush moved again. Allex squinted his eyes, trying to identify what was the matter. The movement adjusted to become three shapes, three figures, concealed in the dark, part of the shadows, faced away from him, watching the camp activity intently. A burst of barely audible radio chatter came from one of the figures, unintelligible to Alex from that distance. One of the figures turned toward the other two, what was clearly apparent was the yellow lettering across the back...AFP. Australian Federal Police.

# CHAPTER 32

The water was starting to get cold. Clara wished they would hurry up. Crowther was back aboard, and his two crew were now in the dinghy, alongside the boarding ladder as Crowther passed down the bags for Troy and Mendez to place in the tender. The bales were plastic wrapped with heavy tape around them, stacked neatly at the yacht rail, awaiting transfer ashore.

Her legs were getting tired. Something bumped her under water, she stifled a scream, but did not let go of the anchor chain, nor try and climb up it to the deck, which all her instincts told her to do. She forced herself to stay still.

Finally, they must have loaded what they thought was enough, and pushed off from the hull, the outboard burbled as Troy steered the inflatable toward the shore, Mendez in the front, leaning over the packages protectively.

It was time. Clara moved around to the boarding steps in the water at the stern. She placed her foot on the bottom step, hoisting herself up. Water dripped from her clothes pooling on the transom. Vaughn Crowther appeared from below, stepping up into the cockpit, another bale in his hands, when he saw her. He stopped still, looking quizzically at her, squinting his eyes in the dark to get a better view.

'Who the fuck are you?' he demanded. He wasn't alarmed but seemed more put out by the inconvenience of her presence. Clara didn't reply.

'I know you,' he said at last. 'You were at the yacht club. Are you lost? What are you doing swimming around here in the middle of the night, there's sharks in these creeks you know.'

'You don't really remember me, do you?' She asked. 'A *contabandista* like you should always know who they have tried to kill.'

He stood still...looked at her till his eyes widened in recognition.

'Shit,' he stiffened, reality dawning on him. 'You're that policewoman from Havana.' He looked ashore, looked around the boat before facing back to her. 'What are you doing here?'

Clara couldn't answer...she knew what she was supposed to do, what the Ministry had ordered, her hand hovering above the Baretta in the back of her jeans. But now that she faced him, she hesitated, unsure of her next move.

'What the fuck do you want?' he said angrily.

'You shot me.' She finally said.

'You tried to come on my boat.' He answered as if that was a perfectly good reason to do so.

'It was my job!' she hissed. 'You were smuggling drugs. You shot me and left me for dead, floating in the harbour.'

'I didn't mean to shoot you,' he retorted.

'Yes you did.' She said, she finally gripped the handle of her Baretta, pulled it clear and levelled it at Crowther.

'Why did you come here? To arrest me again?' he said, looking around, the first hint of nervousness to his voice.

Clara couldn't answer that, at this point she didn't know herself. She had no idea how she would react when she faced him. The Ministry expected that she would kill Crowther, revenge Major Colomè's death. It's what they wanted, what was expected of her, it was what she had been ordered to do. She held the pistol steady, aimed directly for Crowthers chest, released the safety and slowly took up pressure on the trigger.

Her hand shook just a little, a hesitancy that manifested itself in her grip. She couldn't. She was a policewoman first, an investigator, she wanted answers, not more deaths. She removed her finger from the trigger.

'Why did you shoot Colomè?' Clara asked.

At first, he didn't answer, Clara could see that he was trying to regain some composure, he knew that he had been close to death.

'Who's he?'

'Major Colomè of the Tropas Guarda Fronteras, our Customs police. He was aboard your boat in Havana, he was going to search it, remember. You shot and killed him, just after you shot me.'

He didn't answer but looked shoreward.

'Is anybody with you?' he asked.

She ignored his question and pressed with her own.

'Why did you shoot me? Why did you kill Colomè?' As far back as Cuba, as far back as the time in the water under a wharf in Havana, nursing a bullet wound in her shoulder, she wanted to know if what she had heard that night was not her imagination.

'Did he want money?' She pressed him. 'Was Colomè in on the smuggling too? Was he there for a pay out?' She said forcefully, demanding an answer.

Crowther didn't say anything at first. He started to fidget, his head bobbed a little, Clara could see him working toward something.

'He wanted too much,' he said. 'I'd already made the arrangement with his boss, but he wanted more.' Crowthers voice dropped in resolve.

'Arrangement with who?' she pressed him.

'Who do you think? That upstart's boss. And what about you? Do you want a payout too?' He began to coerce; money would solve this predicament. 'Do you want some of this?' he waved his arm expansively at the drugs stacked against the rail, then narrowed his eyes and jutted his head forward. 'Or do you want revenge?'

Clara stood her ground, still unsure of which way she wanted to go.

'Revenge is worth nothing,' he said. 'Don't fuck with me...I've been there before...revenge is for suckers; money is the only thing that's worth killing for.' He began to edge backward, his hand reaching up under the cockpit awning as he spoke. But Clara had been there before, she'd seen that move and shook her gun at him. He stopped.

'I want a deal,' she said, and then the world exploded in a blaze of light.

A searchlight beam ripped the darkness apart and speared the two of them standing in the cockpit. Crowther spun around, silhouetted against the intense light coming from a boat only 20 meters away. Villi had come good, he was here as a distraction, but then a voice called out from across the water, and it wasn't Villis.

'This is Australian Federal Police, stay where you are, both of you. Don't move, anyone. We are coming aboard.'

Clara stood still, watching Crowther intently. He stood with his hands fidgeting at his side. His home was under siege from without and within, and there was nothing he could do about it. The police boat was moving slowly toward them. He seemed resigned to his fate, he'd been caught, had nowhere to go. He turned back to her.

'So, you lived hey!'

'You tried to kill me.'

'I only shot you in the shoulder you know. If Id wanted to kill you, I could have. What's your deal?'

'I want justice.' Clara stated.

He began to edge sideways, glancing at the water.

'I could go over the side...right now.'

'I'd shoot you first...and I won't aim for the shoulder.'

'Then you wouldn't have your deal,' he said, a slight smile on his lips.

She looked hard at him and nodded before slipping the gun into the back of her jeans as the Customs boat bumped alongside.

'Don't scratch my boat you cunts,' Crowther yelled, his eyes still locked on Clara.

'Police and Customs. We're coming aboard. Don't move from where you are, keep your hands in sight, I want to see your hands, both of you.' The voice of authority came from the spotlight.

The first officer into the cockpit was in full uniform. He scrambled aboard ungainly, but once there, placed his hand on his holstered gun and asked Clara and Crowther to move back to make room for the next two men. The second aboard was a Customs official by the badge on his sleeve, while the third man was dressed in a bright tropical shirt that brought a guffaw from Crowther.

'What's this? Hawaii five O?' Crowther laughed merciless in his ridicule.

'Federal Agent Cunial, AFP. Under Maritime Law 185, we are searching your yacht for probable containment of narcotics and drug trafficking purposes. Thank you for inviting us aboard.' Cunial recited.

'I don't remember inviting you.' said Crowther sarcastically.

'I do,' he said, then he turned to the uniform. 'Check him for any weapons and mobile phone.' When that was done, and the officer came up empty, Cunial pointed to the deck. 'Sit' he ordered Crowther, then turned to Clara,

'Now you,' he said.

Clara held up her hands in protest.

'I'm Lieutenant Ramirez of the National Revolutionary Police Force of Cuba.'

'What the fuck are you doing here lady? You are a long way from home. Have you been swimming?' he asked incredulously, looking up and down at her dripping clothes.

She stammered a reply that sounded less than convincing. 'I swam here, yes, I'm...I've been following this yacht... for drugs.'

'I don't know anything about that.' He shook his head. 'Search her.'

'Ask Agent Hughes, he's with your police,' she blurted. 'We've been investigating this boat, in connection with drug smuggling from Fiji. It has to do with this man, and this boat.'

'Hughesy?' Cunial stated. 'He's in there.' He pointed toward shore. Shouts of authority echoed across the water as torchlights wavered around the camp. Calls of Australian Federal Police were intermingled with orders to stay still and lie flat. It looked and sounded chaotic. 'He's got his hands full at the moment. You better have a good explanation for being here. Till then, you sit down with this bloke, and don't move.'

She started to protest, but he just pointed to the deck. At least he hadn't included her in the search, and she still had her gun, an asset, or a liability, she didn't know which yet. But Crowther knew she had it hidden and had said nothing, that made her complicit.

'Watch these two,' he said to the first officer and indicated for Customs to follow him down into the cabin. He looked at Crowther as he spoke to make his intentions clear. 'Are there are any more crew present or any surprises waiting for us below? You can tell me now.' Crowther shook his head. With that, they disappeared down the companionway.

Clara twisted around to look at the shore. Figures moved back and forth in the torchlight, seemingly at random. She wondered where Alex was.

# CHAPTER 33

Both Alex and the AFP officers were startled by the explosion of light from the creek behind them. He could see the figures of Crowther and Clara transfixed by the spotlight flooding the yacht, while a voice reached out across the water for them to stay where they were, that they were being bordered. Reflected light revealed a large Customs launch closing in to come alongside the *Cosmos*.

The effect on the camp party was instantaneous. Voices cried out in surprise and figures started to move in the shadows.

'Fuck, too early!' He heard one of the officers exclaim. 'We're not ready.!'

'Shit, we have to go now.' Another shouted into a microphone he held up to his mouth. 'Now! Now!' he yelled. They burst out of their hide near Alex bludgeoning their way through the scrub toward the camp. Alex stood up from behind a melaleuca, watching them closely to see what transpired, but too much undergrowth just contorted the figures and showed a ghostly dance as they dashed around the campsite. More figures appeared from the track to his right, flashlights stabbing in the dark with cries of AFP and orders to stay still were shouted and ignored. It was pandemonium.

Bodies pushed through the bush, some in the lead, some in pursuit, torches strobed and flickered between the trees. A truck door slammed, and an engine started, until bangs on the bodywork and shouts for compliance brought that to a halt.

Alex was transfixed. The Feds must have been watching all the time, hiding out, waiting for everything to be in place before springing the trap, the yacht, the dinghy, the truck, all the players engaged in the smuggling in one spot. If only he had known earlier. He glanced in the yacht's direction; Clara was on her own with that lot. He wondered where Villi was. Maybe they didn't get them all in one place after all, but Villi could wait. The camp was still in an uproar, but for now he had to push his tendency for schadenfreude aside, he needed to find Dittman.

A policeman passed close to him on the track, his torch waving up and down, hurrying toward the action in the camp. Alex waited for it to pass and was about to leave his hiding place when he noticed a dark figure detach itself from the shadows ahead, cross the track and disappear into the scrub just in front of him...Tiger Dittman. Alex ducked under some low branches to follow him as silently as he could.

The bush was thinner here, less undergrowth, taller trees, but more dropped branches, all of which, Alex stood on. Ahead he could hear Dittman blundering his way through, he was making little effort now to hide his passage, it was too hard to rush in the dark without making the noise of twigs snapping underfoot. Tiger must know he's being followed. Ahead, heavy footfalls were now added to the noise of snapping underbrush, Tiger was speeding up, no longer worried about a quiet escape. Alex increased his speed to match in pursuit, his feet stubbing and buckling from the sharps underfoot. Shrubs and light branches whipped at his face and tried to drag him back, he ducked and stumbled over fallen boughs, and the cabbage palms opened the skin on his arms as he brushed against them. But he was gaining on him, he could tell. There was no direct route that Tiger was following, no path, the noise he made in escape twisted and turned as the vegetation dictated, but Alex knew where he was heading, the boat ramp. Ahead of him Tiger kept ploughing on, the camp and Police far behind.

Alex burst into the carpark and tripped over a log that defined the parking area, sprawling in the dirt, stirring his anger further. He struggled to his feet, the weak glow from a light pole illuminated the boat ramp and carpark. Tiger was at the car door of his Holden utility only metres away, trying to get the keys in the lock. He glanced around at Alex and quickly renewed his efforts. Alex heard the lock release and the door handle lift as he crossed the space between them at a run and charged into Dittman before he could get into his car.

He dropped his shoulder at the last second and hit Tiger in a tackle, bending him over double. Tigers arm caught on the partly opened car door, twisting him with the weight of the impact, throwing them both into the gravel. The hard ground of the carpark didn't absorb any of their fall, they bounced and rolled apart, and it was Alex who got to his feet first. Dittman cried out in pain and clutched at his arm. He tried to rise but couldn't. Alex stepped over him and snarled for him to get up. Dittman rolled onto his back, clutching at his shoulder.

'Get up.' Alex jeered, his fists balled ready to hit Tiger again. Beneath him, Tiger screwed his eyes closed and rolled from side to side as he tried to control the pain. Alex glanced back at the car to see the door partly open, the keys still in it, then back to Dittman at his feet. Dittman wasn't going anywhere, it was over. Alex's anger began to subside, he stood back and left him where he was, strode across to the car and looked in. A small overnight bag was open on the front seat, some clothes bundled in the top, but under the bag, poking out from beneath it was the laptop, the reason he had come in the first place. He reached in and retrieved the computer and the bundle of notes with it, backed out, put them on the roof of the Holden before he walked back over to Dittman.

It wasn't the powerful developer, or a cunning drug smuggler that looked up at him from the dirt, instead was an old man. He looked feeble, lying on his side, covered in dust. There was no malevolence in his eyes, gone was the arrogance and bluster, only defeat, loss and pain. Alex wanted to feel the hate but couldn't. Fuck it, he bent down and offered his hand to help get Tiger to his feet. He pushed him toward the car, Dittman stumbled and came up against the bonnet, turned and leaned back against it, breathing hard from the pain of his busted shoulder.

'You know,' he said to Dittman, trying to put into words his feelings. 'I so wanted to hurt you. When I got you, I wanted to beat you to a pulp. I would have run you down if I had the chance you pathetic heap of shit. You sent Woods to kill me, to assault Megan, steal my stuff, all my evidence, I owe you big time. But now that I've got you ...I just don't care any more. I got what I want just here.' He nodded to the stack of evidence on the top of the cab.

'I didn't try to kill you,' Dittman croaked. 'That was Woods.'

'Bullshit,' Alex spat. 'He was under your orders, he told me.'

'He was only supposed to scare you off.'

'Well, he tried to kill me. He shot me. Then he nearly killed Megan when he robbed us. Your orders mate.' Alex paused. 'He's dead you know. Wood's is dead.'

Tiger looked up sharply. 'How?'

'He was shot. Bled out.'

'I didn't know.'

'You saw him last night, didn't you? He dropped my stuff off to you, at your house. All my evidence against you that he took. Gloria saw you and him. You must have seen he was wounded.'

'It was dark...he didn't get out of the car.' Dittman winced again. 'Shit, this hurts, can I sit down?'

'No!' said Alex. 'So, what gives here? You into drugs now too?'

'I only got the track graded for them, that's all.'

'More bullshit Tiger. If you only graded the track, why are you here now? In the thick of it.'

'They weren't going to pay me till tonight. I had to be here, till the job was over, before I got paid. If I didn't show, I wouldn't get paid. I didn't know it was drugs.'

'That's a lie Tiger, what did you think it was?'

'I'm not with them, I'm not part of it, believe me. They have me over a barrel. I need the cash now...for the Cedar Vale project, any more hold ups and I lose the lot. I wouldn't do drug smuggling.'

'But you would do murder, wouldn't you! I'm not believing you Tiger.'

'What do you mean murder? I haven't murdered anyone. You're making stuff up now Holmes.'

'You tried to have me killed...and you killed Barry Crinns, the body in the dunes, your stepson. It's all there.' He pointed at the laptop on the roof. 'You killed that kid a long time ago, Clarry Woods all but said you did, and I've got the transcript of his confession.'

'I didn't kill the boy, I swear to you, he was already dead when we found him. He'd been there for months. It was a shock when we dug him up, but there was nothing I could do, he was already dead, so I just covered him up again, that's all.'

'Then why the fuck didn't you report it? He was your wife's son, your stepson for Christ's sake.'

Tiger was silent for a few moments before he slumped down to the ground, leaning against the front wheel.

'He was a shit,' Tiger declared, looking up at Alex. 'He was a fucking shit. An evil little prick. I'm not sorry he died. He showed up demanding money. He only came to the coast for money, tried to blackmail Gloria...and me. But I sent him on his way, dropped him off at Hideaway beach and I never saw him again...until he showed up in the dunes, dead.'

'And he just went away because you asked him to? Doesn't ring true Tiger. Nope, not good enough, it's all pointing to you still.'

'Alright, alright,' Dittman pleaded, 'he did get money.'

'How much?'

'About $5000. He stole it.'

'From you?'

'Well, not directly. I sometimes kept land sale deposits in my real estate office over at Hideaway Beach, and I might have told the kid where it was, and how to break in. He took it. The money was insured, losing it didn't cost me anything, only the break in.'

'The police didn't say they found any money on his body.'

'They wouldn't have. I went looking for it when we found Crinns. It wasn't there, wasn't in his pockets.'

'You slimy bastard, you checked the dead body of your stepson for money. '

'I'm not proud of it you know,' he said miserably. 'But I didn't kill him.'

Alex didn't know whether to believe Dittman or not. Everything he had gathered led to his guilt, but for some reason, his impassioned pleas rang true. If what Clarry Woods had said was the case, Tiger may not have been responsible for Crinns death. He was certainly a callous slime bag, but it didn't necessarily make him a murderer.

'If you didn't kill him then, then who did?'

'I don't know. But whoever did it, they took the money.'

'And you never told Gloria?'

'She didn't need to know. She thought he had just moved on, she didn't know he was dead...and I didn't tell her.'

'No wonder Gloria is leaving you,' Alex said in disgust.

Dittman said nothing to this, perhaps he already knew. He was shutting down, his head dropped, maybe he'd realised he'd said too much already, he'd confessed to what he could, and now came the remorse, but he didn't think Dittman knew what the word remorse meant.

Alex turned away, nothing more here. Dittman was a figure of misery but not worthy of any pity that Alex could show for him. He reached in the cab and emptied Dittman's carry all on the seat before putting his laptop and notes in it. He thought about taking Dittman's utility, but figured it could be too much trouble, so closed and locked the door. He cast a look back at Tiger before throwing the keys far into the bush, leaving Tiger Dittman to wallow in pain, the cops will find him soon enough. Down the road was Tunkumba, he started walking.

A car swept past him before he'd reached the turn off. It's break lights lit up the bush a vivid red as it came to stop in a cloud of dust, whined in reverse, hurtling back toward Alex, stopping next to him. In the front were two men in Hawaiian shirts, a blue police light on the dash.

'And who are you?' asked the driver.

# CHAPTER 34

A mound of taped up bales off the yacht were already stacked on the bank by the time Clara came ashore. She and Crowther were closely watched as the inflatable covered the 20 meters from the *Cosmos* to dry land. Both Agent Cunial and the armed officer sat either side of them, and although they weren't cuffed, they were clearly under close guard, the officer never took his eyes off them. Torches arced out toward the dinghy as it ran up on the sand.

Clara followed Vaughn Crowther up the bank, guided by the glow of a torch over the exposed tree roots. Beyond, the Federal Police were finally bringing some semblance of order to the raided campsite. A powerful arc light had been set up illuminating the campsite while as torches moved around, slower, with more purpose, inspecting the open truck. Three figures were crouched against its rear wheels, a policeman standing over them. She recognised Troy, the young one, and Adam, the crewman from Havana and the caravan park shop. She didn't know the third one.

They were led across the clearing, to the opposite side where a log lay facing the creek. Cunial indicated that they were to sit on it. Clara was concerned that she and Crowther were being treated as one entity.

'I'm not with him.' She stated.

'We'll see about that. Till then, stay here.' ordered Cunial.

'I want to speak to Agent Hughes,' she demanded.

'You'll have to wait.' Cunial turned away to watch two men dragging a squirming bedraggled figure out of the bush. Hughes dressed in another loud floral shirt, alongside a uniformed officer, frogmarched a short thick set man across to the log. Clara recognised him from the *Cosmos*, one of the crew from Nerimbah, Mendez.

'Sit down,' Hughes ordered, his hand resting on his holster under his shirt. 'I've had enough of you.'

'*Que te jodan*.' Mendez spat at Hughes. For his trouble, Huges pushed him down into the dirt in front of Crowther.

'What did he say?'

'He said for you to go fuck yourself,' explained Clara, standing up to be noticed.

'How original,' quipped Cunial.

Hughes swung the torch into Clara's face.

'Ramirez. What are you doing here?'

'Do you know her?' Cunial asked.

'Yeh. She's with the Cuban Police.'

'I was on the *Cosmos*...'Clara began to explain.

'She was with this bloke on the boat when we boarded it.' Cunial pointed to Crowther.

'What were you doing there? No don't tell me, I got too much to do right now. Sit here with the others until we can sort this mess out. Keep an eye on them,' he instructed the uniformed AFP Officer standing guard. 'Cunial, with me.' Hughes turned and strode down toward the creek bank, shining his torch on the stacked bales of narcotics.

'What's with all the Hawaiian shirts?' Crowther remarked, striking up a conversation with the officer.

'They've been undercover here for the last few days, watching you lot.' The officer replied.

'I'll bet the mosquitos loved that,' he quipped. The officer chuckled.

'Crowther makes jokes, but he killed a Customs officer in Havana earlier this year.' Clara remarked. The guard stopped chuckling. Clara went back to watching Hughes and Cunial, trying to hear the snatches of conversation that floated up to her.

They leaned over the bags, Cunial lifting one in both hands.

'About 20 kilos I reckon.'

'And how many are left on the yacht?' Hughes asked.

'Heaps. Much more than this. When I went below, they were piled under the floorboards, into every hold. I left the Customs guy counting them.'

Hughes withdrew a pocketknife and opened it, sliced through the plastic protective wrap and dug the blade into the contents, lifting some of the brown sticky substance up to his nose and tongue.

He turned and called out for all in range to hear. 'Well, its confirmed, we got the right yacht, it's high-quality resin.' A ragged cheer echoed around the camp site. Hughes looked around at the groups under guard; she heard him order Cunial to get the three prisoners at the truck and bring them over to join her group at the log.

She looked down at Mendes who was squirming next to her and was shocked at the malevolence in his stare.

'You fucking police bitch.' He sneered.

Clara tried to ignore him, but he kicked out at her from where she sat. Though it didn't connect, he hawked up a glob of phlegm and spat it at her.

'Fuck you *comemierda*,' she replied to the insult.

Crowther chimed in. 'Heh Mendes, she's the one who dobbed us in, she got us into this mess.'

'*Gilipo*.' She snapped. '*Mierda Crowther Tu lo que eres es una comemierda*, you are such an asshole. I followed you all the way from Cuba. You made your own mess.'

'*Que te jodan*,' Mendez hawked at her.

'What's he saying?' the officer demanded, nervously stepping away from them.

'Same as before. He's nothing but a Columbian *mocoso*.' Clara jeered, 'a little prick who got caught.'

'She did it Mendez, she told the police when we were coming, that's how they knew, she did it.' Crowther egged Mendez on, leaning forward, hissing in his ear.

'*Perra*.' Mendez snarled as he launched himself at Clara, pushing her over the back of the log, his body following as he reached for her neck. Crowther was knocked sideways. Mendez landed heavily on her, he tried to circle her throat with his rough hands, before she lifted her knee and jammed it into his groin. He released her throat and began to pummel her with his fists, rolling them both in the dirt until he was hauled off her.

'Cut it out,' Hughes yelled, dragging Mendes to one side.

Clara struggled to her feet, pulling her shirt down and dusting herself off. She checked for her gun in the back of her jeans... but it wasn't there. She looked down, scuffed at the ground, sweeping her foot around, trying to feel for it in the dark. Mendes was just getting to his feet, he had her Baretta in his right hand. His first shot took the officer squarely in the chest of his armoured webbing, his pistol barely out of its holster fell to the ground as he was thrown off his feet. Mendes swung the gun toward Hughes and loosed off a shot, before bringing it round to bare on Clara.

It all happened so quick, she hadn't moved. Crowther twisted from the ground and swept his legs over the top of the log, hitting Mendes' legs out from under him as he pulled the trigger, the shot went wild. Crowther got to his feet and sprinted off into the bush. Clara woke from her freeze and automatically leaned down to pick up the fallen officer's gun. Mendez recovered and tried to bring up his gun again. She had fired a police Glock at the academy, at targets, she was good, her shots didn't miss then. She squeezed the trigger twice. Mendes collapsed, fell in on himself, crumpling to the ground, she didn't miss now either.

Without a second thought, she took off after Crowther. He'd got away once but it wasn't going to happen again.

Ahead she could hear him charging through the scrub in blind panic. She caught a glimpse of him ducking and weaving between the low-lying shrubs. She wasn't gaining on him, but nor was she dropping behind. The undergrowth slashed mercilessly at her face and sticks in the soft leaf litter underfoot eventually slowed her down. She lost sight of him in the moonlight; she stopped and listened. Nothing. He had gone into hiding. *Mierda*. Behind her, the shouts and torchlights of the AFP chase were distant and coming closer.

She moved quietly out to the left, the bush looked thicker there, more shadows, more appealing if you didn't want to be found. A grove of melaleucas opened before her, she swept it with her periphery vision, all trees, tall shadows...but maybe not.

She raised her gun at the central trunk, mostly white with intermingled low hanging branches, one had a tall streak of burnt bark on one side.

'You run again, and I'll shoot you.' she said out loud. Initially she thought she was mistaken, until Crowther carefully detached himself from the shadow of the tree, raised his arms and stepped out into the light.

'I saved your life,' he said. 'I saved your life back there.'

'You ran. You've done it before; you'll do it again.' Her gun hand began to quiver; she firmed her stance. He had tried to escape, she had a valid excuse to shoot him now, she would be protecting fellow police from a fugitive who had killed before. Her instructions from the Ministry would be complete. There may some trouble from the Australian Government, but in the end, they would back her, she was a policewoman, whatever police force she represented. Her time here would be over, she could go home to Cuba, to her mother and her brother, absolved of her moral dilemma.

She firmed her grip on the pistol and straightened her shoulders in preparation.

'What was your deal? Your deal on the boat,' Crowther pleaded. 'You said you wanted a deal?'

In the distance, the pursuers were crashing through the scrub, coming closer. She so wanted to pull the trigger and be done with it.

'I'll let you live if you'll do something for me.'

He nodded.

'Say it,' she said.

'I'll do whatever you want.'

'Good. Now get on the ground.'

Vaughn Crowther lowered himself onto the soggy floor of the tee-tree swamp, lay on his stomach and put his hands behind his head. She knelt down and put the gun against his head, whispering quietly in his ear. When she finished, she stood and called loudly.

'Over here! He's over here.'

She took her finger away from the trigger and lowered the gun to her side. It didn't take long for the trailing AFP officers to find them both.

# CHAPTER 35

Alex knew straight away that these guys were Police, probably Federal Agents, the short back and sides haircut, the direct manner, and the gaudy Hawaiian shirts as some sort of tropical camouflage gave them away. He'd already rehearsed a plausible response to being questioned when distant popping sounds echoed from the bush behind him. The police driver froze. It wasn't till later that Alex realised that what he heard was gunfire. A radio on the seat between the two men lit up with urgent squarks.

'Fuck,' the driver blurted. His passenger grabbed the radio and responded that they were on their way to provide a blocking force. The flashing blue light on the dash lit up as the driver planted his foot, spinning the tyres as he headed down the road toward the boat ramp.

Alex stood spitting and wiping at his eyes as the dust settled. Darkness filled the space where the car had just been, it enveloped him, and he suddenly felt small and isolated. There had been shooting, and he was alone on a stretch of dirt track with a fugitive drug trafficker in the bush somewhere behind him...and probably coming closer. He stood silently, still, listening intently, till he detected the first indiscernible sounds of human movement coming from the bush. Then as suddenly as it came, it abruptly stopped.

Alex wasn't going to hang around to find out what came next. He tucked the bag firmly up under his arm and headed toward Tunkumba at a quick pace. He was nearly at the Goldston turn when the car came back, no flashing lights, less in a hurry. For the second time that night, the car pulled up alongside him. Only this time they stopped, and both got out, flashing their Australian Federal Police badges.

'Mate where are you heading?' the driver asked.

'Tunkumba Caravan Park.' Which wasn't entirely incorrect, he was really after the phone box on the footpath in front of the office.

'I think you'd better come with us.'

'Have I done something wrong?'

'Don't know that yet, do we. What's in the bag?'

'My laptop, a folder, notes.' He held it open for the first Agent to see. A torch was shined inside and he seemed satisfied.

'Not sure if or where you fit into any of this, but we're taking you to the station for a statement of your where abouts tonight.'

'Into what?' Alex asked innocently.' What's going on?'

'Nothing!' one of the Agents said.

'Drug bust,' said the driver. He stood back and indicated that Alex should lift his arms out to the side. He had no reason to object. They frisked him, and held the rear door open for him to get in.

In the back seat was Tiger Dittman, he sat hunched in the corner, turned away from Alex, which was fine by him.

They drove past the track that led from the main road into the camp, Dittman's track. Flashing police lights lit the side of the road and car lights bumped down the track in the direction of the camp. Overhead, a helicopter circled, casting an eerie glow, like a wartime scene from Apocalypse Now. An ambulance passed them in the other direction as their own car continued toward Goldston.

'Was someone hurt?' Alex asked.

'A couple, one of them an officer.' The driver replied. His partner looked across at him, shaking his head in reproach.

'A policewoman?' asked Alex.

'Don't know.'

'How did the drugs get here?'

'Can't tell you that.'

'So, what's with the Hawaiian shirts, why aren't you in uniform? Surely you can answer that.' Alex prodded.

'It's Queensland. We've been in undercover surveillance for a couple of days.'

'Mate, even we don't wear Hawaiian shirts up here,' stated Alex.

'Look, enough with the questions, shut up till we get to Goldston will you.' The driver said, his voice thick with finality.

Alex leaned into his own side of the back seat, watching the landscape whisk by in the glow of the headlights. How much do I tell them? Alex thought, I bet Dittman's wondering the same thing. He gripped on to the shopping bag even harder, his bundle of evidence against Dittman, and swung around in his seat to look back over his shoulder. Where was Clara? Shit.

The police station at Goldston was the last time he saw Tiger Dittman. On arrival at the front doors, he was led away to an ambulance, ignominiously holding his arm. Miserable wretch, whatever they do to him, I hope it hurts. Alex was led inside and told to wait on the bench in the entry way until they got to him. The station was lit up and preparing for the onslaught from the night's operation.

The desk sergeant allowed Alex to use the phone and make a call, but it was close to midnight before Megan arrived. Till then, it was chaotic. Federal agents came in, leading in members of the smuggling syndicate, one at a time. Alex recognised some of them, like Crowther, but not others, watching them get processed at the front desk before being taken away to different interview rooms or stacked into the holding cells at the rear of the building. At one point a scrum of officers led by Agent Hughes came in, Clara amongst them. She caught his eye but was bundled past before anything could be said. She looked tired, drawn, bedraggled. Behind the front counter, Police vied for home turf dominance with the interloping Federal Agents. Calls were made, phones rang and were answered while shouts for paperwork to be completed were ignored. It was chaos.

An agent in a dirty Hawaiian shirt came back out and flopped down onto the bench next to him. Alex thought he recognised him.

'I'm Agent Hughes, AFP. Do you want a coffee?' He offered.

'Yeh, I know you. God, I'd love one,' said Alex.

'Good. If you find a decent one in town, bring me one back. I've got a long night ahead.'

Alex looked at him perplexed, not understanding.

'You are Alex Holmes, aren't you? We met last week at the hospital,' he said, in a matter-of-fact tone. 'My guys tell me they picked you up near the boat ramp. Investigator Ramirez told me about you.'

'Clara, she's alright?'

'She's fine.'

'I heard there were shots, a police officer down?'

'He's OK, only bruised, the bullet hit his body armour. It wasn't Ramirez.'

'Who shot him?'

Hughes ignored the question.

'We're going to be here all night, we can't interview you for a statement at the moment, got more pressing people to deal with. Ramirez was adamant that you were with her from the start and not any part of the smuggling operation. You're not a flight risk but can you report tomorrow afternoon for an interview and written statement with that guy, Agent Cunial.' He pointed to another floral shirted officer leaning over a desk. 'He'll be down at Nerimbah Police Station tomorrow. No point in hanging around here waiting for your Cuban Lieutenant either, she has a lot to talk to us about, she's going to be tied up here for a while, OK?'

'Understood.' Alex conceded, 'I'm waiting for my wife to arrive.'

'Now that's a good thing, go home with her. Forget about Ramirez for the moment.' Hughes remarked as he stood up and glanced back behind the desk.

'Not sure what you mean?' Alex queried.

Hughes was slow in his response, as if choosing his words carefully.

'Investigator Ramirez...she was very concerned for your safety...overly concerned, I would say.'

'You must have a very active imagination.' Alex said.

'Yeh, well,' he sighed. 'We don't deal in imagination, more interested in facts Mr Holmes. I'll be waiting to read your statement when it comes.' He turned and disappeared into the chaos behind the front desk.

Half an hour later, Megan walked in the door.

# CHAPTER 36

### Tuesday

'You're famous,' Megan said, perching next to him on the bed in the morning sunlight. He took the coffee cup she proffered. 'It's all over the news, well, TV and radio anyway. A drug bust at Tunkumba last night. The yacht *Cosmos* seized in a joint operation between the AFP and Customs, boats, helicopters, a huge drug shipment. Apparently, the AFP had the yacht under surveillance since it left Fiji, waiting for it to show up. Apparently, the cops were undercover, blending into the local community as tourists. The media are having a field day.'

Alex was still waking up but tried hard to listen to everything Megan was telling him. His head was still in the mangroves of Tunkumba creek, Villis boat, flashes of dark, the fight with Dittman, all resurfacing from his dream state. He shook his head to clear it as much as he was able.

'Yeh. I thought that might be the case,' Alex said, smiling at the memory of the AFP agents in their battered floral shirts. 'Any names?' He queried.

'None mentioned yet.'

'What about shootings, any reported?'

'No. Nothing. You said last night that there had been a shooting at the creek, but they haven't mentioned anything in the news about it, maybe it's too early.'

'Maybe they don't want that to come out. I wonder if it was Clara?' He swung his legs out of bed and stumbled out to the main room, turning on the TV to the local channel. He stood quietly watching it reel through the morning show while Megan showered.

She joined him at the TV, towelling her hair dry as the half hour news update confirmed everything Megan told him, nothing new from the lead of the drug bust, until the next story unfolded.

*...And in further news to hand, the body of a 59-year-old local man, Clarence Woods, was found dead in his car on a property in the hinterland this morning. Police have confirmed he died of a gunshot wound. They are at the crime scene and have sealed off the area. There are no further details at this time.*

'So now they've found him.' Alex stated. 'It had to happen, I suppose.'

'What an awful thing to say!' Clara murmured. 'Talk about him as if he was an annoyance, something that got in the way.'

'I didn't kill him. He was dead when we found him. I told you that last night.'

'It's not what you say Alex, it's how you say it. As if he didn't really matter, he was a living human two days ago, and now he's gone.'

'He assaulted you, if you remember, and tried to kill me. I'm not going to shed any tears for his passing.'

'You said he bled out in the front seat of his car outside his house. Died of his wound from Clara's gun, and you left him there. That man's dead. He died by himself, alone, have you thought about that? A cold lonely death. And all you can say is that it had to happen.'

She sat down gingerly on the couch, looking up at him, accusing him of...he didn't know what.

'I'm sorry if that sounded a bit harsh. I can't say that he deserved it, but he put himself in the wrong situation in the first place,' he said, thinking back to what Clara had said to him when he was confronted with Wood's body.

'I'm not sad for him...I'm sad for you. You treat his death so off handedly. And this is not the first time, is it. I can't be so matter of fact about it like you.'

Alex realised she wasn't used to death at such a close range. He'd seen it up close when he was younger, when the drug barons of the coast ruled, and were taken down. His *Cold Cases* television programs dealt with it all the time, and since then, he was able to compartmentalise it, and whenever possible, keep death in a locked box in his mind. He liked to think that he was keeping it in perspective, but that was a cruel excuse for its true horror.

He sat down on the couch next to her. She had a point, Clarry Woods died a lonely man, in pain. He shouldn't be so easily passed off as a 30 second news item, no-one should be passed off so quickly.

'Woods told me that he had no choice. I said everyone has a choice, but perhaps events out of your control limit those choices. I think he was under Tiger Dittman's control for much of his life. but he made that choice to assault you, knock you out, just to get the laptop...he didn't have to.'

'Yes, I know that. It's just...' Megans voice petered out as she tried to explain how she felt but couldn't find the words. Alex felt the same, was it remorse? He didn't know. He reached across and picked up her hand in his, she didn't pull away but squeezed his hand in return. She sighed and turned to him.

'We talked about Dittman a lot yesterday while you were gone,' she said. 'He was around as a property developer when Nerina and Villi first got together. Nerina's from a strict Methodist family. They didn't approve of Villi at first, he was a fisherman on the trawlers. He could be away for long stretches at a time, but he used $5000 from his Aunty in Fiji as a down payment on a shop to start his own Chandlery, and that impressed her parents to no end. They weren't married then, but soon after. She talked about her extended family a lot, especially Kami, the doctor. I told her about all the things we are doing to stop Dittman from blocking the creek at Cedar Vale, and why we are trying to find evidence against him.'

Alex bit his lip, unsure how to begin.

'Well, Tiger Dittman is well and truly in the shit now. I don't know where I'm going with this, but...Villi turned against us last night. I can't figure it out, but he did everything to stop us getting ashore at Tunkumba. It was like he was working for them. He might even be the Fiji connection for all I know. Did she talk about Villi going back to Fiji recently, or why he had to see his nephew in hospital last week?'

'No, nothing of that. We were just talking.' Megan sat looking expectantly at Alex.

'I honestly thought he was helping me and Clara get to get Dittman and also Crowther, but at the last minute, he turned. Wouldn't take us in, he was going to leave us stranded out on the boat. I need to know why before I make my statement to the police this afternoon. If he's part of the smuggling syndicate, that's his problem, I'm not going to dob him in, but I won't lie for him either.' He struggled with the disquiet he felt. Villi was his old friend, he couldn't readily believe that he was mixed up in drug smuggling, it wasn't really in his nature, he didn't need it, his business appeared to be doing well, why dabble in drug smuggling? Tiger Dittman was the same. But if it wasn't the drugs, what was it?

'I'm getting dressed,' he said. 'We're going to see Villi...find out why he ratted on us!'

Alex and Megan stood outside of Villi Tanoas house. He'd driven past the chandlery on the way, but it was closed. The sign on the door said Villi was taking a short break for personal reasons. Well, he had his own personal reasons for fronting Villi Tanoa. A shadow passed in front of the glass in the door at the top of the stairs. It opened slowly. Villi stood in the doorway, Nerina behind him. Villi didn't say anything, Alex climbed the steps and pushed the door open, walking past Villi down to the kitchen. They all followed.

'I'm in a pickle,' Alex said, turning to Villi. 'I have to make a statement to the police this afternoon, about a mate of mine and

I'm not sure what I will say about him. Did you see the news this morning?'

'I did.'

'Your friends have all been arrested.'

'They're not my friends.'

'Didn't seem like that yesterday, when you deliberately kept us away from shore. What happened after I went overboard?'

' I saw the Customs launch go past, so I left.'

'I'll ask you straight Villi, I want the truth. Are you the Fijian connection here?'

'You don't get to accuse me of that Alex. Of course I'm fucking not!' He objected.

'But when I asked you yesterday, you didn't say no, you didn't say anything. I don't care if you are in it or not. You knew I wasn't on some vigilante drug bust or revenge like Clara wanted,' Alex said, exasperated. 'I was only after Dittman and the laptop, all my evidence. I didn't give a shit about the drugs. You knew that, but you tried to keep me on the boat.'

Villi didn't say anything. He looked at Alex blankly. If silence means consent, then there was only one conclusion.

'So, it's really that you didn't want me to get Dittman or the evidence? Alex concluded.

Villi looked at Nerina, still silent, no denial.

Alex couldn't let it go. 'Why didn't you want me to get the evidence against Dittman? It's got nothing to do with you, it's to get Dittman for the murder of Barry Crinns twenty years ago.'

'Did you get it?' Villi asked quietly.

'Yep. I got the laptop, and all my notes.'

'And what about Dittman?'

'We had a fight at the boat ramp. He confessed, I let him go.'

'What did he confess to?' Nerina asked quietly.

'When I had Dittman on his knees, he was adamant that he never killed Crinns, that someone else did. The last he saw of Crinns was when he dropped him that night at Hideaway Beach. He gave him $5000 to leave.' Alex turned his gaze to Villi. 'He also told me that when he and Woods first found Crinns body, the money, the $5000 was gone.'

The table was silent.

'So, he was killed for the money.' Villi stated.

'Maybe,' said Alex. 'Do you know?'

Villi was silent. Nerina was looking at Villi, her hands clasped tightly in her lap.

'What's he saying William? What's he meaning about the money? Does he know?' she whispered.

'Do I know what Nerina?' Alex asked.

Villi's lips moved wordlessly, a big man, always so confident, yet this time, at a loss for words. He looked at Nerina, then at the floor.

'Dittman didn't kill Crinns, I did,' Villi murmured.

Megan sucked in a breath and looked expectantly at Alex. In the back of his mind, Alex wasn't surprised. Nerina had given it away talking with Megan the day before. Not directly, but enough to raise his suspicions. Alex said nothing but waited for Villi to explain.

'The night he disappeared, I was with Nerina, at a party at Hideaway Beach,' said Villi, looking directly at Alex. 'There were a lot of us, another party on the beach, we were all drunk. The sort of one we both used to go to before you left for Uni. Nerina wasn't drinking much, nothing really, she didn't like me drinking so much. She was disappointed with me, said I was making a fool of myself, so she went for a walk. Later I got up and followed her. Maybe I was bit pissed off, but I wanted to say sorry. Down the beach I heard Nerina crying. I found that prick Crinns trying to, you know, he was assaulting Nerina, in the dunes, he was trying to...you know...' Villi couldn't say it.

'...rape her? He tried to rape Nerina?' Megan quietly completed the sentence for him.

Villi nodded.

'Nerina was crying, and her clothes were all messed up, his pants round his fucking ankles, so I beat him and beat him. I didn't stop. I beat him in the head, squeezed his neck, I was so mad.' Alex thought of Villis big hands, his natural strength, he could imagine it. He looked at Nerina, she sat saying nothing, looking down in her lap, her eyes screwed shut. The memory too strong. 'Nerina's a good girl; she didn't deserve that.'

'And then what? Alex asked quietly,

'I stopped. He wasn't moving. He hadn't moved for a while. He had no pulse. That's when I knew I'd killed him.' Villis voice petered out in the silence of the kitchen.

'I was still a bit drunk, I know it's no excuse, and I live with that, I have done for twenty years. We could have gone to the police, but our parents would never have understood, they would have been so ashamed, ashamed of Nerina, even though it wasn't her fault. Where's the justice in that? So, we buried him, together, as deep as we could so that no one would find him. It would be our secret.'

'And it would have stayed a secret if the storm hadn't uncovered Barry Crinns skeleton twenty years later.' Alex ventured.

'And then Alex started investigating Dittman, and you had to find a way to stop him.' Megan quietly surmised.

'Why did you have to keep digging, Alex?' Villi asked. 'You kept looking for evidence to get at Dittman. Uncovering more about him and Barry Crinns. At some point, you would end up at me. I tried to stop you, persuade you to leave it to the Police, bury whatever evidence you had in a Police storeroom, but you wouldn't give up, you were obsessed.'

'Dittman was my prime suspect until last night,' Alex revealed. 'Then he mentioned the money. He all but gave Crinns $5000 to leave town, but it wasn't on him when they discovered the body, someone had taken it. What happened to it Villi?'

'I think you know.' He looked across at Nerina then back at Alex. 'I took the money, the $5000, and brought the lease on the shop with it.'

Alex nodded, that made sense of Dittman's confession.

'You said you got it from your Aunty in Fiji!' Nerina remarked.

'I had to think of something.' he said lamely. 'You would never have approved. I didn't want you to ever think that we've profited from that boy's evil.'

He reached across and grabbed her hand in his. Seeking forgiveness through touch. For the next minute they were lost in each other's depths, the silence of shame and redemption. It seemed that confession also gave rise to great tenderness. Villi looked back at Alex.

'So, what happens now?' he asked.

Alex leaned back in his chair, looked around the walls at the photos of boats and Villis family, the carved wooden implements and the cross on the wall. A crime is a crime, but what part does justice play he thought. He looked at Villi and Nerina Tanoa wondering how little would be gained by punishing them more than they had punished themselves already. Alex collected his thoughts.

'Villi, you've been living with that secret for twenty years now, how much longer you want to live with it is up to you, not me. Look, the police might find their way to your door one day, but it won't because of anything I have said or done.'

'Thankyou' said Villi with a sigh of relief.

'Trust me,' Alex said. 'We all have secrets. I know where you've been, I've been there myself.' He helped Megan to her feet and pushed both their chairs in under the table before facing them. He looked directly at Villi. 'And now, I'm going to take the advice from a good friend of mine and stop rooting around investigating cold cases that should stay cold and buried. I'm going to have a holiday like I came here for instead.'

They left Villi and Nerina at the kitchen table and let themselves out. At the bottom of the stairs they bumped into Xavier who greeted them warmly before he headed up the steps.

'Now that's a good enough reason to keep a secret. He's a good boy, the whole family. No-one needs to know.' Alex nodded toward Xavier as he disappeared through the front door.

Megan turned to him.

'But what about your statement to the AFP this afternoon?'

'Oh, I'll think of something, I usually do. They don't want me, or Villi, they're just crossing the 'T's' on their own operation.'

# CHAPTER 37

Alex wasted no time winding down. He and Megan shared a crumbed fish burger for lunch at the picnic table overlooking the beach discussing Villis revelation. It wasn't a burden for Alex, he had enough questionable actions in his past to know that everyone had secrets, some more burdensome than others, but most secrets were not to see the light of day, and Alex was OK with that. Now that he had made that decision, his mind felt free, the contortions of 'what ifs' had disappeared. There would be no cold case after all, he couldn't do it without hurting Villi and Nerina and he had given them his word. Dittman would get whatever he had coming to him for his involvement with the drug traffickers. He would leave the authorities to sort that one out.

'Alex,' a voice called from behind him. He and Megan turned to see Clara Ramirez striding down the grassy slope toward them. 'I thought you would be here. No one was home, I think the beach is your second house.'

Alex rose from the bench, passing the remainder of his lunch to a scowling Megan.

'You look terrible,' he chided her. Her hair was loosely piled on top, her eyes red rimmed and cheeks hollow. She had on a fresh T shirt and jeans but still bore the battering from Tunkumba creek, mud splattered her temples and still smeared the underside of her arms. 'What happened to you last night? You look like you haven't slept.'

'I haven't, but I'll have plenty of time on the plane for that. Agent Cunial is taking me to the airport after I get my things from the hostel.'

'Are you being deported?' Megan asked from her seat, barely concealing her glee.

'I'm being sent home, same thing.' She answered Megan, then turned back to Alex and lowered her voice, glancing around to see if anybody else could hear. 'Last night I shot the *contabandista*, Mendez, the Columbian. He took my gun, and shot a policeman with it, then he tried to kill me and Agent Hughes, but I shot Mendez in defence; Hughes knows that I saved him.'

Alex looked thoughtfully at her. He was thinking back to her reason for coming here in the first place.

'You didn't get Crowther, the skipper?'

'No, not him. In the end I had the opportunity, I could have but I didn't. I'm a policewoman Alex, not an assassin. I don't care what the Ministry want, if I did that, I'd be tied to them forever. No, my job is finished here, I can go home now, still a Police Investigator.'

'Will it be a problem when you return? For you or your family?'

'No. I don't think so, I have some... insurance.'

'Can't you stay for a few more days, the least they owe you.'

'Let's just say that Agent Hughes would prefer me out of the way as they untangle the legalities of a Cuban policewoman shooting a Colombian criminal on Australian soil with a gun taken from an AFP Officer. That is how Agent Hughes described it anyway.'

Alex had to smile at that. Hughes' pragmatism shone through.

'But your gun?' he asked seriously.

'It's untraceable. It has Mendez's prints on it now, so it is his gun that killed Mr Woods, and shot the policeman, not mine. And Mendez is dead. The only people who know different are you and me, and I won't tell if you won't.' She paused. 'They don't care about us Alex, you can tell them anything you want, they got their drug *contabandista's* and their success is all over the news. They don't want anything to upset that; it's why they're getting rid of me so quick.'

She turned and looked back to where Agent Cunial was waiting by his car, pointing at his watch. She turned back to Alex.

'I must go. Oh! One last thing, Agent Hughes said to tell you that your friend Tiger Dittman is filing charges against you for assault.'

'That dickhead,' Alex chuckled. 'I can hardly wait.'

'Neither can I,' Clara said seriously, offering both her hands. Alex took them in his. She leaned in and brushed his cheek with a kiss.

'Come to Cuba,' she whispered, 'Tell me how it ends, *te estaré esperando*.'

With that, she smiled sweetly down at Megan, turned and walked up the grass toward the waiting car.

Alex sat back down at the table, retrieved his half-eaten lunch, noting how his wife looked particularly pleased now that Clara had gone.

Alex lay on the bed after lunch, his body still recovering from last night, his muscles ached. He stretched and tried to focus on what parts of his body hurt the most. Outside the afternoon sun was trying to burn its way through the blinds. Megan lay with her back to him, so he shuffled across tentatively, and reached his arm over her, pulling himself a little closer. He sensed her waking with a start. She turned into his arms and pressed her body against his, lifting her shirt so that her skin joined with his, her breasts pressed hard against him, reaching around to caress his head then down to his buttocks to pull at his shorts. Alex smiled and pulled her bare back in tighter.

Their love making was cathartic, at first gentle and caressing, until the urgency took over and they lost themselves in each other. Later he didn't bother pulling the sheets back up, but lay on his side, his leg draped over hers, each lost in their own thoughts.

'I'm glad you're back.'

'Me too,' he agreed.

'Yesterday everything moved so fast.'

'You were still concussed; I couldn't take you with us. We were on the chase.'

'I know that. You were gone all that time. It scared me.'

He reached over and swept her hair away from the bruise on her forehead. In turn, she touched at the scabs and cuts that littered his arms and face.

'I had a mangrove mud pack just for you. Can you tell?' He joked.

'Not a chance. As ugly as ever.' She paused before continuing. 'When do you go in to make your statement?'

'Later this afternoon,' he said, hesitantly.

'You're not worried, are you? Agent Hughes exonerated you.'

'Clara Ramirez exonerated me; it was Agent Hughes who let me go.'

'Did you have to bring her up.'

'I owe her. She cleared me, but I know where Dittman fits in now, and I don't have to bring Villi into it.'

'Dittman's in enough trouble already.'

'Here's hoping,' he said, grinning widely. 'Couldn't happen to a nicer guy.'

'It's good to see you smile again,' she said.

'I guess that's the end of the Cedar Vale development as well.'

'A win for both of us.'

'I'm going for a swim.' He declared, glancing out the window at the sundrenched beach below.

'Not yet you're not,' she said as she rolled across on top of him.

He was still smiling when he entered the surf half an hour later, swimming strongly onto the waves, taking pleasure from the pain of his cuts stinging with saltwater healing. The small waves suited his playfulness perfectly.

He was still smiling when he ordered a coffee at the surf club, joking with the barista and tipping his regulation sugar into the cup with an exaggerated flourish. Megan strode across the grass toward him, waving furiously, one hand behind her back, swaying her hips cheekily from side to side.

'We don't have to be back in Melbourne till Monday,' she said. 'We've still got three more days.' She pushed the coffee to one side and brought two cold beer bottles out from behind her back and placed them on the bench. 'What do you want to do now that everything's wound up?'

'I think we need to give Villi and Nerina some space.'

'It doesn't stop us being friends.'

'Knowing what we know now, doesn't make it any easier though. We've become the keepers of their secret.'

They both fell silent, considering all that that implied.

'And what about us, are we friends?' Megan asked.

'The best of,' he replied.

Alex looked long and hard at her, the last week had taught him much about what he wanted in life, what he cherished, and what he would forgo to keep it.

'So, no Cold Case about *The Boy in the Dunes*?' she asked.

'No, definitely not, we won't be touching that one. I'll let the Police figure that one out.'

'What about *The Great Tunkumba Drug Haul* or *The Platypus of Cedar Creek*?'

'They're not a cold cases, and the titles are a bit long for a TV program don't you think,' he chuckled.

'I know, but have you heard about Podcasts?'

'A Podcast. I hadn't thought of that. See, this is why I love you,' he said in mocking jest.

'Do you?' she said in a quiet voice. 'This last week I wasn't so sure.'

'This last week made me realise that I was never so sure in my whole life.'

'Absolutely?' she asked seriously.

'Absolutely,' Alex repeated back to her grinning, chinking the neck of his beer bottle against hers.

# CHAPTER 38

**Havana, Cuba**
**Thursday**

It took her two days to get home to Cuba. The Air America jet flew into Havana, landed and stopped just short of the terminal, and waited. The jet spent nearly as much time on the tarmac as it had getting there from Mexico City. Clara looked out the window, watching other jets pass hers and dock at the terminal, wondering if the delay was on purpose because the plane was American. She rested her head against the glass, how petty.

In the main concourse, Clara spotted Sergeanto Paulo Vasquales from Policia Headquarters standing at customs talking to one of the girls at her booth. He detached himself from the counter and sauntered across the tiled floor.

'Heh Ramirez,' he called. 'Colonel Perez wants to see you, now.' He pulled into step with Clara, taking great pleasure in being the bearer of bad news.'

'Yeh, sure,' Clara said. 'Here, take my bag.'

'Take your own bag Ramirez,' he objected. 'You're not that much of a big shot that you don't carry your own bags. It doesn't hold here, this is Cuba, remember.'

She smiled, expecting nothing else, secure in the knowledge that she had returned from a world that he could only imagine, and will never experience.

'That's Investigator Ramirez to you *pendaho*,' she corrected him, adding that he was an arsehole. Vasquales slowed down behind her at his own pace, reaching into his pocket for a cigarette.

'You may find this hard to believe Vasquales,' she called over her shoulder, smiling as she exited the terminal building, 'but it's good to be home.'

Vasquales stopped short, making her wait while he lit his cigarette and took the first few drags. She opened the rear door of the Police Lada and squirmed in over the hot vinyl seats, breaking into a sweat in the stifling heat of the Police car. Good to be home?

The Ministry of the Interior building still reflected the heat of the mid-afternoon sun. It drenched the front steps and baked the outside walls, while the air conditioners struggled to cool the inside.

Clara forced herself to sit still. She desperately wanted to be in uniform, but the jeans and shirt from the flight home put her at a disadvantage straight away. She was nervous and desperately in need of a shower, but she knew what she had to do. Her career was on the line, and this was Cuba, champion of the people, and it was now or never she thought. She sat across from Colonel Perez in his office, filled with apprehension.

The Colonel held out his hand. 'Please give me your travel authorisation, your passport and temporary appointment as Investigator.'

She rummaged in her bag, passing only the first two of them across to him.

'And the other please,' he clicked his fingers at her. She held on to her appointment as an investigator.

'Don't test me Ramirez, hand it over.'

'No. I earned this,' she said waving the paper in the air.' Nowhere on here does it say the word temporary.'

He opened the draw and dropped what he had inside before turning back to her. He drummed his fingers on the desk, as if looking for a way to start.

'You have some serious explaining to do. My sources upstairs tell me that you failed to complete your orders.'

She expected this and had prepared her defence in the long hours of the flight home.

'No. I didn't fail, Colonel Perez. I brought a criminal to justice. I could not extradite him to Cuba to stand trial for murder, I had no warrant to do so, I had no official capacity, you know that, so I did what I could. He is being punished for a crime he has committed, and no longer a threat to the people of Cuba.'

She was stone cold resolute, she could not afford to get emotional, could not show the fear eating away inside her.

'Those were not your instructions from the Ministry.'

'I was sent to bring justice to the man who murdered Major Colomè. I did that. He is in a jail awaiting trial. I upheld the honour of the National Revolutionary Police force and brought a fugitive to justice. That is the job of the Police, to uphold the law, not to deliver punishment. The last time I looked that was what the Police force stood for here.'

'Don't lecture me Ramirez, I might remind you that you are an officer in the National Police force of Cuba only as long as I wish it to be so.'

'And I might remind you that both our positions are reliant on the successful completion of my assignment, and I believe I did that.'

Perez was quiet, drumming his fingers again on the desk as he contemplated what she said. Clara went on the offensive straight away.

'Why was I sent to kill Vaughn Crowther? You sent me to find him, but the Ministry sent me to kill him. I want to know why. Did you ask yourself why? Or do you already know?'

Perez stopped finger drumming, his eyes narrowed. Clara continued.

'Major Alberto Colomè of the Guarda Fronteras was accepting bribes to allow yachts to pass through Cuban waters and thereby, avoid US border patrols. Those bribes were arranged with the FULL KNOWLEDGE of the Ministry of the Interior prior to the yacht arriving. Major Colomè is the Ministers nephew, but he just collected the money. He was killed because he was extorting more than had been arranged from Vaughn Crowther, the captain of the yacht *Cosmos*... he told me so. Silencing Vaughn Crowther would be the only reason they sent me to kill him...to remove the evidence and protect the Ministry from allegations of corruption. Am I wrong Colonel?'

Perez leaned forward.

'Do you have proof of this?'

Clara nodded, barely able to speak.

'What proof do you have?'

'I'm not ready to tell you yet.'

'If you put this accusation to the Minister, with or without proof, you open yourself up to reprisal...you would become the only link between the Minister and your so-called corruption charges. A dangerous place to be.'

'That is why I am telling you.' She pointed out. 'I'm not the only one who knows now.'

'And you think that was a good idea? That you are safe here. Have you considered that I too may be in on the 'so called' corruption. We are inside the Ministry of the Interior building, only one person saw you come in, no one would know if you did not leave. Seargent Vasquales is just outside the door, he would do anything I tell him.'

'I have considered this,' she said blandly, hiding the fear inside.

'And still, you claim the Minister of the Interior is corrupt?' He raised his eyebrows.

Now was her gamble, it all hinged on her judgement, her hunch...her gut feeling...the one thing she had told Alex that Police did not act on.

'I believe you are first and foremost a policeman, Colonel Perez. You swore to protect the principles of the revolution and the Cuban people. Like my father, you fought against corruption, and I believe you still do.' She looked directly at Perez, wishing desperately to believe that she was right, that her belief in him was not misplaced.

Perez looked straight back at her. Silence. The clock on the far wall echoed the time in seconds, but they did not pass so quickly. The silence stretched to minutes. She closed her eyes to await her fate.

'What do you want to do, Investigator Ramirez?' he asked her.

'First, I want a shower,' she sighed.

The receptionist at the top floor of the Ministry told Perez and Clara to go in, they were expected. Clara was in her dress uniform, impeccable, her damp hair swept high in a bun, her blue shirt ironed and epaulettes stiff with the insignia of First Lieutenant.

Minister Ibarrio, a small, weathered man, sat behind a desk that befitted one of the most powerful men in Cuba. Given his position and reach, some thought of him as second only to Raul Castro. He had fought alongside Fidel, was a hero of the Revolution, small in stature but formidable in reputation.

General Abelardo was much taller, in the uniform of the Security Division. He stood to one side, watching them both approach the desk. There were no chairs for the visitors.

'I've brought Lieutenant Ramirez to see you as requested,' announced Perez. Minister Ibarrio waved him aside and pointed for Clara to step forward. He leaned back in his seat and nodded to General Abelardo.

'Give me your report on your operation in Australia.' said the General sternly.

Clara faced the Minister and started to speak.

'Not to the minister, to me.' Abelardo asserted.

'Very well,' she said, turning to face the General. 'The investigation is complete. I found the murderer of Major Colomè in Australia. His name is Vaughn Crowther of the yacht *Cosmos*, currently in jail for drug trafficking. He poses no further threat to the Cuban people; justice has been served.'

'Justice has not been served Lieutenant Ramirez. You knew what your orders were,' Abelardo stated.

'I did.' Clara chose her words carefully. 'I served the Cuban Government in a foreign country, to the best of my ability as a Police Investigator. If I had done as you ordered, I would be on trial in Australia for the murder of the yacht captain, which would not be in the best interests of the Cuban Government.'

There was no response to this, perhaps they hadn't considered that eventuality, she thought.

'The consulate reported that a Columbian national was killed in the operation to bring Crowther to justice.' Minister Ibarrio observed, holding up a folder marked Cuban Consulate, Australia.

Clara inclined her head in agreement. 'That's true, he died in a firefight, resisting arrest during a drug smuggling operation I was a part of. I shot him.'

'Did the opportunity come up for you to do the same to this Crowther?' The General interrupted.

'It did. But I chose not to'.

'Why didn't you?'

'Because I am a Cuban Policewoman, not an assassin. I didn't join the Police for that. And you threatened me,' Clara said, turning to Minister Ibarrio so there was no doubt as to who she was addressing. 'You threatened my family.'

''You do not talk to the Minister that way.' The general exploded at her, moving around the desk to intercept her.

Ibarrio held up his hand for the General to stay where he was. He looked directly at Clara; she almost withered under his gaze. He opened a second folder and quickly glanced at its contents before turning to her.

'Your brother...he is an agitator, under investigation,' Ibarrio stated, 'and your mother has a record of anti-revolutionary sentiments.' The underlying implication was evident.

'That may be so, but neither of them deserves retribution for my actions.' She stood still, facing Minister Ibarrio, and stole a sideways glance across at her superior Colonel Perez. He showed no signs of his interfering, but she was buoyed by the fact that he was watching Ibarrio and the General...not her.

'You realise that this could have major implications for your career and your family's future?' Ibarrio pointed out.

Clara was shaking, inside she quivered but managed to keep her voice clear, firm, confidant. 'I'm not an assassin for your revenge, Minister Ibarrio, I know that Colomè was your nephew and taking bribes. Nor am I going to stand by and let you harm my family to protect the corruption coming from this office.'

'You do not get to accuse me of corruption.' Ibarrio said coldly. He turned to Perez. 'She is your officer Colonel Perez, as such, your responsibility.'

Clara continued before Perez was able to answer, her voice loud with conviction. 'Vaughn Crowther was paying Major Colomè bribes for safe passage of his yacht, the *Cosmos,* through Cuban waters, and it was with the full knowledge of the Ministry of the Interior. I had Crowther sign and date this statement in the presence of an Australian Federal Agent.'

The room fell silent.

The dice had been rolled, and there was nothing more for her to add. This was her insurance. Now her life was totally in the hands of the men in this room.

'Do you have the statement on you?' Ibarrio asked.

'I do. It is a copy of the original.'

'May I see it.'

Clara slowly removed it from her breast pocket and handed it across the desk to Ibarrio. He unfolded it and read silently. When he finished, he placed it on the desk in front of him. The General reached for it, but Ibarrio waved him away.

'I take it that you don't have the original on you?' he asked Clara.

She shook her head. He turned to Perez.

'Have you read this?' he asked the Police Colonel.

'No, Minister.'

'Perez, were you aware of these corruption charges?'

'No Minister. Lieutenant Ramirez only brought it to my attention just before this meeting, I did not have time to warn you.' Clara shot a look at Perez, was he turning on her or covering his arse?

Ibarrio looked to Clara. 'Do you realise that you are implicating all three men in this room with these charges of corruption?' Clara's throat constricted, she was aware that all three men surrounded her, watching her.

'Somebody here is,' she croaked.

'*Eres una puta mentirosa*,' the General spat, accusing her of lying.

'*Que te Jodan*.' She exploded, the tension unleased, aiming her abuse at the General, she hated him and all he had put her through. 'I nearly died because of of you...or all of you.' Clara yelled at him, twirling around, unable to control her nerves, accusing them with her glare.

'Silencio!' Ibarrio shouted. He leaned forward in his chair, and placed both hands on the desk, speaking in a cold, calculated voice. 'You wait outside Ramirez.' He pointed at the door.

Clara didn't know what to do, she couldn't figure out what it meant. She looked at each of the men in turn. Finally, she squared her shoulders in defiance and retreated to the far side of the room, opened the door and looked back.

'It's Investigator Ramirez, Minister.' Clara corrected him as she backed out of the office, slamming the door behind her.

Outside in the hallway, she collapsed against the panel wall, her legs shaking, arms squeezed over her breasts, trying to regain some control. She had just accused the third highest Office in the country of corruption. Clara didn't know if Minister Ibarrio was part of it or not, or the General...or Perez for that matter, but she didn't care, she had done what she had come for.

Muffled voices rose and fell from inside the Ministers office and a short time later, Seargent Vasquales with two uniformed officers appeared at the head of the stairs. He marched quickly over and stood before her. She steeled herself ready for arrest.

'What did you do in there?' Vasquales questioned, a hint of respect in his voice. He turned away from her, knocked and opened the door to the Ministers Office and disappeared inside, the uniforms close behind him.

General Abelardo's voice rose dramatically in indignation before it was cut off abruptly.

It was time she went home.

Clara parked the Police Lada hard up against the wall opposite her apartment building, scratching the winged mirror as she did so. The sun was nearly gone for the day, and the heat evaporated from the pavers. Zaya Bernal, her oversized neighbour stood up from behind his precious red Studebaker, wringing out the last of the suds from a washcloth with his huge hands, beads of sweat glistening on his muscled skin. The rich red duco gleamed from its daily bath.

He sat down on the front steps of the apartment, and pulled out a cigar, lighting it, puffing furiously till a belch of thick smoke enveloped his bald head. Clara crossed over the street and loosened the collar of her Police shirt as she sat down next to him on the step. The surprised look on his face only deepened when she reached across and snatched the cigar from his fingers. She put it to her own lips, drawing in the fragrant smoke, before exhaling it with an exaggerated breath.

'*Niceto*.' she said, as she handed the cigar back to him. He nodded in agreement and took another deep pull on his cigar, all the while admiring the paintwork of his gleaming car. Clara leaned her elbows back on the step behind her, letting the tension unwind from her body as she studied Bernal with renewed interest.

This was Havana after all, she thought.

# Also by Alistair Hume

Dinnan Rocks
Tunkumba Creek

# About the Author

This is my second novel that shares with readers my love of Australian coastal communities.

The town of Nerimbah and Tunkumba Creek are not real places, though many of its geographical characteristics bear the elements of any number of Australian seaside fishing towns, especially those in South East Queensland. To help me establish and maintain a geographical identity for my story, I created fictitious maps for my own reference, filling them with my own place names, some of which are derivatives of traditional languages. The maps helped me immensely to keep track of my character's movements and logical timelines of action. However, Cuba is another matter, and there really is a town called Australia near the Bay of Pigs.

Alex and Clara's story is not based on any real person, though what happened to them could be associated with real events of December 1996, contributing to the themes of crime, justice, and mercy. There is no doubt that drug trafficking has had a significant impact on what were once innocent coastal communities, and that has been well documented.

I love the process of writing and am indebted to my family, my wife Debra, and daughters Anika and Chloe, for their continued encouragement and editorial input. The cover photo is mine, depicting a well-known mangrove tree at Poona. I thank Col, my son-in-law, for his work on my cover design. Many thanks to my friends who offered encouragement at every step, and their interest in the Arts in all its forms.

www.ingramcontent.com/pod-product-compliance
Lightning Source LLC
LaVergne TN
LVHW091029080826
845145LV00002B/416

* 9 7 8 1 7 6 4 5 8 7 3 3 4 *